THE RELUCTANT CHARTIST

M. K. Jones

A CASE FOR
MAZE INVESTIGATIONS –
THE GENEALOGY DETECTIVES
BOOK 7

CW01497037

Cover design: Alison Morgan at AliCat Design
Cover Photo: With permission of Gwent Archives

First Edition: 2022

Category: Historical Thrillers/Private Investigator Mysteries

ISBNs
Paperback: 978-1-80227-846-0
eBook: 978-1-80227-847-7

Chapter 1

Nick Howell sat back from his computer, whooped three times, and clapped his hands in the air.

The whooping was both loud and unusual. Nick wasn't a man given to boisterous expressions of happiness. So, on hearing him his Maze Investigations colleagues, Maggie Gilbert and Zelah Trevear, came running to the office from the kitchen to find out the cause of this rare expression of joy.

He spun his seat around as they entered and as soon as she saw his face, Maggie Gilbert knew what had happened. 'You've done it!'

He nodded. 'Taken me a year, but, yes, we have our first connection to royalty, and Welsh royalty at that.'

Maggie walked over and hugged him. 'Well done, my friend. Our client is indeed descended from a Welsh prince. Are you going to tell him?'

'I'm going to call him now.'

'Just a minute there,' Zelah Trevear intervened, putting up a hand. 'You'll need to remind him of the clause in the contract that says he gives us full permission to use this discovery for marketing purposes. There's nothing that needs to be hidden in this one, is there?'

'No, and he'll be fine with it. He's been so sure, and so patient. You'll have to agree the text with him, Zelah, that's all. But he's going to love the publicity.'

'As are we,' Zelah smiled and went back to the kitchen. Zelah's role in the company she owned was marketing and publicity as well as genealogy research. She was the most experienced researcher of the three partners, and so proficient in spotting a marketing opportunity that Maze Investigations had developed a glowing international reputation. Maggie Gilbert now specialised in the most difficult brick wall cases, whilst Nick Howell, the quietest of the three, was a dogged investigator who, over the six years they had been in business, had developed an enviable database of genealogy resources.

'This is superb, Nick. We've been quiet for so long. It's good to have some really exciting news. The second best news this year, of course.'

He gave her a cheesy grin, also very unlike him, but this time tinged with pride and happiness.

'Stella will definitely agree with you once she's awake. Max is doing the honours this morning whilst she gets some sleep.' He turned back to his computer and picked up his phone. 'Anyway, here goes. Do you want to be on the call?'

'No, I'll leave it to you. I picked up something new, or rather, a case returning to us, this morning. I was just talking to Zelah about it.'

'Which one?' he asked as he punched in numbers.

'Do you remember that enquiry we had about a year or so ago, a man saying one of his ancestors took part in the Chartist Rising in Newport? Said the ancestor had left a story about a valuable treasure he had stolen as he came down the valley, that he hid close to Newport, at the Cathedral?'

'Yes, we turned him down, didn't we? I checked it out but I couldn't even verify the name he gave us, never mind any story about someone having lost precious goods to the Chartists. Shame, as it would have been a great story if it had happened. Why is he back?'

'Because he says he's found something new…' but she didn't get any further as Nick's client answered the call and the conversation began. Back in the kitchen she could hear the excited shouting.

'How's it going in there?' Zelah asked, looking up from some papers on the kitchen table.

'With great delight; I can hear. You'll have to get your teeth into the story pretty quickly before the client calls every newspaper in Wales.'

Zelah grinned. 'No problem. I'll arrange a call with him and Nick as soon as this first call's done. How's Nick? He looked tired this morning.'

'Hardly surprising,' Maggie said. 'They aren't getting much sleep. I can barely remember that far back, but …' She paused as Nick joined them at the table.

'He's unbelievably excited. I've stopped him from calling the newspapers, and the BBC. I told him we need a discussion to agree on who does what. I can manage it in about an hour, Zelah if that's OK with you?'

'Fine,' she replied. 'But don't you want to get off home?'

'I'll go as soon as the call's done. Stella just texted me. She's awake, but Max is going to wait for me to get back.'

'He's as thrilled as you are,' Maggie said. She turned her head as the sound of thumping footsteps on the stairs announced the imminent arrival of her son Jack. He glanced around the kitchen and sitting in a vacant seat, grinned at Nick. 'How's the princess?'

Nick grimaced. 'Fine, thanks.'

Maggie shot Jack a look, before turning to Nick.

'Nick, you have become a father again, unexpectedly we know, but you don't have to hide your delight. And she is a little princess.'

It had been beyond a shock when, six months earlier, following a period of worry about the health of Nick's partner, Stella, the tests and examinations had resulted in the news she was pregnant. Their immediate reaction was, of course, shock; Stella being in her mid-forties and Nick in his fifties. But, three months ago, on New Year's day, the safe arrival of Flora Gwendoline Howell had been a cause for a wonderful celebration.

She had turned out to be a healthy, happy baby with startling blue eyes and a shock of white hair similar to Stella's. Of course, they knew that could change, but for now, she was the Princess and they all adored her, none more so than her half-brother Max who, at twenty, had become her biggest fan. He and Jack had become friends since Max had come back into his father's life the previous year.

'Is Max still on babysitting duties?' asked Jack. He was also taken with the baby but didn't admit to it, especially in front of his mother.

'Can't keep him away,' Nick replied. 'He's a great help for Stella during the day. She's already trying to keep an eye on the Manor, can't help herself.'

'She's done a great job keeping it going, and now, at last, they can visitors back. It was her first baby, Nick,' Maggie said.

He smiled. He had met Stella at Llanyrafon Manor, a sixteenth-century farmhouse that had been taken over by a local group and supported by EU funding. The group had turned it into a popular visitor attraction with meeting rooms, a café, and a small museum depicting life as it would have been when the farm was an Elizabethan family home. One of the early Maze cases had brought them to the Manor to investigate Nick's family history. There, he had met the Manager, Stella Bell.

'At least it's a quiet period for them. April usually is, and she's cutting down the opening times. She has good staff, who'll take care of the place. She's also planning to take Flora with her when she's feeling up to going in.'

'That's the beauty of having flexible working arrangements,' Maggie said. 'Having the Maze office here in the house gave me the opportunity of a lifetime, to work and bring up kids at the same time. We have Zelah to thank for that.'

Zelah waved them away. 'You had the room, we had the need. Nothing more to it. Right, let's get ready for this call, then Maggie, you can give us more updates on this client?'

Maggie nodded and was about to start when the doorbell rang.

'Are you expecting anyone?'

'No, Zelah. It's probably just a parcel delivery. Jack's addicted to ordering stuff online.'

Jack grimaced, but stood and walked towards the door. 'I haven't ordered anything. But I'll go, don't you trouble yourselves.'

They heard muffled voices from the hallway, then Jack returned.

'Mum, it's for you. There's two policemen at the door. They're from London and they're asking for Mrs Gilbert of Maze Investigations.'

Chapter 2

'I'm Maggie Gilbert. How can I help you?' She was looking at a man and a woman, the former fortyish, tall, with greying dark hair. The woman younger, also tall, had bottle blonde hair pulled into a ponytail. They held up warrant cards. Maggie took a look at them, long enough to ensure they knew it wasn't a perfunctory glance.

'We'd like to speak to you about a case we're investigating, in Soho,' the man said. His accent was difficult to determine, being a London twang but acquired from immersion in the capital, not native. The woman didn't speak.

'You'd better come in.'

From the hallway, she turned right into the former dining room that had become the Maze office. 'This is where we work. Please take a seat.' She indicated the conference table, adding, 'Just a moment, please,' and walked out of the door. 'Nick, Zelah, I could do with someone in here, please.'

They both came to join her and sat down.

'Now, how can we help you?'

'We wanted to talk to you, just you,' the woman said.

'Well, we are Maze Investigations, all three of us, so anything to do with the company can be said to all of us. Perhaps you could begin by introducing yourselves to my colleagues and tell us why you're here,' she added with a smile.

The two officers looked at each other, and the man nodded. 'I'm Detective Inspector John Finch, this is Detective Constable

Olivia Abbott. We're part of a unit that investigates homicides and unexplained deaths, where there may be suspicious circumstances. We're hoping you can help us with an enquiry into a death, Mrs Gilbert.'

'Of course, if I can.'

Does the name Anthony Bandon mean anything to you?'

Maggie nodded. 'Yes, it does. I had a discussion with him just recently.'

'How recently?'

'A few days ago actually, and I had a message this morning. He's a client … or are you telling me that something has happened to Mr Bandon?'

The officers looked puzzled, then DC Abbott nodded. 'Yes, I'm sorry. Mr Bandon was found dead in his hotel room three days ago.'

It was Maggie's turn to look horrified and puzzled. 'Oh no! That's terrible. It must have been just after I spoke to him … hang on, Anthony Bandon is Australian. He was speaking to me from Melbourne. He emailed me this morning.'

The Inspector bit his lip. 'I see. Well, Mr Bandon was actually in London, at the First Point Hotel in Soho, which I have to tell you, is a one-star dive.'

'It didn't look like a hotel room on our call,' Maggie replied. 'It looked rather homely. You know, pictures on the walls, knickknacks on display. This is odd. Besides, I was in London three days ago but he didn't make any attempt to contact me then.'

So, when you say you had a discussion with Mr Bandon, it was on camera, Mrs Gilbert?'

'Yes, a video call.'

'Could you take a look at this for me?' The Inspector, reaching into his pocket for his phone brought up a headshot of a man appearing to be asleep, which Maggie knew was a shot taken after death.

'Who is this?'

'This is Anthony Bandon.'

'No, it isn't, or at least this isn't the Anthony Bandon I spoke to. I mean, it's a bit like my client, a little older I would say, same colour hair, but it's not him.'

'What were you doing in London, Mrs Gilbert?'

'I was researching, at the London Metropolitan Archives.'

'Was that anything to do with Mr Bandon?'

'No, nothing at all. It was for another client,' Maggie replied.

Zelah leaned forward. 'You haven't explained why you're here wanting to speak to Maggie,' she said. 'What's this man's death got to do with her?'

The Constable replied. 'Mr Bandon's room had nothing in it to identify him, no wallet, no passport, no personal effects of any kind, apart from a business card found in the lining of his overcoat hanging in the wardrobe. It's your business card, Mrs Gilbert.' She reached into her briefcase and took out an evidence bag, which she handed over to Maggie.

Maggie took the card, as Nick said, 'When you say your division works on homicides and unexplained deaths, which is this?'

'We're not sure yet. We're waiting for an autopsy report. There's nothing obvious, no evidence of anything malicious, but we have to wait and see. However,' he took the plastic folder back from Maggie. 'You must have met this man at some point, Mrs Gilbert, and handed him your card. Are you sure you don't know him?'

Maggie shook her head. 'All I can tell you, Inspector, is that I do not recognise the man in that picture. He is **not** our client. He's older than the Anthony Bandon on my video call. And at events like conferences and shows, I hand out hundreds of business cards.'

'I see. Well, thank you for your time. Here's my card. If you remember anything else, please get in touch.'

'OK. Will you let me know if you find out who this man in London is, and what happened to him?'

'I may have to ask you to account for your whereabouts in London, Mrs Gilbert. Did you stay overnight?'

'Yes, I did. At the Victoria Palace Hotel. I arrived around seven o'clock at Paddington and made my way to the hotel, where I had dinner. The following morning I went to the archives when they opened at ten and spent the day there. I had made a reservation. You have to do that for now, because of Covid. I then caught a train home at around five that afternoon.'

'Thank you. And just for the record, what's the case you're investigating for Anthony Bandon in Australia?'

'It's an ancestor he believes was a Chartist, involved in the Newport uprising in 1839, who he says was tried and transported to Australia, and who had a secret involving something stolen, something immensely valuable, but we've not found any proof. He first contacted us about a year ago.'

'So why the video call four days ago?'

'Mr Bandon said he had new information to share with me, something significant.'

'Did he tell you what it was?'

'No, he needed to check out one more thing first, then we were going to speak again; he's due to let me know a date and time. The message this morning told me he had more information, but nothing further about another discussion.'

'I'd be interested in that call, Mrs Gilbert. Please let me know when it's going to take place.'

'Of course.'

The two detectives stood up. 'Thank you for your time. We'll head off now.'

'Well, that was a bit disconcerting,' Maggie said after she had shown them to the door and returned to the office. 'Nick, what's up? You're scowling.'

'Not sure. They were both dark.'

Maggie waited, knowing there was more to come. Nick's ability to perceive energy was rarely misplaced.

'Doesn't mean too much, given their jobs,' Zelah intervened. 'They work with dead bodies and the circumstances around suspicious deaths. Enough to make anyone dark.'

Nick shook his head. 'I don't understand why there was nothing identifying this dead man in the hotel room. That's odd.'

'Well, I'm going to get in touch with Mr Bandon in Melbourne, tell him about this,' Maggie said. 'No point waiting for him to call now. Do you both agree?'

They nodded. She turned to walk out but paused in the doorway. 'There's something niggling at me, about that conversation; about the pair of them.'

'I agree,' Nick said. 'Not sure either what it is, though. Did you pick up anything, Zelah?'

'No,' she replied. 'Come on, let's get back to work. If there is something, you two will figure it out.'

**

Nick and Zelah left at lunchtime, Nick taking Jack with him to meet up with Max.

Maggie had sent a message to Anthony Bandon but had not yet received a reply, but as it was now late evening in Australia she couldn't really expect anything until the following day. She kept going back over the discussion with the two detectives. She was alone in the office just after seven when her partner returned home. Bob Pugh was in a grumpy mood which, Maggie knew, was due to an ongoing difficult discussion with his boss.

As a Detective Chief Inspector in South Wales Police, Bob had recently been dealing with a major drugs-related crime syndicate, leading a covert team. They hadn't had the breakthrough they were hoping for and the Chief Superintendent was putting Bob under pressure to either crack it or scale it down.

'Bad day,' he murmured as she joined him in the kitchen, putting her arms on the top of his shoulders and squeezing taut muscles.

'No progress?' she asked, knowing the answer.

'Nope.'

'How much longer has she given you?'

'A week.'

'Sorry, Bob.'

'Not your fault; what have you been up to today? Anything interesting?'

He had been putting dishes into the microwave as he spoke, now putting them on the table with plates and cutlery. 'I'm assuming you were waiting for me?'

'Yes, thanks. I have something I want to tell you about.'

As they ate, she told him about Nick's breakthrough in his case, then about the visit from the two detectives from the Met. He stopped eating.

'Why did they tell you they were here in person?'

'Because they can't identify the man other than the name he gave when he checked in and they found my business card; that was it, really.'

And they travelled down here just to ask that? They could have phoned.'

'I suppose. Maybe that's what's bugging me. Something is, but I can't put my finger on it.'

'Give me their names again.' He scribbled them down in his notebook, took out his phone, and walked into the conservatory. Maggie could hear the muted one side of the conversation.

After a few minutes, he returned to the table.

'Maggie, there are no detectives in that Division of the Met called John Finch and Olivia Abbott.'

She put her cutlery down. 'Damn it! There was something about the pair of them that didn't sit right.' She reached into the pocket of her jeans, to take out the business card the man who called himself Finch had given her and gave it to Bob. He took it, raised an eyebrow, then took out his phone, put it on speaker, and dialled the number. Maggie pushed her plate aside and sat forward.

The call was answered immediately. 'Finch speaking.'

'Good evening, Inspector Finch. This is Detective Chief Inspector Robert Pugh of South Wales Police. You gave your business card to my partner, Maggie Gilbert, and…' The line went dead. Bob dialled again. It rang twice, then stopped.

'Definitely not from the Met,' Bob said. He was about to say something more when the phone rang. He checked the caller's number. 'It's him. Odd.'

'Answer it, then.'

Bob didn't bother with niceties. 'Who are you and what do you want?'

'My apologies, Chief Inspector. My name is John Finch. I am associated with the Met, but they wouldn't have told you that.'

'Tells me nothing.'

'I am with special security services, Miss Abbott is a Met officer.'

'Still not enough.'

'You met another associate of mine last year, as did Mrs Gilbert, who I assume is listening to this conversation.'

'Who would that be?'

'His name is Will Sharpe.'

'Maggie drew in a quick, loud breath. 'The man from the Vice squad.'

'Exactly. We could do with your help.'

'Then why didn't you ask today?' Maggie said.

'I wanted to ascertain how much you knew about Anthony Bandon, which was not much, from what you told us. However, in this case, Anthony Bandon, or whoever our unidentified corpse turns out to be, will be the subject of a parallel investigation. I'm interested in someone else.'

'Who would that be?' Bob growled. 'I'm not liking the sound of this.'

'Someone Mrs Gilbert will know, or rather, know of. Look,' he softened his tone to be conciliatory. 'I don't want to discuss this over the phone. Can we meet?'

'If you're prepared to come to the station tomorrow morning and if you give me the name of this person. Maggie deserves to know.'

After a moment's hesitation, the man answered. 'We'll be there at nine. The name we're interested in, in this case, is Sir Henry Camberwell.'

Maggie's mouth dropped open. 'No! No! No! That man is evil.'

'Indeed he is. We'll see you tomorrow morning.'

The call ended.

Chapter 3

Zelah and Nick's reactions were as she expected. Zelah exploded. Nick remained silent.

'The question is, though, should I meet them in the morning?'

Zelah's instant response was, 'No. Under no circumstances. This client is dodgy and your work last year proved there was no substance to the Chartist story.'

'Nick, what do you think?'

They waited the usual few seconds. 'I do not want Maze to be involved in any way with Henry Camberwell. I have nothing further to say on that subject. However, the client said he had more information. I would be interested to hear it before we make a final decision.'

'Good luck with that,' Zelah snapped. 'Given he's dead.'

'I still don't think the client who's calling himself Anthony Bandon and the body in the hotel is the same person,' Maggie replied. 'How about I go along, hear what they have to say, but make no commitments. I can also confirm one hundred percent that we will not engage with, or be involved, directly or indirectly, with Camberwell?'

'Works for me,' Nick replied.

'Well, reluctantly, OK with me,' Zelah added. 'But you make our Maze position crystal clear.'

'Will do,' Maggie said. 'The meeting is at nine; shouldn't take more than an hour. I'll meet up with you in the office as soon as it's done.'

She ended the call and turned to Bob. 'You heard that.'

'Fine with me. If the dead man is your client, then the case goes nowhere. I've got too much on to be side-tracked by this. I'll hear them out, but that's it.'

**

Maggie and Bob sat opposite John Finch and Olivia Abbott in an atmosphere of polite tension.

Finch began. 'First of all, thanks for seeing us, Mrs Gilbert, and I apologise for telling you we're with the Met. Genuinely, Olivia is. I am attached. Olivia is with the Art and Antiques Unit. My interest is in Camberwell for a different reason, and I know of your brush with him last year.'

'It was more than a brush,' Maggie said. 'A woman called Helen Redland died and the son of my associate, Nick Howell, took a great risk in working with Bob to end an attempt to bring young foreign girls into the country to be deposited into brothels, all organised by Helen Redland. Perhaps you are the person who can confirm what we believed, or rather suspected at the time. Helen Redland's partner in that appalling venture was Henry Camberwell?'

'Yes. I can't say more than that.'

Maggie shrugged. 'I talked to my colleagues last night. We'll have nothing to do with Camberwell, but we are still interested in our client, Anthony Bandon, who hasn't responded to the message I sent yesterday. So, do you know yet if the person you found in the hotel is Anthony Bandon?' She turned to Abbott. 'Is the so-called treasure stolen by an ancestor that he commissioned us to discover, why you're part of this?'

Finch held up a hand before Abbot could reply. 'I can tell you our part of the story before we go any further.' He turned to Bob. 'If that's OK with you. I know you're busy.'

Bob glanced at his watch and nodded. 'I have a briefing at nine-thirty.'

'Then let us get on with it. I'm going to ask Olivia to give you a quick precis of her involvement.' He turned to the unsmiling Abbott and nodded.

'In 1838 there was a major theft from the British Museum. Several artefacts were stolen. The majority were recovered, eventually, by various means, except for one piece. That was a vase, Chinese. You'll probably have heard of the Ming dynasty. People think it's all valuable. It isn't, but other pieces are. The stolen piece, which was never discovered, was an eighteenth-century reticulated vase made for the Emperor Quinlin by a man called Tang Ying. It was traced via two buyers, to a man in South Wales. Recently, papers of a South Wales Iron Master, a man called Samuel Fathergill, have been released to the public and are on the internet. They include a diary, in which he describes a visit to a man called Prosser, on the night of the Chartist uprising in Newport. Prosser showed him a vase he had bought. He had been told it was an excellent piece for a collector, which Prosser aspired to be. Fathergill recognised it as the piece stolen from the British Museum and advised Prosser to get rid of it. There's no further information about what Prosser did.'

Maggie frowned. 'Is it that important? And if the theft took place in 1838, why would you care? I mean, it can't have survived intact, can it? It's probably in pieces somewhere by now.'

'From an individual point of view, I don't care. I've been brought in because a group, including Camberwell, is trying to

17

find this piece. You are aware he has a semi-legitimate business in rare antiques?' Finch said.

'I know he's well connected,' Maggie replied. 'But I still don't understand.'

Abbott sighed. 'The last time a vase from this particular ceramicist, for the same Chinese emperor, was sold, a couple of years ago, it achieved forty-one million dollars.'

Maggie gasped.

'Exactly. This one could be worth that much and more. If we find it, it will go back to the British Museum. If Camberwell finds it, it will be sold illegally to the highest bidder.'

'And you think it still exists?' Bob asked.

Abbott shrugged. 'I don't know.'

'I brought Olivia in because we hope we may be able to draw Camberwell in,' Finch interjected. 'If your client is, or was, genuine and his information is sound, this could be our way of finally bringing him down.'

'Hang on,' Maggie said. 'You have no idea if our client is anything to do with this case.'

Finch put his finger to his neck and pulled at his collar. 'I wasn't entirely forthcoming with you yesterday, Mrs Gilbert, regarding your business card.'

'You don't say.'

'Apologies again. Fact is, we took the card and tested it for fingerprints. We got nothing on the dead man. But we did find a print for …'

'Let me guess,' Maggie interrupted. 'Henry Camberwell.'

He nodded. 'Whoever the body turns out to be, he must have been given the card by Camberwell. There was one other set of prints, but no-one we know. This next part is a surmise and yes, it's a big leap. Camberwell knows your reputation and we're thinking he found out something about your client. He wanted the man to contact you, under the guise of being Bandon.'

'But I still don't get it. Anthony Bandon is in Australia and he's just come back to us. Why would Camberwell be confident this dead man could pretend to be our client and get away with it?'

'There's more,' Bob said, tersely. 'Either you tell us everything, or this meeting ends now.'

Finch sat back and folded his arms. Abbott didn't move.

'Everything,' Bob repeated. 'Not just the edited version you're working out right now.'

Finch sat forward again. 'Anthony Bandon is missing. I've been in contact with the Melbourne police. He disappeared two days ago. And they've confirmed the man in London is not Bandon.'

'So, what this sounds like to me is that Anthony Bandon has been taken out of the picture and the man in London put in to contact me,' Maggie said.

'That's my guess, yes, Mrs Gilbert.'

'Well, that's ridiculous. As soon as I saw him in person I would have known he wasn't our client.'

'Perhaps you weren't meant to meet him. I suspect …' Finch's phone rang. He looked at it and stood up. 'Excuse me, I must take this.' He walked out into the corridor.

Olivia Abbott didn't react.

'What do you think about all of this?' Maggie asked. The woman looked like she had a straitjacket on underneath her business suit.

'Not my business,' she replied. 'I'm here to consult on the vase, should you find it.'

'What does that mean, *should you find it*? I have no instructions from our client about anything right now, never mind finding this object. I, no I should say we, have no …' she paused as Finch re-entered the room.

'The man in the hotel died of natural causes. A heart attack,' he said, sitting again. He looked at Maggie. 'What's the matter?'

'Your associate has just talked about Maze finding the vase. I was just telling her, we have no instructions and we aren't looking for it. Not now, not ever, now that Camberwell might be involved.'

Finch turned to Abbott, whose cheeks had reddened. She muttered 'Sorry', turning away from Finch's angry stare.

'OK, I'll cut to the chase. I want you to continue with the client's case. We'll pay your usual fee.'

'No.' Maggie stood up and walked to the door.

'Mrs Gilbert, please. Hear me out.'

Bob glanced at his watch again. 'Last chance, Finch.'

'Mrs Gilbert, we have to stop Camberwell, by whatever means. You know what he does. This piece of pottery – sorry, Olivia, but that's all it is to me regardless of however many millions of dollars some uber-rich crackpot might be willing to pay for it – is the sprat to catch the mackerel. If you get back on the case, Camberwell will home in on you. If he hasn't already, and I suspect he has, because of the business card.' He leaned forward and put his hands on the table. 'You are the best hope we have, right now. I've seen your reputation. With Maze on the case, Camberwell will be assured there's a chance of finding it.'

Maggie stood with her back against the door, arms folded. She wanted to walk out, but her disgust of Camberwell's activities held her back. 'How are we supposed to proceed, with Camberwell's man dead – I'm taking it that's who he was – and with our client missing?'

'Good question. I believe you already have enough information. Anthony Bandon gave you the name of his ancestor, didn't he? And I've given you the details from the papers of Samuel Fathergill, which potentially names the man Prosser as the last known buyer. Can you take it from there?'

Maggie shrugged. 'The original information from the client gave us nothing. That's why we stopped investigating a year ago. It was too vague and the genealogy couldn't be verified. Yes, he did come back to us a couple of days ago to say he had something new, but he didn't give us any clue as to what that was.'

'Would you at least talk to your colleagues? Bandon is missing and the police in Melbourne are actively searching for him after we asked. He might turn up.'

'I have to go,' Bob interrupted. 'Maggie, what are you thinking?'

'I'll talk to them. Best I can say.'

Finch stood up. 'Thank you. Olivia and I are driving back to London. We'll wait to hear from you.' Maggie stood aside as they left the room.

'Up to you, love.'

'I know,' she replied. 'I will speak to Nick and Zelah. But I can predict what their responses will be. Bob, what do you think, honestly?'

'I think it's entirely up to you. But whatever, you must keep away from Camberwell.'

'That's a no-brainer. Right, I'll text them now to let them know I'm on my way back.'

Bob grinned. 'Bonfire night. Light the blue touchpaper and stand well back.'

Chapter 4

Zelah and Nick had said little during Maggie's report on the meeting with Finch and Abbot, but their unsmiling, stony-faced expressions told her she was heading towards a blasting.

'Well, what do you think? Should we talk about this?'

Nick stood up. 'No. And if you two decide to go ahead, I will resign from this Company.'

'Oh, don't be so melodramatic,' Zelah snapped, waving a hand at him to sit down. 'I don't like the idea of it any more than you do, but I would like to see that bastard Camberwell taken down. Nick, think of the misery he's caused. He's a trafficker. Think of the girls.'

'I'm thinking of my girls. That man wouldn't hesitate to hurt any one of us or my Flora and Stella and Max. What about Alice and Jack, Maggie? And Mischa and the boys in Ireland, Zelah.'

Maggie ran an agitated hand through her hair. 'I know, Nick. You're not being melodramatic. Zelah shouldn't have said that. Look, you're a good man, Nick, and I know you'd like to see Camberwell go down. But none of us would think even for a second of putting our families in danger. Can't we just talk about how we might do this? If there's any way we can help?'

Nick paused. 'I … I don't know.'

'Do you want to talk to Stella?' Maggie asked.

He nodded. 'I'll go speak to her. But don't expect her to agree.'

When he had gone Maggie turned to Zelah. 'You shouldn't have said that.'

Zelah sighed. 'I know. But you know me. Mouth open, foot straight in. I hate the thought of Camberwell being able to do what he does. How about I speak to Mischa and the boys? They have as much right to be a party to the decision as us.'

Maggie nodded. 'I'll speak to Jack. Bob didn't seem averse at the meeting this morning, but I'd like to talk to him here, away from the station.'

'What about Alice?'

'She's just sixteen. I'll have to tell her, although she still doesn't seem to have developed any sense of danger about the world.'

'Maybe that's a good thing,' Zelah replied. 'She's an incredibly brilliant young woman.'

'I still think of her as a child. She isn't, though. I wonder …'

'I've had the same idea. Matthew.'

Alice's best friend, Matthew Parker, the son of a senior intelligence chief, had security protection whilst the two teenagers attended college in Cardiff. Matthew and his mother lived in an apartment in the city from Monday to Thursday, not far from the sixth form college. Alice lived at home and travelled daily. She and Matthew had been friends for five years whilst they attended a school in Cheltenham for gifted children, before they finished their GCSE exams and transferred to Cardiff.

'If she could stay at the apartment while this is going on, I'd feel much better.' Maggie stood up. 'I'll call Matthew's mother, explain to her, see what she thinks.'

'Good idea. I'll call Mischa. It's almost Easter, so she'll be back at Rosscarbery next week, for three weeks. I can arrange security for her, Niall, and Stephen.'

'How's the medical training going?'

'Hard work, apparently, but she's busting it. Now she and Niall are engaged he's great support for her,' Zelah replied. She couldn't hide her pride in her unofficial ward and the progress she'd made since the death of her father Kennet Quinn.

'Good for her. What about her mother and the steroid kid?'

Zelah grinned. They still referred to Gerry Quinn in pejorative terms despite his, so far successful, efforts to turn his life around and support his mother in running the Quinn property business on a legal basis, which had not been the case when Kennet was alive and in charge.

'I suppose we should warn them. Michelle will turn to jelly and wail, as usual. Gerry might actually step up. He asks me for advice on the business on a weekly basis now. His brain seems to be working better since he stopped looking like the Incredible Hulk.'

'I almost like him,' Maggie replied, grinning. 'On a serious note, they do need to know.'

Zelah nodded. 'Well, you and I are willing to give this a shot?'

'Provided we have everyone's agreement. If anyone is opposed, then no. Let's start tackling them.'

'I'll call Mischa,' Zelah said, but Maggie felt a hint of reluctance, which was unusual for Zelah.

'Everything OK over there?'

'Yes, and no. It's Stephen. He wants to make a major investment in Rosscarbery, by building a new accommodation block. I'm not so sure it's the right direction or timing. He's given me a plan and an estimate. It's a lot of money. Not that I don't have it, but he can't understand why I won't just give him the green light.'

'Why are you hesitating?'

'He hasn't thought it through. The new block would take an additional twelve children. But the dining room isn't big enough, so we'd need another extension. And more staff, and more horses. He's included it all in his budget, but, I don't know, I'm just not sure. I've said I'll consider it and go over to Cork to discuss it with him and the architect.'

'Is he OK with that?'

'No. He's taken umbrage. He's cross with me. Says he'll get the money elsewhere if I don't put up.'

'Zelah, has he ever accepted you as the rightful owner of Rosscarbery? It's been his family home since he was born. Maybe some part of him still resents the way his father and grandfather died. Maybe he feels he should have an equal share in the big decisions.'

Zelah shrugged. 'I understand that. I'll be gentle with him.'

Knowing Zelah, Maggie doubted that Zelah's interpretation of "gentle" would be the same as hers, but for now, it wasn't her problem.

**

They reconvened the following morning at nine. As well as Maggie, Nick, and Zelah, Nick's son Max and Maggie's son Jack joined them, together with Stella and baby Flora. Also present, to everyone's surprise, was Gerry Quinn.

'Your mother not joining us?' Zelah asked, tongue in cheek.

Gerry grinned at her. 'Did you expect her to, Zelah?'

'Nope.'

Given the way Gerry and Zelah had loathed each other throughout the year of confrontation between Maze and the

Quinn family, Maggie and Nick gave each other a quick, furtive grin. Max and Jack didn't react. Neither yet trusted Gerry Quinn.

'Well,' Zelah continued, 'you'll be pleased to hear that your sister and the McCarthy Miller boys are joining us by video.'

Gerry gave a quick nod. His relationship with his sister was repairing, slowly, but was not yet warm enough for him to be anything other than wary.

'What about Alice?' Nick asked.

'She's not going to be here for the next couple of weeks. She's staying down in Cardiff with Matthew and his mother. She'll be safe there.'

Nick nodded.

'Let's get going, then,' Maggie said. 'Zelah, can you start the video call?'

Zelah brought up the call on the whiteboard and the faces of Mischa Quinn and Niall, along with Stephen McCarthy Miller, appeared in the office at Rosscarbery House on the outskirts of Cork. They greeted each other, with a nod of the head between Mischa and Gerry.

'I'll start,' Maggie said. 'Zelah and I contacted each of you yesterday, to give you the details of my – our – meeting with Finch and Abbott. Bob sends apologies, by the way. Big case on. So, they are prepared to pay us a sizeable fee to see what progress we can make in finding the "treasure". Which we now know is a Chinese vase that disappeared on the night of the Newport Chartist uprising in 1839. Zelah, can you share the screen with the photo you found?'

A picture appeared of a small vase, no more than eight inches high, slowly revolving to show the detail of its circumference.

'This isn't the exact one, of course,' Maggie said. 'But it was made for the same emperor by the same ceramicist, so it will be similar. And they are unique and precious. There aren't half a dozen left in the world and the last one sold went for forty-one million dollars.'

There were gasps of 'wow' and 'no way' from the Irish group and 'that's crazy' from Max Howell.

'For that ugly little thing?' Jack Gilbert said.

'Wouldn't want it on my mantlepiece,' added Stella.

'Me neither,' said Gerry Quinn.

'You don't have a mantlepiece; you don't even know what a mantlepiece is,' Zelah growled at Gerry. 'And whether we like it or not, or believe anything is worth that kind of money, it is what it is.'

'Moving on,' Maggie intervened. 'If you look closely as it turns, you'll see it's in layers, with the underneath layer one complete picture. Apparently, it was commissioned by an emperor called Qianlong and made by a master porcelain creator called Tang Ying. This emperor liked novelty and each creation was unique. Look at the detail. Once the design was in place, each element was separately glazed, enamelled, and fired. There was a huge risk of collapse, so the firing had to be perfect to stop the structure collapsing or distorting. Quite amazing, if you think about it. Incredible craftsmanship, for its time.'

They all stared again at the revolving vase, as it revealed intricate details of a path lined with trees, water, a small bridge, and overhead a sky with a fiery Chinese dragon.

'And you say the Newport vase will be similar?' Nick asked.

'I don't really know, Nick. Abbott is supposed to be providing a sketch of what the British Museum put out when it was stolen, in 1838.'

'So, you've been asked to carry on looking for it, in an attempt to flush out Camberwell?' Stella asked.

27

'Yes. That's the challenge and also the problem. Our previous interaction with Camberwell was one meeting. But we know that he was behind the importing of girls for the brothels, etc.'

'And the death of Helen Redland,' Max interrupted.

'Yes,' Maggie said. 'He's a dangerous man. We need to be exceptionally careful and wary.'

'He's bound to find out soon, if he doesn't already know, that his man posing as Anthony Bandon is dead. When he can't reach him, he'll go looking, won't he?' Mischa asked.

'Again, yes. We don't know what he'll do when he finds out. Finch will keep us informed. It also means that Finch is our new client, so we can return to looking for the ancestors of Anthony Bandon, which I've told him is what we might – and I emphasised the *'might'* – be prepared to do, but only if all of us agree. Over to all of you now. Pitch in.'

For a few seconds, there was silence.

"So, what you're saying, Maggie,' Max began, 'is that you're going to re-instate the search for Anthony Bandon's ancestors.'

'Yes, that's the idea.'

'Why did you stop last year?'

'Good question,' Maggie replied. 'In 1838 there was a major theft from the British Museum. Several artefacts were stolen. The majority were recovered, eventually, by various means, except for one piece. That was a vase, Chinese. You'll probably have heard of the Ming dynasty. People think it's all valuable. It isn't, but other pieces are. The stolen piece, which was never discovered, was an eighteenth-century reticulated vase made for the Emperor Quinlin by a man called Tang Ying. It was traced via two buyers, to a man in South Wales. Recently, papers of a South Wales Iron Master, a man called Samuel Fathergill, have been released to the public and are on the internet. They include a diary, in which he describes a visit to a man called Prosser, on the night of the Chartist uprising in Newport. Prosser showed him a vase he had bought. He had been told it was an excellent piece for a collector, which Prosser aspired to be. Fathergill recognised it as the piece stolen from the British Museum and advised Prosser to get rid of it. There's no further information about what Prosser did.'

'You read all of them?' Max asked.

'Yes, he means all of them,' Maggie said. 'That's several thousand pages of notes, all in the original handwriting.'

'You really are a nerd, dad,' Max said.

'I am, son. I also checked the lists of transportees to Australia in the months following the uprising. That's where I found William George Evans. But, like I said, he was a thief, with a well-known reputation for thieving, nothing to do with the Chartist march.'

Zelah sat forward. 'Did you check any details of his conviction? Or where he came from? Or what happened to him when he reached Australia?'

'No, there was no need at the time. He was convicted for the theft of two silver candlesticks. The complainant was a man called Pritchard. But,' he paused, putting a finger to his chin, 'he was arrested in Newport a month or so after the marchers who were caught, and he was taken to Monmouth gaol.' He shook his head. 'Maybe, I could have missed something.'

'Before anyone else says anything, here's what I'm proposing,' Maggie said. 'We know that Anthony Bandon said he had new information. So, although he's not able to tell us in person, let's go back and see what we had then and what we have now. Nick can start with William George Evans, the thief who went to Australia aboard the convict ship, and George Evans, who was with the marchers but who was let go, to find out if there was any relationship between them. Let's give it a week, then see what we've got. Personally, I want to read these papers and diaries by the man Fathergill. If we haven't got any further by the end of the week, we give it up. We won't mention the theft of the vase, so as far as Camberwell is concerned, we're just re-looking at the genealogy. What do you all say?'

There were several nods. No-one objected.

'Nick?' Maggie ventured. 'Are you in?'

'A reluctant yes, as I can see Stella nodding. But the minute we get so much as a sniff of Camberwell, I'm out.'

'Fair enough. Right, that's it then. But before we finish, everyone – you must be careful. Be watchful. And if anything, even the slightest thing out of the ordinary occurs, let me know immediately.'

Zelah said goodbye to the Irish group and stopped the recording. 'Time to get to work.'

'Not today,' Nick said. 'I'm taking Stella and Flora home. Max, you coming?'

'I am.'

'I have to go to work tonight,' Jack added.

'Let's leave it there until tomorrow, Zelah. I want to talk to Bob and let Finch and Abbott know that we're going to carry on, for now,' Maggie said.

'OK. I have a report to finish, so I'll be here for the next hour.' She paused. 'You are sure, aren't you?'

'Yes, but with nerves jangling just a bit,' Maggie replied. 'Let's hope we can at least settle the issue of the genealogy quickly, this time.'

'Don't hold your breath,' Zelah replied. 'I've got a feeling we missed something last time, which was not our fault, maybe because Mr Bandon held out on us, or just got it wrong himself.'

'Maybe he's OK and he'll turn up.'

'Don't hold your breath. But if he does turn up alive, he'll have some explaining to do – to Maze, as well as other interested parties.'

Chapter 5
November 1839

They had dined well, Samuel Fathergill had to admit.

He had been surprised to find he was the only guest of the lawyer turned coal mine owner Mervyn Prosser. Despite the unrest and the rumours of gatherings of Chartists in the valleys around his own town of Merthyr Tydfil, he hadn't been able to refuse the invitation, when Prosser confessed he had come into possession of an interesting piece of art and wanted his opinion. Fathergill had an excellent reputation as a collector and expert, particularly of fine pottery, and when Prosser wrote that his new piece was, he believed, Chinese, Fathergill set off to Malton Court with some excitement.

He hadn't had any great expectation of the dinner amongst what Prosser had described as 'a small gathering of likeminded friends'. Prosser was known to have no interest in the epicurean arts, as he had experienced some months ago when several of the iron and coal owners had come together at Prosser's newly built home. However, the temptation of examining a potentially rare piece of Oriental pottery was too great to ignore, so he travelled with two arms servants, just in case.

He wasn't surprised to discover, on arrival, that Prosser also had armed servants patrolling his estate.

'I have no belief they will dare to come near us,' Prosser said as he led Fathergill into the hall of the great house. 'But, best to be safe.'

Fathergill noticed that the house was otherwise silent. 'Your wife? I thought we were to be a small gathering?'

'I sent my wife away earlier in the day, to her brother, over in Bristol,' Prosser replied with a smile. 'I can assure you, my dear Fathergill, we are perfectly safe here. My men are more than able to defend my property. As for the other guests, they were not able to be with us.'

The speech intensified Fathergill's concern, rather than assuaging it. 'The talk is of hundreds assembling. Frost and Williams have been active these past days.'

Prosser would have spat on the carpet if it hadn't been another of his prized possessions. 'That man is a disgrace to his class. My friend Phillips, the Mayor, will deal with him as soon as this nonsense is over. Now, let me show you around.'

For the next half an hour Fathergill managed polite interest as Prosser conducted him around the main rooms of his new mansion. The house wasn't quite finished and the smell of paint and wood was strong. Fathergill made the expected comments of congratulation, before the two men entered the dining room.

The dinner was better than the previous occasion, but Fathergill couldn't help but notice the worried looks on the faces of the servants and the furtive glances exchanged between them, as the courses were served. On two occasions a man entered the room, whispered to Prosser, then left.

'A problem, Prosser?' he asked, after a third visit, when they had retired to the library.

'None,' Prosser replied, but his smile seemed forced.

'Perhaps we should get on with the business of the evening. Your new acquisition.' Fathergill was becoming alarmed at the background sounds of doors slamming and running footsteps.

'Indeed, let me fetch it.'

Prosser stood and walked across to a chest sitting in the corner, took a key from a drawer in an escritoire and opened the chest. He carefully brought out a small package, unwrapped the layers of cloth covering it, and turned around.

If he had expected to see delight and amazement on Fathergill's face, he was stunned by the expression that greeted him. Fathergill reached out and took the small vase in his hands, with immense care, but with anger.

'Where did you get this?'

'I … I bought it, from a most reputable dealer, in London, a man of known esteem, an expert in fine works,' Prosser blustered.

Fathergill took his eyes off the vase and gave Prosser a look that chilled him. 'I think you know that is not quite the truth, Prosser. And if you are so sure of it, why is it locked up in a chest and not on display in your fine new home?'

The quietly spoken words were enough. Prosser threw himself back into the chair he had vacated. 'He assured me it was genuine. Are you telling me it is not a true piece?'

'Oh no, not that. This is indeed a true piece. A true stolen piece.'

Prosser jumped up, took a few paces, then turned back to Fathergill, mouth open.

'Taken from the great Museum in London three weeks ago. Surely you read of the theft?' Fathergill added as he slowly rotated the centre of the vase and gazed in amazement as the scenes appearing under the top layer. 'This is the most beautiful thing I have ever seen. You must return it. Immediately.'

'But … but I paid a fortune for it,' Prosser blustered. 'I assure you, the man was genuine. I was introduced to him at a bona fide meeting, at a good club. You must be mistaken, Fathergill,' he said, now firm. 'Yes, it's you who are mistaken.'

'I am not mistaken. Look at the markings.' As he spoke Fathergill turned the vase upside down. 'This was made around a hundred years ago, for a Chinese emperor named Qianlong. The markings are clear.' Fathergill continued to gaze lovingly, with the vase now close to his face as he examined the detail.

Prosser didn't care about Chinese emperors or anyone else. He had bought the piece to impress his friends and fellows, once he was quite certain of it, that being the only reason he had invited Fathergill, whom he knew considered him not in the top echelon of South Wales iron and coal masters. He was about to rebuff any suggestion of returning the vase when a man burst into the room.

'Sir, they are marching in their hundreds, maybe thousands. They are already at Pontypool and will come down this way, towards Newport. William Jones is at their head, whipping them up,' the man said breathlessly.

'We must leave, immediately,' Fathergill said, jumping out of his chair and handing over the vase to Prosser, somewhat reluctantly. 'If they come upon you, they could do you – us – harm, or take us as hostages.'

For a moment Prosser looked bemused, then he nodded. He wrapped the vase in its swaddling, locked it in the trunk, and put the key back in the drawer.

He turned to the servant. 'Pritchard, I shall go with Mr Fathergill. Make sure they don't enter my property. You have weapons.'

'I do and I will, Sir.'

The two men left the house and launched themselves into Fathergill's coach, which hurtled down the drive at great speed and onto the Newport road, with the armed servants watching for any movement on the road. They didn't know how much time they had, but encountered no opposition before arriving some hours later at Fathergill's estate in the countryside on the outskirts of Merthyr.

For the next twenty four hours, as they waited for news from Newport, eventually receiving confirmation that the uprising had been defeated, there was no further discussion of the vase. Prosser decided he would deal with it on his return. It would be tricky, but he was uncertain now of his great prize and had no intention of becoming a laughing stock amongst his peers. He would find a way to quietly dispose of it and recoup some of his precious guineas.

Neither man had any idea that, throughout their discussion in the library they had been observed. The hidden watcher had seen the vase, and the opportunity.

Chapter 6

After Zelah had finished her report and left to go home, Maggie telephoned John Finch to let him know they had decided to return to the genealogy of Anthony Bandon, this time with a starting point of William George Evans.

'We couldn't prove he was Bandon's ancestor,' she explained. 'But we don't know if that was a genuine mistake on his part, or an attempt to mislead us.'

'But you weren't misled.'

'No, thanks to Nick's nerdity. And I know that's not a word, but it works for us.'

'Quite a good one, actually. So, you start working tomorrow?'

'Yes. We'll begin with more knowledge than last time, but we'll try to not let your issues interfere with or influence us. We're going to carry out a genealogy project.' She paused. 'And not without a lot of discussion and some fears. As you know, we held a get-together to make sure all our families are OK with us proceeding. This was the outcome. Genealogy only and for a week. When we've done all we can, I'll get back to you.'

For several seconds there was silence on the other end of the call.

'No, I need more than that.'

Maggie tensed. 'What does that mean?'

'I want someone there with you. I want the information as you find it. I said I would fund your research and I will, but I want my own person on your team. He or she, I haven't allocated an individual for the job yet, will report directly back to me, in real-time.'

'Then you didn't hear me. I said no interfering. I meant it.'

'My appointee won't be there to interfere, just to observe and report.'

She hesitated. 'I can't agree without running it past Zelah and Nick.'

'Then do so, and call me back once you have a decision.' After a few seconds of silence he added, 'You know, there are other genealogy investigators who could take the information and run with it.'

Maggie took a few seconds before she replied in what she hoped was a calm voice. 'Mr Finch, if you have somehow been led to believe that threatening me is a way to get what you want, then someone has thoroughly deceived you. And more fool you for believing whoever that was.' She hit the button to end the call.

**

Bob Pugh stopped dead in the kitchen doorway. He knew that expression. 'OK, what's happened?'

At speed and with much gesticulating, Maggie told him about Finch's requirement, before finishing with hands on hips.

'Right. Give me a minute, I'm just going to don my virtual riot shield and armour.' He took up a stance of a man ready to repel an advance. 'If I was him, I'd have done exactly the same.'

It took a second before she exploded, but just as she got started Jack appeared. 'Bob, why are you standing like that? Is it charades?'

'It's me repelling a full-on attack from your out-of-control mother.'

Jack glanced at Maggie. 'See what you mean. I'm going to stand behind you.' Once there he stuck his head out to the side. 'What's up, mother?'

Bob explained and Jack pulled his head back in. 'I can't see the problem, either,' came the voice from Bob's back. 'If whoever it is, just sits, watches, listens, and makes notes, how does that affect you?'

'Not funny. You don't understand, either of you,' she muttered, pushing past them and disappearing into the office, slamming the door shut.

Jack stood in front of Bob. 'You going to try to talk to her?'

'No.'

'Me neither. Cooking our own dinner, then?'

'Looks like it.'

**

Nothing had improved by the following morning. Bob left for work shortly after six, leaving Maggie asleep. By seven thirty she was in the office, reading more of the Fathergill papers when her phone rang. John Finch. She listened to his information and ended the call without speaking.

When Zelah and Nick arrived at eight-thirty, she pounced on them before they could draw breath.

'Do you want the bad news, or the even worse news?'

'Go on,' Nick said.

'Finch has insisted we have a member of his team with us at all times, so they can report back to him in real-time instead of waiting for a report like a client usually does.'

Nick shrugged. 'As long as they don't get in the way, or offer "helpful suggestions",' he replied. Maggie stared at him in disbelief. 'You don't mind?'

'Not really, as long as we set the rules and he, or she, sticks to them. What about you Zelah? Do you care if we're being watched?'

'Yes, I do. Whoever it is will have to keep well out of my way. Let's hope it's someone who can transform themselves into a fly on the wall and not ask any questions.' She gave Maggie a piercing gaze. 'You didn't tell him to sod off, I'm presuming.'

'Not exactly. I said more or less what you're saying. The even worse news is – Finch called half an hour ago. The person is Olivia Abbott.'

'Well, she'll have to get used to being ignored,' Zelah said, as the front doorbell rang.

'That's probably her now. I'll get it,' Maggie said.

She showed Olivia into the office and pointed at a chair. 'We're about to start our morning meeting. You're welcome to take notes.'

Today Olivia was dressed in a black business suit with a white blouse, her hair fashioned into a plait wrapped around her head, her face perfectly made up. She carried a briefcase from which she took a notepad and pen. Nick noticed that the pen was a well-known and expensive make of fountain pen. She removed the gold top and sat poised.

'Would you like something to drink? Tea, coffee?' Nick said.

'No, thank you.'

'Then we'll get going, but before we do, Olivia, there are a couple of rules, which I have already explained to Inspector Finch. We have agreed you can join us, as an observer. Genealogy is our business and our expertise. We don't expect input from you. And of course, everything you hear in this room is confidential. We know you're going to share it with Finch, but it goes no further beyond him.'

The frozen smile didn't leave Olivia Abbott's face. She gave the slightest tip of her head.

They quickly glanced at each other. 'Right, who's going to start?'

'Before we get down to the detail, I'd like more information about what happened on the night of 4th November 1839,' Zelah said. 'I don't know enough about the events of the uprising and what actually happened when the marchers reached the Westgate Hotel, nor the aftermath. I do know it was a rout. Nick, can you give us a quick precis?'

'I'll sum it up as best I can. Well, there had been restlessness and unease for several months, on account of the Charter.'

'What exactly was the Charter?' Zelah asked. 'I don't know that, either.'

'It was a demand to the Government, comprising six points. It came about because of the manner in which the Iron and Coal Masters had control over every aspect of their workers' lives. The wages were delivered in company coin that could only be spent in the company shops where the prices were inflated, meaning most families were always in debt. Massive poverty, long working hours, and so on, whilst the Masters raked in the money. Of course, this was considered by the middle and ruling classes to be a God-given right with everyone in his anointed place. But, the working people didn't agree. The Chartist movement came about to give the workers political rights and some influence. It was almost the equivalent of the French Revolution, grown out of the perceived injustices of the growing industrial influence. The Charter had six points: male suffrage …'

'What does that mean?' Olivia asked.

'It's the right of every man to have a vote,' Maggie replied. 'It was only men at the time, not women.'

'Carrying on,' Nick said. 'Then, there was a secret ballot to elect representatives, annual parliaments, paid members of Parliament, equal electoral districts, and the abolition of the requirement to own property as a means to a vote.'

'We've got all that,' Olivia interrupted again.

'None of it was available, back then. Only men who owned property could vote and the senior ones chose their candidates, with the votes publicly recorded. That was the Charter. It was presented to Parliament, which rejected it out of hand. That's when it began to get more physical. One of the main leaders – a man called Henry Vincent - had been imprisoned for making inflammatory remarks. That was in May 1839 and in August he was sentenced to a year in prison, where he was denied all books and writing material. This was seen as unjust and agitated the Chartist movement. In part, it gave rise to the uprising that culminated in Newport, where the crowd wanted Vincent and others freed.'

Olivia muttered something under her breath.

'What was that?' Zelah demanded.

'Nothing.'

'It wasn't nothing. What did you just say?'

Olivia realised that Zelah had caught her remark. There was no point in prevaricating. 'I said: *bloody Marxist agitators.*'

Maggie opened her mouth, but Nick got there first. 'Well, Olivia, perhaps we should have insisted you take a History 101 course before joining us. Karl Marx was born in 1818, so he was just twenty years old when the uprising happened. And at the time he was a student in Germany. So, if you want to remain with this team, keep your ignorant opinions to yourself.'

Maggie closed her mouth. It wasn't often that Nick let rip, but she could see red spots on his cheeks, and his lips were pressed shut.

Olivia had also reddened, with narrowing eyes and pursed mouth projecting deep anger in Nick's direction.

'Olivia, we agreed that you should be here to observe, as I thought I had clarified,' said Maggie. 'Any more remarks like that and I'll show you the door. We don't need this project; we have plenty of work.'

'For now,' Olivia said. 'That could change.'

Zelah stood up. 'That is a direct threat to my – our - company. OK, Maggie, let's stop everything now. Please get on the phone to Finch and tell him we're done.' She turned to Olivia. 'If you are suggesting you and your boss could damage our business and our integrity, then think again. Now, pick up your belongings and get out.'

Olivia remained seated and stared at Zelah, a small smile forming on her lips. 'I don't think so,' she said in a quiet voice.

Maggie was already on the phone to Finch. She took the call into the hallway, as the silent standoff continued in the office. A few minutes later, she returned. 'He's on his way,' she said. 'You are to remain here until he arrives, but you will not stay in this room. Move yourself into the living room. Now. If you don't I will ask Nick and my son, who is upstairs to assist you.'

Olivia stood up, picked up her notepad and pen, and left the room. Maggie closed the door once she was in the living room and returned to the office.

'Well, that went well,' she remarked. The tension broken, Nick grinned and Zelah chuckled.

'Seriously though, what are we going to do when Finch arrives?' Nick asked. 'I'm sorry I said what I did, but there's something about her that worries me. Her energy is dark.'

'That's always a worrying sign,' Maggie replied. 'You're right Nick, we can't have her here, but I suspect Finch may try to smooth things over.'

'I'm not for being smoothed,' Zelah snapped. 'He's already said there are other genealogy companies. Let him find one that could move as fast as we can on this case. And as for her, no way is she staying.'

'Why don't we get on with talking about the case,' Maggie said. 'Zelah is there any more history you need to know?'

'I want to hear more about the marchers and what happened to them,' Zelah replied. 'If Bandon's ancestor did get transported, why did that happen?'

'In the end, there were only three who were actually transported as a direct result of the Newport uprising,' Nick replied. They were the leaders, John Frost, a former Mayor of Newport, Zephaniah Williams a master collier, and William Jones, who was a former actor and at the time of the uprising also a watchmaker. They were originally sentenced to be hung, drawn, and quartered for treason, but the sentence was commuted to transportation after massive national appeals to Queen Victoria. There were three more who were sentenced to transportation, for what was called the "drilling of men in the use of firearms". They weren't from Newport, but from Montgomery. And it was earlier in the year. They were Abraham Owen, Humphreys Lewis, and John Ingram.'

'Could Bandon's ancestor have been one of those?' Maggie asked.

'Possibly. I didn't check the first time around. Others were sentenced to transportation as a direct result of Newport, but in the end, they weren't transported. I'll have to go back into the records to find out what happened to them. I think there were also another four a bit later on. That gives us seven to check out immediately.'

'That's where you and I can start, Zelah,' Maggie replied. 'Nick, can you make a start on the others who were sentenced and what happened to them?'

'Just hang on a minute. Why are we talking about pursuing this? We just said we won't work with Olivia Abbott so, aren't we going to tell Finch where to shove his money?'

'I wasn't aware we said we'd stop, Zelah. Just that we won't work with Olivia if she's going to be an interfering nuisance.'

Zelah shrugged. 'There's to be no negotiation about her. That's my line and I'm not crossing it.'

'I'm not arguing,' Maggie agreed. 'Nick, are you prepared to carry on, if it works out with Finch?'

He nodded. 'As long as she's not here. I'm not comfortable around her. Anyway, first I want to get on with the full story of William George Evans and how he ended up on a convict ship.'

'Lots to do, then. I can also give you a quick update on the Fathergill papers if you like. I read them yesterday afternoon and this morning.'

'We need everything we can get,' Zelah said. 'And there's another issue that we haven't addressed. How many of them came back to Britain?'

'I'll research that one, too,' Nick said. 'It could be the key to this vase story.'

The doorbell rang, three times.

'Finch,' Maggie said. 'Let's find out if it's worth starting anything.'

Chapter 7
November 1839 Newport

George Evans couldn't hold in his tears of pain a minute longer. He had decided on a plan to burst out of the cupboard, praying the surprise would momentarily shock Fathergill and Prosser into giving him the vital seconds to escape from the room. He drew in a deep breath and put his hand on the door ready to push when the servant entered the room.

Saved!

Two minutes later the men were gone. He heard the sounds of shouting as they gathered overcoats and sticks and headed out of the building. Slowly, tentatively he opened the cupboard and crawled out. His knees, which had been tucked up behind him for two hours, screamed with agony as he unfolded them. He realised he would never have been able to tumble out and run, as the pins and needles slowly subsided and he wobbled to his feet.

Listening carefully, he heard only a door slam in the distance. Holding onto a chair as life and muscle power returned to his cramped legs – he hesitated. The story of the vase had been fascinating. Fathergill said it was worth a small fortune but, it was stolen. Ha! So much for the mighty Mervyn Prosser, now the possessor of illegal goods. George had to take a look.

Guessing from the sounds he had heard of a drawer opening and closing, he quickly discovered the location of the key. It was weighty, but given the size of the trunk sitting in the corner of the room, the only piece of furniture with a lock, it must be the right one. He crept over to the door, opened it an inch, and listened. No sounds. Back to the trunk. The key turned once. He carefully held up the lid. There was one item inside. He took it out. Smaller than he had expected. He unwrapped the layers. The vase was no more than eight inches high. He wasn't impressed by the patterns and scenes. Foreign stuff. Still, he knew a good fence in Cardiff who would likely take it off his hands for a fair sum. He wrapped it up again, tucked it into the deep inside pocket of his overcoat, specially designed for holding his takings, re-locked the trunk, then returned the key to the drawer. No need for Prosser to realise right away that his treasure was gone.

Returning to the cupboard he picked up the sack of food he had taken from the kitchen where he had broken in. No need to leave that behind, either.

Back to the door. No noise. He walked stealthily across the hallway, where the sound of rain hammering on the glass ceiling window muffled his footsteps, past the stairs, all his senses on alert. Pausing again at the front door, he opened it slowly. A slight creak made his heart jump. Stepping outside he closed the door and began to walk rapidly down the driveway.

'Oi, you! What are you doing!'

The servant. Damnation! He began to run. At fifty-five he was still fit enough to put on a good turn of speed. Multiple footsteps behind him meant there was more than one person. He glanced around as he ran, looking for somewhere to conceal himself but there was nowhere. Panting now, lungs straining, he could see the gates leading out onto the Newport road. There were some lights, perhaps a building where he could shelter, and shrug off his pursuers.

But, the lights were moving. Too late, as he ran through the gates and along the road he found himself confronted by a crowd of men, torches held aloft, many carrying pikes and wicked looking long sharpened sticks. He stopped in front of them.

'Who are you, then?' said the leader. 'What's in the sack, brother?'

George Evans couldn't speak. He put his hands on his knees and panted, then stood up. 'Food,' he panted. 'I've just taken it from the kitchen at Prosser's house. They're chasing me.'

Prosser! One of the hated names. 'We'll share that with you, brother, and you'll come with us.'

George began to protest. 'It's for my family.'

'We're your family tonight,' the leading man said, pushing him into the first rows of the crowd. 'We're for Newport, to join Frost. You'll come with us. Oh, look, brothers, what have we here?'

The servant had arrived, followed by two old men, both of whom were wheezing and panting.

'More recruits to join us, indeed. Sent by Prosser, eh?' The surrounding crowd laughed and jeered.

'John Pritchard, Mr Prosser's personal manservant. You will not lay hands on me,' Pritchard replied.

'And what about these two?'

The two older men raised their heads. 'Gardener and coachman, we are.'

'Then you can accompany us too.'

They protested, but to no avail. Pritchard, seeing what was about to happen, turned and ran. A few of the men from the crowd went to run after him, but their leader stopped them.

'Leave him.' He turned to the two old men. 'Is Prosser at home?'

They shook their heads.

'Run away, eh. Man's a coward as well as an oppressor of good working people.' He signalled to two of his companions. 'Put them in the centre, where we can keep an eye on them.' He turned back to the old men. 'You are for the Charter, now. We're going to protest and free our compatriots, that Mayor Phillips has taken - against the rightful law – and held at the Westgate. We're to meet up with Frost and Williams tonight. Let them find out how much the Charter means to us. Let's go!'

Their enthusiasm was great, despite the unrelenting rain. George Evans realised they must have been on the march for hours and there was some dissent about which was the best way to progress. Some wanted to wait for further instructions. Others wanted to divert across the canal and follow the path via Bettws to the agreed meeting place at Cefn Most were soaked to the skin, but their eyes and expressions were determined and fervent. His best bet, for now, was to go with them, until he could find a way to get away from them. He had no care or concern for the Charter. The workers would always be under the yoke of men like Prosser, Phillips, Crawshay Bailey, Homfrey, and the rest. His way, stealing from them, was better. To his right he could see the gardener and the coachman, muttering, angry, but watching him. He'd have to move further away from them. In the end the group split in two. George, the gardener and the coachman were taken with the group that had decided to make for Cefn.

After an hour's marching George hadn't yet found a way to extract himself.. And, he had discovered, he wasn't the only reluctant Chartist that night. From the conversations around him, he learnt they had taken men wherever they found them on the march down to Newport. At a stop outside a public house, where the leaders entered and took food and beer, one man tried to escape. He ran as far as the canal and jumped in, but had been chased and dragged out, and brought back to the march.

By dawn, they had reached the hamlet of Cefn, where they found a crowd of thousands already assembled. George Evans had never seen the leader of the Chartist movement – John Frost. Yet, here he was, walking amongst them, encouraging, in a quiet voice, urging them to remember what there was to gain. George could only think about what there was to lose. Despite a couple of possibilities, there had been no means of escape. He became more fearful that he would have to go all the way, down into the town. Perhaps he could keep to the back of the crowd. There had to be a way out. A hundred yards away he spotted the roof of a sizeable farmhouse and began to walk towards it. One of the men who had been appointed a group leader went to stop him, but George shook him off.

'If the house is empty we can shelter there.'

The man nodded. 'Bring any food you find, and drink. Elias, go with him.'

George growled, but he couldn't protest. The man Elias had a pike and he prodded George ahead of him. They fought their way through a hedge, entered the back of the house, and found it empty. There was little food to be found, but they took what was there and returned to the crowd where the food and beer was divided up.

More Chartists arrived during the night. Before dawn, they set off again, now a crowd of around five thousand men from the valleys of South Wales, the iron works, and the coal pits, all united in their determination to see the Charter succeed. The final phase of the march on the Westgate Hotel in Newport had begun.

Chapter 8

Maggie stood in front of a grim-faced John Finch on the doorstep.

'Before I let you in, I want to be clear about two things. One: we did not provoke this. Two: there is to be no shouting and recrimination. Now you can come in. Nick, Zelah, and I are in the office. Olivia is in the living room.'

He walked past her, into the living room. Ten minutes later he entered the office.

'Olivia is sorry for her comments. She wishes to apologise.'

'Big deal,' Zelah said. 'We had an agreement. She broke it less than a quarter of an hour into our first discussion. We don't need that, nor do we need you. But,' she gave him a piercing look, 'you need us. And don't think your threats to go to another genealogy company bother us. See if you can find someone else to take this on from scratch. Camberwell will be so far ahead you'll never catch up.'

'Is she speaking for all of you?' Finch said.

'Of course she is,' Nick snapped.

'Mrs Gilbert?'

Maggie didn't reply, but stared at him, arms folded and scowling.

'OK, OK, I give in. What do you want?'

'What – exactly – is she sorry for?' Maggie asked.

'For interrupting. Her views are her views. But I have made it clear that if – and I mean if – you allow her to stay, she observes.

The next time she opens her mouth, she's out.' He paused. 'I don't think she will. The prospect of recovering the vase, however small a chance there is, is too important to her to not be here. Second chances, please.'

'Give us five minutes,' Maggie said. Finch nodded and left the room.

'Straw poll,' Maggie said. 'I've calmed down, so I'll give her another chance.'

'No,' Nick said. 'There's something else going on with her.'

'On the fence,' Zelah said. 'However, if Nick's right, maybe it's better to have her close, where we can keep an eye on her. She thinks she's watching us. We can watch her, whilst she's trapped in here. What do you say, Nick?'

He gazed up at the ceiling and around the walls. Zelah sat back with her arms folded. This was Nick. No point trying to hurry him.

After a couple of minutes, he said, 'OK. I don't know what she's up to, but we should be guarded in her presence. Business only.'

'Works for me,' Maggie replied. 'I'll let Finch know.'

Finch and Olivia accompanied her back into the office.

'I apologise,' Olivia said, through gritted teeth. 'I will not be commenting in future on anything you say or do.'

'How very heartfelt,' Zelah snapped.

'Like one of my kids when they were little,' Maggie added. 'Sorry – not sorry. Whatever, we accept your apology.' Olivia tensed, her hands balling into fists. *Serves her right*, Maggie thought. 'We need to get on. This has been an unhelpful interruption.'

'The price just went up,' Zelah aimed at Finch. 'And fifty percent upfront. Just like a normal client.'

He remained stone-faced. 'I'll leave you all to it.'

They took their seats around the table.

'OK, we all know what we're doing. Let's get on with it,' Maggie said.

'Just a minute,' Olivia interrupted. 'I don't know what you're doing.'

'Tough,' Zelah replied. 'You'll just have to watch and work it out. We share our information as we go along when we're all working on the same case.'

Olivia's cheeks flushed the colour of a ripe beetroot, but she held in the burst of abuse they could see was straining to get past her lips. With a grin, Maggie, Nick, and Zelah took up their positions at their computers, leaving Olivia sitting at the conference table with her notebook and designer pen.

**

Two hours later, as Olivia scribbled furiously, Maggie called a halt. She stretched her arms and shoulders. 'Time for a break. Lunch?'

'Actually, I'm ready to get out. How about a field trip?' Zelah said.

'What did you have in mind, Zelah?'

'I'd like to go down to Newport, walk down Stow Hill from the Cathedral to the Westgate Hotel, take a look through the eyes of a Chartist marcher.'

Maggie and Nick looked at each other and nodded.

'We can go to a local pub for lunch, after. Let's go, then. Olivia, are you coming with us?'

'No, thank you. I don't see the need.' It was the only time she had spoken in the past two hours.

'Suit yourself. You'll have to find somewhere to go, then, because you aren't staying here,' Maggie said. 'Please give me your phone number and I'll call you when we get back.'

Olivia scribbled the number on a post-it note which she flung onto the table, then stood, took her coat and bags, and left the room, slamming the front door as she let herself out.

Maggie picked up the note and entered the number into her phone. 'Are we being mean to her?'

'No,' Zelah and Nick said in unison.

Maggie chuckled. 'Fine with me. Let's go. I'll drive.'

They parked at the base of St Woolos Cathedral, which stood on a small but steep incline leading onto Stow Hill. The wind, which had been sharp when they left Maggie's house, had picked up and chosen the Cathedral as a target for some serious gusts.

'Let's get this over with,' Zelah said, as they buttoned coats and tightened scarves.

'We'll start with a visit to the memorial to the ten Chartists buried in the grounds,' Nick shouted over the wind. 'It's not the actual grave. No-one knows where it was, or who most of them were.'

'If we must,' Zelah muttered.

The memorial was a stone plaque, with an inscription. Maggie took a photograph. 'Should we go inside?'

'No, it doesn't look open and anyway, we need to get on so we can get warm again. I can't feel my toes.'

Nick led the way around the graves and onto the road. 'The marchers came past here,' he indicated where the main road continued, and marched down the hill. Let's go.'

They used the raised walkway on Stow Hill to follow the marchers' route down into the town.

'People in the houses lining the walkway would probably have watched, fearfully, from indoors. And down there,' he pointed to the impressive catholic church, 'St Mary's Catholic Church was being built. Stories tell of the workmen on the roof watching the marchers, but refusing to down tools and join in when they saw the marchers coming. John Frost was at the front, easily spotted due to his red scarf, urging the men on. It must have been an incredible sight.'

'Are there any buildings left from that time?' Maggie asked.

'I don't know,' Nick replied. 'I've seen a list of buildings that were here, in a directory of 1848. It was a mixture of shops and private residences. It was fairly affluent, with solicitors, engineers, boot makers, drapers, and so on. The Union workhouse was also here, plus a number of private offices for agents of local companies and iron masters.'

At the bottom of the hill, they crossed the road and turned right into Commercial Street towards the Westgate Hotel.

'This is where it all went down. And went wrong,' Nick said. 'The battle lasted about twenty minutes. The Mayor, Thomas Phillips, had had soldiers brought in from England and they were well armed. Plus, they were better prepared than the marchers, despite their numbers and weapons. Naively, Frost thought with the numbers he had, he could negotiate a surrender.'

They stood in front of the hotel, staring at its portico.

'I don't see any bullet holes. Are they really there?' Maggie asked.

'Lots of opinions for yes and no,' Nick replied. 'Historians were divided for a while over whether they are actual bullet holes or just the remains of metal stanchions, but now it's mostly believed that they are, indeed, bullet holes from the confrontation. However, this portico was added at a later date. The bullet holes are inside, behind the front door.'

'It must be a real mess inside,' Maggie said.

'They say it's still beautiful. It has Grade II listed status. Work has been going on with the current owners, to open it occasionally for some events. It's the site of the last armed rebellion in British history, so it should be taken care of.'

'How many died, Nick?' she asked.

'Twenty-two dead, and dozens injured, maybe hundreds. I suspect they panicked.'

'So, they ran in all directions from here,' Zelah said, rubbing her hands together and blowing on them.

'Yes, some back up Stow Hill, some down the High Street, others towards the castle and the river. Some were caught, and others got away but were captured later. There was a huge effort to catch as many as possible and put them on trial. It really was a major national event.'

'What did Bandon have to say about his relative and whatever was his part in the march, if he played any part?' Zelah asked.

'Nothing, he didn't have that level of detail.'

'Nick, do we know where the supposed relative lived in Newport?'

'Not yet, but I'm working on it.'

'Right,' Zelah said, rubbing her cheeks now. 'Let's get out of this freezing cold. It must be time for lunch. Where shall we go?'

Maggie looked around. 'How about going back out towards home? There's the Greenhouse Inn out at Llantarnum. Wasn't it supposed to have been one of the stopping places for the marchers?'

Nick nodded. 'Yes, and the food's good.'

**

57

Over lunch, they made plans about how to continue, but Zelah was pessimistic about what they could achieve.

'If you haven't found any more confirmation about Bandon's relative, Nick, I can't see how we're going to proceed until we clarify and confirm who he actually was.'

'Difficult without Bandon,' Maggie replied. 'Well, we said we'd give it a week, so let's keep going. And if we can't get any further, so be it.'

'Agreed,' Zelah said. 'Time to get back.'

'I'll let Olivia know we'll be home in ten minutes,' Maggie said, dialling the number. It rang but wasn't answered and she left a message. 'Up to her, if she bothers to pick it up,' she said as they left the pub.

When they arrived at the house, Olivia was already there, sitting in her car, engaged in an animated conversation on her phone.

'Wow, look at those jabbing fingers,' said Zelah. 'She's not a happy bunny.'

'Must be on the receiving end of another diatribe from Finch,' Maggie said as she went in, leaving the door open. 'None of our business. She took off her coat, and sat at the table without speaking.

She was about to say something else when an incoming email took her attention.

'OMG! I don't believe this!'

Nick and Zelah turned around in their chairs to face her.

'It's from Anthony Bandon. He's alive and well. And, more to the point, still in Australia.'

Chapter 9
Newport 1839

George Evans was running, as fast as he could, to get as far away as possible from the Westgate Hotel.

Disaster! He had managed to remove himself towards the middle ranks of the marchers and thought he had lost the gardener and the coachman, when the front of the march reached the Westgate Hotel, spreading out, facing the entrance. George was still on the hill, just past the new church of St Mary where he had seen men who had been putting tiles on the roof scrambling down and running away. There was a roar of shouting voices, then screaming, then shots.

'They're killing our men,' someone shouted. 'Let's kill them.'

Some in the crowd shouted back, but many looked uncertain. They edged forward when suddenly, a group of men came charging back up the hill. 'We're done for!' one shouted. 'Our men are dead! Soldiers are killing them!'

That was enough. The crowd dispersed with screams of anguish and despair, many throwing down their weapons as they made their way back up or further on down the hill. In the chaos, George had to think quickly. He needed to get away, not be caught, for how would he explain the vase hidden inside his coat? He must get rid of it. Hide it somewhere safe.

His house was at the bottom of Pillgwenlly, close to the river Usk. He made a rapid decision and began to run down the hill. As he crossed the road opposite the Westgate, he glimpsed bodies lying on the ground, bleeding and moaning. He ran along Commercial Street, taking advantage of the chaos and mayhem.

He ran for five minutes amid a group of desperate men, as the crowd around him lessened, past closed shops and boarded-up houses, until he reached the church of St Paul. He was in pain from the effort, barely able to catch his breath. Inside the church gates, he glimpsed a small hut. Letting himself inside, he carefully closed the iron gate behind him and jammed it shut with a plank of wood lying against the inner wall, then hid behind the hut.

He could hear running footsteps on the road beyond the gate, with manic shouting. A few times the gate rattled and he held his breath, but the plank of wood did not break and the person moved on.

As his breathing slowly returned to normal, he glanced around the churchyard. The church had been open a few years earlier but had no graveyard. Nothing for him here. After another half an hour, or so he judged, the sounds of running had stopped. Tentatively he peaked around the hut. No-one in sight. Letting himself out he started to walk. It took every ounce of discipline he had not to run. Ten minutes later he sauntered around the corner of High Street Pillgwenlly and strolled up to the front of his house. A gathering of neighbours stood in the middle of the street, talking in low voices. Keeping his face neutral, he approached.

'Been some big happening, up in the town,' he said conversationally. 'What's been doing?'

'Haven't you heard? Frost and his men have taken the Westgate for the Charter. They'll be here soon.'

'What will they do, then, Morris?' George asked, feigning concern.

'Don't rightly know, George,' said his next-door neighbour. 'I reckon we should stay at home, wait to hear ...'

They turned as two men came running around the corner, clothes in tatters, one of them bleeding from a head wound.

'All lost,' the bleeding man panted, wiping tears from his face. 'All lost. They'll be coming to find us, and anyone else there.'

The second man looked at George. 'You was there,' he said.

'Not me,' George protested. 'I've just arrived, come from the Cardiff Road. Saw a crowd running. You didn't see me. Must have been someone looked like me. Not me.' He looked at his neighbours, in a mute appeal to speak up for him.

'He didn't know what happened,' said the man Morris. 'We all thought you'd won.'

The man, still directing a sharp look at George, said, 'The soldiers began to shoot. Some of our men shot back, but we was outnumbered with guns. There was panic. We got away, but everyone around here knows we've been for the Charter.' He turned to the bleeding man. 'We can't stay. We'll have to run. I have a brother up in Dowlais. We'll go there, until the fuss dies down.' He turned to George. 'You coming?'

'Me, no. Why should I? I tell you, I wasn't there.' He turned away and shouted over his shoulder, 'I'm going home. I want nothing to do with you and your Charter.'

He stomped up to his house, head held high until he was inside with the door closed behind him. Then, he stopped in the dark hallway, panting, using the wall to keep him upright as his legs shook, before grabbing onto the bottom of the stair rail.

Soldiers would be coming and probably the special constables. He could protest he wasn't there, unless they could find someone to identify him. The coachman and the gardener! He had to find somewhere to hide the vase. Without it, if he was taken into custody he could claim that he had been kidnapped on the road, forced onto the march, as they had been. He would say he had taken food and drink from Prosser's house. The man Pritchard might know by now that something else was missing, if Prosser had returned home. But if not, then he still had time. But what to do with the vase? He supposed he could throw it in the river, be rid of it. But his avaricious nature wouldn't allow him to let go of an article supposedly of immense value. Maybe there was somewhere along the river he could hide it. The river was tidal, its banks muddy. Could he find somewhere, a place he could return to and retrieve it when peace had been restored?

He thought and thought. That was it. Bury it in the river, near to one of the pills where the ships came into unload and load again. If he wrapped it carefully, it should survive. There were places along the river …

He kept to himself throughout the following four days, not going outside, jumping at every noise from the street. On the fourth evening he ventured out to the Ship and Pilot Inn in Commercial Street. This had been the scene of meetings of both men and women supporters of the Charter in previous months, when Henry Vincent had addressed a crowd gathered there. This would still be a venue for Chartist supporters. There might be some useful information.

This evening the mood was sombre. George heard that soldiers had been on the streets, questioning, searching houses. He shuddered. The vase was in a sack under the bed. If anyone mentioned his name and they came to search, it would be found and he would be done for.

'What say you, George? George?' His neighbour had shaken his arm and laughed.

'Just thinking. What's happening in the town, then?'

'They say the Constables are rounding up anyone who might come under suspicion and putting them in the Union. They started examining them today, I hear.'

George shuddered. 'I heard some died.'

The neighbour leaned in and whispered. 'They say a group who died was taken up to the church at St Woolos and buried there. No names given.'

'There must have been many wounded,' he ventured.

'They say they're running home, back up to the valleys. If they can run, sheltering where they can. Those that can't run will get buried, quietly, I should think.'

'Bad days to come,' George said shaking his head. 'I'm for home.' He stood and walked to the door without looking back at the neighbour, who shook his head, then turned back to the group of men sitting at the table. 'Something bothering him, no doubt. Think he was there? He said he weren't.'

'Nah,' said another. 'Not George Evans. He don't believe in the Charter. He believes in himself. Don't have enough room in his head for anyone else.' There was a ripple of laughter and the conversation moved on.

At the door, George looked around, listened, and waited. No sound of footsteps in this or the nearby streets. He ran along Commercial street and around to his front door, let himself in, then barred it behind him. An idea had begun to expand itself in his head. Something in the conversation. He shook his head. He went up to his bed, tried to sleep, but failed, kicked his snoring wife, then returned to the kitchen, took out the gin bottle, poured a glass, downed it in one, all the time listening. He needed to make the vase safe, somewhere. What had they been discussing?

It came to him, as he sat in the darkness. The perfect answer. He laughed. No-one could ever find it, where he was planning to put it.

At midnight George Evans left his house. He was away for two hours. His wife slept and asked no questions. She had learned long before that questioning his business resulted in a beating.

Someone else was awake in the house in the darkness, listening. His daughter Mary Ann heard him pace around, return to the bedroom for a few minutes, then back down the stairs, along the corridor, and out.

She thought about following him but decided against it. Plenty of time to question him in the morning. Mary Ann Evans had no fear of her father. She knew he was up to something and that something would not be anything good. She would find out, whatever it was.

Chapter 10

With Nick and Zelah on her shoulder, Maggie scanned through the email from Anthony Bandon.

Hi Maggie, sorry for not getting back in touch. Family emergency in NSW so had to be away for a couple of weeks. As I said, I have new information. Can we have a Zoom, please? Tomorrow at 9 am for you? Anthony B.

'Well bless his little Aussie heart. He's OK,' Zelah said. 'Strange he doesn't mention the police have been looking for him.'

'If he's only just returned home, maybe he doesn't know yet,' Nick suggested.

'I'm going to accept. I'll set up the call and we'll find out tomorrow morning.'

'Just a minute. You can't do that.'

Maggie turned around. 'Yes we can, Olivia. This is our client.'

'No, Mr Finch is your client. You'll have to get his permission.'

Maggie saw Zelah's hackles rising. 'No, Olivia. Both are our clients. We are looking at aspects of the same case, that's all. I'm going to set up the call. If you feel the need, you call Finch.' She turned back, indicating to Zelah to zip her mouth, which was met with a glare, but with acquiescence.

Maggie typed a response, then set up the video call. She glanced at the time on her laptop. 'It's almost three. Time for a re-cap?'

Zelah and Nick both moved to the table, as Maggie swung her chair around. Neither looked at Olivia.

'I'll start. I've been reading the Fathergill papers. One of the issues we originally had was that there was no report anywhere of an important and – or – valuable item being stolen at the time, as Anthony Bandon claimed last year. From what I've read, Fathergill made it clear to Prosser that the vase was stolen, which may account for why Prosser never publicised its disappearance. From the diary, it also appears that Fathergill himself didn't tell anyone Prosser had it. He decided to keep schtum. Probably didn't want the awkwardness of being associated with it, especially after Prosser's involvement with the aftermath of the uprising.'

'Makes sense,' Nick said. 'Entirely possible Prosser either moved it on or destroyed it.'

Can't see him destroying it,' Zelah put in. 'From historical evidence and those accounts, he was a man who wanted his worth to be known. Despite knowing the vase was stolen, he might just have kept it to show it to close friends.'

Nick shook his head. 'From what Anthony Bandon told us, the "valuable item" that dated from the time of the uprising could well have been this vase, and it could have been stolen from Prosser by his relative. How else would a man who was transported have got his hands on it?'

'Is there anything on record about a man being transported for stealing from Prosser?' Maggie asked.

'Not that I've found, yet. I'm still going back over witness statements. There are several men called Evans, and, as we know, the only one put on trial was George Evans who was forced into the march and subsequently let go. ' He paused. 'I wonder if Anthony Bandon got the wrong man? That would make more sense, now. Perhaps that's what he's going to tell us tomorrow.'

'You didn't search widely enough last time, then, did you?'

'We did what we could with the information we had, Olivia. And you aren't supposed to comment.'

Olivia shrugged and smiled pointedly at Zelah, then picked up her phone and left the room.

'She's bloody infuriating,' Zelah muttered. 'I don't know if I can stand much more.'

'What do we do now?' Maggie asked, deciding to avoid being drawn in, as much as Olivia annoyed her too.

'I think we wait for Bandon, in the morning,' Nick said. 'If he's found more detailed information, it will save us time and effort.'

'Inspector Finch gives you permission to carry on,' Olivia said, as she walked back into the office, giving Zelah another smug smile.

Zelah jumped up and Maggie decided this might be the time to physically intervene, but Zelah said, 'I'm going home. I'll see you all back here in the morning.'

She picked up her coat and bag, swept past Olivia as if she wasn't there, and let herself out.

'You can go, too,' Maggie said to Olivia. 'We've finished for the day.'

As soon as the door closed on Olivia, Maggie turned to Nick. 'I don't know about you but I'm going to put in another hour. I want to know as much as possible before we speak to Anthony in the morning.'

'Me too. I want to get more into who William George Evans and George Evans were. Was there any biological relationship between them?'

'Unlikely. Too many men at the time called Evans. And George and William. I'm going to re-examine Anthony Bandon's line of descent. I want it ready in the morning. I remember we had some problem finding out the provenance of his three times great grandparents around the time of the uprising.'

'Yes. He gave us the name William George Evans and he was convinced it was correct. But that's looking less likely.'

'Let's get to it, then,' Maggie said.

**

Nick finally left at six, just before Bob arrived home. Maggie greeted him warily.

'How was your day?'

'Not good,' he growled. Then, 'Sorry. Our surveillance is turning up nothing at all. Another two days, she who must be obeyed says. Then, we have to pack it in.'

'I thought you had a week?'

'So did I, but with nothing at all to report, she's decided it's not worth the budget. Two days.' He slapped his hands onto the office table, palms down, then lowered his head, stretching his neck muscles.

Maggie walked up behind him and put her arms around his waist. 'Sorry,' she said.

He stood up and turned around, smiling at her. 'Good job I've got you to come home to.' He leaned down and kissed her. The tender moment was broken by Jack bursting into the room. 'I'm off to work – oops, sorry.'

They broke apart, laughing.

'Have a good shift,' Maggie said. 'What time do you finish?'

'Midnight.'

'Be careful, then,' Bob added.

Jack grinned and left them.

'Come on,' Maggie said. 'Let's get something to eat and I'll tell you about my day.'

After dinner, they sat in the living room, where Maggie had piled logs onto a roaring fire. Each had a glass of whisky, which they sipped as the flames crackled and hissed.

'Do you want me to speak to Finch?' Bob said.

'No. Olivia's a pain in the arse, but as long as she keeps quiet, I can put up with her. Not sure about Zelah and Nick, though.' She paused. 'I can't understand why she's baiting them. Because that is what she's doing. What could she hope to gain?'

'Maybe she can't help herself,' Bob said, putting his arm around Maggie's shoulders. 'How are you going to handle having two clients on the same case?'

'Not sure. Depends on what Anthony Bandon has to say in the morning.' She yawned. 'I'm going up. You coming?'

'Bit early for me.'

She gave him a quizzical look.

'Then again …'

He stood and put his arms around her. 'I changed my mind.'

**

The following morning Zelah and Nick arrived shortly after eight. Maggie had only just finished breakfast.

'You're early,' she said, yawning, as they sat at the kitchen table and helped themselves to coffee and tea.

'Two minds, single thought,' Nick said. 'We wanted to get here before Olivia.'

'Are you still concerned about her, Nick?'

'Yes. Something's not right.'

'Well, let's see how this morning goes with Anthony Bandon. I'm going to tell him about the dead man in London using his name, plus the police looking for him. Although, when I told Bob last night he rang Finch, who said he was going to contact the police in Melbourne, so I'm hoping by the time we speak to him, he'll already know.'

'Good,' Zelah said. 'I'm thinking about how we can remove Olivia.'

'Last night I went back to Anthony's ancestry chart,' Maggie said. 'I can see where and why we abandoned it last time. This morning, I want to get back into it, if that's OK with both of you.'

'It's crucial,' Nick said. 'Unless his new information is about a discovery on his part.'

'That would be ideal,' Maggie replied.

'I'm sticking with the research of the other Chartists who were transported, just in case they turn up in Anthony's family tree,' Zelah said. 'There's a lot to go through.'

As they walked into the office the doorbell rang.

'She's early, too', Maggie said. 'I'll get it.'

Olivia walked past her and into the office with a nod but no greeting. The tension in the room was palpable, as she took out her notebook and pen, placing them on the table, before sitting back with her arms folded.

Without comment, Maggie switched on her laptop and put up Anthony Bandon's line of descent on the whiteboard.

'Here's what we had last time. Anthony told us his Chartist ancestor, his three-times great grandfather was, according to him, a man called William George Evans, who knew of the existence and whereabouts of a very valuable item. He says this man was transported for his involvement in the uprising and for violence at the Westgate hotel.'

'Which we could not verify,' said Nick. 'We agreed with Anthony's line of descent back to his two times great grandfather, James Evans, but we couldn't find a record of his birth in Australia to a George William Evans. This is on Anthony's mother's line of descent,' he explained to Olivia. 'She was Elaine Williams and she married Walter Bandon, Anthony's father. Elaine's parents were Jonathan Williams and Mary Jane Evans. Mary Jane's father was James Evans and that's where we became stuck last time around. I couldn't find any James Evans born to a convict called William George Evans.

'I've made two major discoveries since yesterday,' Nick said. 'In UK records, in Newport, I did find a William George Evans who married Thomasine Marley and I've found five children, four boys, and one girl. Each of the boys, Samuel, George, Jeremiah, and Owen, died either in infancy or early childhood. The girl, Mary Anne, survived and married a man called Ebeneezer Phillips. Now, here's the part that makes me think that Anthony Bandon got it wrong, or is very mixed up and confused. James Evans was, according to Anthony Bandon, born in Australia in 1850. Anthony believed James' parents were called William and Suzannah, not Thomasine. Now for the second discovery – and it's a big one – William George Evans the thief died on the transport ship, so he couldn't have been James Evans' father.'

'Wow. That's significant progress, Nick. Did you find anything more about the Chartist George Evans?' Zelah asked.

Nick shook his head. 'The only person close to the name I've been able to find is William George Evans, born in Newport in 1784, the one I've just described. He was a thief, a habitual offender who had already done periods of hard labour for small thefts, who was arrested a few weeks after the march and sentenced to transportation. His age on the transportation records is given as fifty-five, which matches the birth in 1784. I'll look at that again. But if this is the William George Evans who died on the prison transport ship, there is no way he can be Anthony Bandon's ancestor in Australia.'

'That was on Bandon's mother's side,' Zelah said. 'What about his father's side?'

'We didn't look,' Nick said. 'He gave us his pedigree chart, but he was only interested in William George Evans on his mother's side. There was no reason to look at his father's ancestors, the Bandons.'

'Could they have been the same person?' Olivia said.

'Who?' Zelah shot at her.

'William George Evans, the thief, and George Evans, the marcher who claimed he was forced to march and was let go.'

Nick looked at Zelah and Maggie, then at Olivia. 'That's what Mischa suggested. I thought not, but now I have to say we can't rule it out, as I can't find any information at all about George Evans the reluctant marcher, being transported. He was let off at the Chartist trials, but I can't find any more about him after that.'

'Well, maybe you should try harder,' Olivia murmured with a patronising smile.

'Time for the call,' Maggie interrupted before Nick could reply.

Two minutes later Anthony Bandon appeared on the screen. Maggie was about to greet him when she saw that he looked pale and agitated.

'Anthony, are you OK? You look worried?'

'The police have been looking for me. They thought I'd been kidnapped. And, my passport's missing.'

'Ah. How much did they tell you?'

'Not much, just that someone in London, with my passport, was found dead in a hotel and there's been concern that something had happened to me. I explained that we had a family crisis and I had to go away with no notice. Is this something to do with you?'

'Yes. Let me explain,' Maggie said.

After she had told him, ignoring Olivia's frowning and head shaking multiple times as Maggie revealed the details, he sat back and blew out a long breath.

'Am I in danger?'

'I honestly can't say, Anthony. If it became necessary, could you go back to your family?'

'I suppose so. Actually, the family I went to see was my great uncle Malcolm, my grandfather's half-brother on my mother's Williams side. As you know, the Evans family joined the Williams's when my great grandfather Jonathan Williams married my great grandmother Mary Jane Evans, the daughter of James Evans. Malcolm'll be a hundred years old next year. He's the only child of Jonathan's second marriage. After Mary Jane died Jonathan married a woman called Jane Moffatt in 1920. The new information came in a phone call with Malcolm. It's a really strange, odd story. Malcolm said that, in his opinion, I was looking in the wrong place, with the Evans side. I should have been looking at the Williams ancestry.

'Jonathan was the son of Timothy Williams. Malcolm said he remembered his grandfather, Timothy Williams, saying his, Timothy's, father came to Australia as a thief. But he wouldn't say any more than that, not even the name. He seemed embarrassed. He did say this thief told a story that he knew about a very valuable stolen item, that was hidden. Anyway, after the call, Malcolm took a turn for the worse and I rushed off to see him, expecting he was about to peg it, which it turns out he wasn't.

'My uncle Roger was also there at Great Uncle Malcolm's house. Roger's in his nineties. I started talking about the family story, about the Chartist and the treasure. Roger stopped me and told me I'd definitely got it wrong. He thought it was on the Williams side, too; when you get back to my great grandfather, Jonathan Williams, the ancestor in question came from his side, not from his wife, Mary Jane Evans, as I believed.'

'So, who was he?' Nick asked.

'Uncle Roger told me the man's name was William Evan Williams. But he wasn't a Chartist, he was just a thief. I don't know much about him, except he was probably born around 1810.'

'Do you know anything, at all?' Zelah asked.

'According to Uncle Roger, he was transported for theft in 1840, when was twenty-nine years old. I haven't checked out anything else.' He paused and coughed. 'Apparently, according to Roger, William Evan was a "wrong un". He was transported for seven years. He got his ticket of leave in 1847 but it was revoked, so he wasn't eligible for his and he never went back to Wales.'

'He was from Wales? Do you know where?' Maggie asked.

'No idea. He was married here in Victoria, to a woman called Roberta McHugh, but he went on thieving and then,' he paused again and licked his lips. 'He was jailed for assaulting her, in 1850. And then, in 1855 he murdered her and was hanged.'

'He must have had children,' Zelah said.

'Yes, according to Roger, one son, Timothy Williams. His son was Jonathan Williams, my great grandfather who married Mary Jane Evans, then Jane Moffatt.'

A few seconds of silence followed. As the others had talked, Nick had been tapping away on his laptop. He sat back. 'Anthony,' he said. 'I've just taken a quick look at the transportation records. William Evan Williams was transported to Australia on the same ship as William George Evans. That is an incredible co-incidence, and we don't believe in co-incidences. I am thinking that something happened, during that journey. William Evan Williams survived. William George Evans died.'

'Like what?' Anthony asked.

'I don't know, yet. Can you give us some time to think this through?'

'Of course. And in the meantime, I'll get back in touch with the family here. I think I'll go stay with them.'

'And now, we can go into greater depth about more branches on your family tree,' Maggie said. 'Is there anything else, Anthony?'

'Not from me. This has all been quite shocking for me.' He blushed. 'I've only ever been interested in the story of the treasure. If I'd done more careful genealogy work, we might have had an answer by now.'

'I'm sorry,' Maggie said.

'Not your fault. But, we'll keep in touch.'

'You're still happy to have us work for you?' Zelah asked.

'Of course. I want to get to the bottom of this. And if you can, please find out more about the story of William Evan Williams. The co-incidences are incredible.'

'There's just one question I have for you, Anthony. How and why did you believe that your ancestor was a Chartist called William George Evans?' Nick asked.

'It was just part of the story, the Chartist, I mean. I found George Evans and the story of his being on the uprising march, against his will, then released, then later on arrested again, in the name of William George Evans for theft and transported to Australia. I've put two separate parts of the story together, haven't I? And amalgamated two men. I've muddled everything up.'

'Sounds like you might have done. We'll do our best to work it all out,' Maggie said, 'but we are now considering that they might have been the same person, although we don't yet understand the details.'

'I agree, it's very confusing,' Nick said, 'so let me try to sum up where we are before we go. There were two men with similar names, William George Evans and George Evans. The latter, George Evans, was forced to join the Chartist march on the night of 4ᵗʰ November 1839. He was subsequently let off. That's all we know about him, for now. That and the fact that there was no-one called George Evans transported as a Chartist. The former, William George Evans, was a thief who stole two silver candlesticks, for which act he was tried, convicted, and transported. I did discover that he had a wife, Thomasine, and five children, only one of whom survived childhood. That theft took place in January 1840. He died on the prison transport and never made it to Australia. We now know Anthony had an ancestor called William Evan Williams who had attacked and stolen from an old man, was caught, and also transported. He and William George Evans were on the same transport ship.

'Now – despite what you've just said, Anthony - I am heading towards thinking that William George Evans and George Evans might well have been the same person after all. It fits with Anthony's original story, with a Chartist marcher and a theft. What's missing is a precious, valuable object. I don't think two silver candlesticks fit the bill. I want to examine whether, when we add in the third person, William Evan Williams, we can make some headway on what really happened to each of them.'

'My head is spinning. Let's leave it there,' Maggie said. 'Let us know how you're getting on, Anthony. And please, talk to the police about everything we've told you this morning – evening. They must take your safety seriously.'

When she had ended the call, Maggie said, 'Well, there's something we didn't expect. That changes our priorities.'

'We need to look more closely into William Evan Williams' criminal records, and any record of his trial. It sounds sensational, so if there aren't any official records, there might be newspaper reports. And, Olivia's point is a valid one,' Nick said. 'I'm going to start on checking that, too.'

'To rule it out,' Zelah said.

Nick grinned.

'I'll start pulling together a family tree for Anthony, diverging at the point of his great grandfather Jonathan's marriage to Mary Jane Evans, and concentrating on the Williams line back from there, to Timothy and his father William Evan Williams, the murderer,' Maggie said.

'Nick, you concentrate on whether or not William George Evans and George Evans could be the same person. I'll take a look at the other crim, William Evan Williams,' Zelah said, 'check out what Anthony said about the murder of the man's wife.'

Before they could turn back to computers, Zelah said, 'Just a minute. I have another issue.' She waited until she had their attention again. 'We now have two clients for the same case. That's not sustainable. Therefore, we need to drop one.' She turned to Olivia. 'As far as I'm concerned, our client is Anthony Bandon. We don't need to be paid by Finch any longer. So, Maggie, please call Finch and tell him what's happened. Olivia, you can go.'

Olivia's mouth dropped open. 'You can't do this.'

'You'll find that I can.'

Olivia turned to Maggie. 'This isn't her decision.'

'Olivia,' Zelah said before Maggie could speak. 'This is my Company, although I rarely make executive decisions, which Maggie and Nick will confirm.' She looked at both of them and they nodded.

'Actually, more often than you realise,' Nick said. 'But I have no problem with this one. Maggie?'

'Works for me,' Maggie said. 'I do think we'll need to keep Finch informed, though. Only fair.'

'We can work out how to do that. Please call him. Olivia, shift your arse.'

Olivia, seeing that she had no support in the room, put her notebook and pen back into her briefcase, grabbed her coat, and marched out of the house, slamming the front door so hard every other door on the ground floor rattled.

Nick stood at the window, watching Olivia, who had stopped at the gate and taken her phone out of her pocket.

'Maggie, call Finch now,' he said.

'I will in a minute, but-'

'Now, Maggie.'

She shot him a surprised look, but picked up her phone and dialled. Finch replied and Maggie began the conversation. Zelah watched as Maggie winced at the shouting coming from the other end until Nick called Zelah to the window. 'Look,' he said.

Zelah saw that Olivia, now standing next to her car and unlocking it, was also engaged in a heated phone call.

'She's furious with someone, too,' Zelah said. 'Just a minute.' She glanced back at Maggie, who was still trying to calm Finch. 'If Maggie's talking to Finch, who's Olivia talking to?'

'Exactly,' Nick said.

Chapter 11
Newport 1839

Success!

George's plan had worked. He had avoided the soldiers and constables on the streets as he made his way towards his chosen place of concealment for his treasure. It was now safe and secure. He hadn't decided how he would retrieve it. That might present some problems, but in six months no-one would make a connection between a strange occurrence and the night of the uprising.

He had just reached the corner of his street when a voice stopped him.

'What would you be doing out and about?' Two special constables stepped out from a doorway that George hadn't noticed was not quite closed.

'Minding my own business,' he growled. 'What's it to you?' His heart was thumping, his palms sweating.

'Just trying to head back home as if nothing has happened, eh? Name.'

'None of your business. I've been out seeing if I can find work. I'm tired and I want to go home.'

One of the men moved to stand behind him, the other in front.

'Name. Now,' demanded the man standing inches from his face.

'George Evans. Labourer. I live just up there,' he said, indicating his front door. 'Can't find no work, though. No thanks to them Chartists.'

'You were with them.'

'Me? No. Nothing to do with me.'

'You're coming with us.'

George made a quick move to dart around the man, but the constable behind him grabbed the back of his coat.

He protested all of the way to the Union Workhouse on Stow Hill, where dozens of marchers who had either been detained during the march or, like himself, arrested in the aftermath, were huddled together. He was thinking desperately, trying for a provable story, when a voice interrupted his thoughts.

'I seen you. You was the man we took out near Malton. You had the food and beer.'

The voice caught the attention of a constable guarding the group. 'You, up.'

Cursing under his breath, George stood. 'That right?' the constable said.

'Might be,' George grumbled. No point denying it now. There would be other witnesses. 'They made me go with them.'

'You can tell it when you're examined in the morning.'

**

The following day in the early afternoon, after a sleepless night, George and a group of six other weary, tattered men were marched down Stow Hill to the Westgate Hotel, where one of the larger rooms on the ground floor had been turned into a courtroom.

A crowd had assembled to watch proceedings, small at first, but growing in number as the day progressed.

One by one the men were questioned by the examining magistrate. A few, still angry and resentful, were committed and returned to the union workhouse to await trial.

George's turn arrived. He had decided on respect, fear, and humility. He told his story to the leading magistrate, Reverend James Coles, how he had been guilty of taking some bread and beer from a local public house – whose name he could not remember – for the purpose of feeding his family and was returning home when he ran into the marchers and was forced to join them.

'I did not wish to join them, Your Worship. I am not a Charter man. I am just a humble labourer and working man. I am sorry for taking the bread. They took it away from me and ate it themselves, then pushed me into the centre of the crowd. I did not wish to go with them, but they gave me no choice. Said they would kill me if I tried to get away.' His voice trembled as he spoke. He put his head down and wrung his hands, but not before a rapid glance at Coles told him the man was hesitating.

Coles had heard similar stories during the morning session. One man with a similar story had brought a witness to verify the tale.

'Can you prove that?' Coles demanded.

George swallowed and looked up. 'One of the men you've just seen, your Worship. He spoke to me this morning. He was there when I was taken by them.' His hands were trembling. This was the moment he feared. The man could confirm his story but might tell Coles that George had been taken running from Prosser's house, not from a pub. He might also tell that two other men, servants of Prosser, were also taken.

'Which man?'

George described him and the man was brought back into the room.

'This man claims you took him by force, forced him to march with you despite his protests. Is this true? If so, where was he taken by you?'

The unnamed man stared for a few long seconds at George, who silently willed him to answer just "yes", without any detail. George held his breath.

'Ay, he was on the run, not far from The Blackbirds Inn. Came straight at us. He had bread and beer, so we took it, and him.'

'And what did he do, when you reached this place? Did you see him attack our soldiers?'

The man spat on the floor. 'Not him, he ran back up the hill.' He gave George a rapid grin. George returned the slightest of nods.

'Very well,' Coles said. He turned to George. 'You are dismissed. Next.'

George's relief was so great his legs gave way and a constable moved forward to hold him up.

'Thank you, your Worship.'

Coles had already moved on to the next man shuffling into the room. The constable walked with George to one of the back entrances onto Stow Hill, pushed him out, and shut the door. George leaned up against the wall, breathing slowly, as relief washed through him, but it was tinged with anxiety. It had been a close shave.

He walked around the corner to Commercial Street, where he was stopped by a crowd and a great commotion. A carriage had pulled up at the main hotel entrance and a man stood there, surrounded by soldiers, shouting to be allowed in. The door was immediately opened and Mervyn Prosser entered the hotel at a great pace. He was accompanied by his servant, Pritchard.

As soon as the door closed behind Prosser, George started to walk but hesitated. Prosser must have returned home. He would know by now that his prize was missing. Was he going to report the theft to the court?

As much as he wanted to run, George walked haltingly back to the hotel entrance. The door had been opened again. A crowd was being admitted. They had been agitating for entry, claiming it was a free country and a trial should not be held in secret. He joined the end of the group of men and walked into the makeshift courtroom, making sure he was hidden at the back of the room.

Proceedings had been halted, as Prosser made his way to Coles and began to speak in a whisper. Coles nodded, then signalled to the soldiers, who departed. The crowd whispered amongst themselves. A few minutes later two older men were led in. One was hobbling, his leg damaged. He was held up by the second man, who had a bandage around his head.

'Are these the men?' Coles asked Prosser in a voice loud enough for George to hear.

'They are. They are my gardener and coachman. They were chasing a thief from my property, one of the band of traitors and villains no doubt, when they were forced to join their misbegotten march.'

'Very well, release them,' Coles instructed the soldiers. 'I am most sorry to hear, Mr Prosser. What was stolen from you?'

George saw Prosser hesitate. 'Nothing,' he said. 'Just some food. My servants found the man in the act and chased him. He was one of them, I am certain. They welcomed him back into their number.'

Liar, George thought. *If I hadn't been let go, you would have them believe I was a Chartist marcher.* Nevertheless, it was interesting. The hesitation told him Prosser wasn't going to admit the vase was gone.

In his concentration on Prosser, he had forgotten about Pritchard. Having leaned out to better hear what was being said he realised that Pritchard was not huddled with Prosser and Coles, but was looking around the courtroom. He pulled his head sharply back in. Had Pritchard seen him? He couldn't be sure, but he should remove himself immediately.

The door to the room was open a few feet away. He pulled his scarf up around his face and shuffled backwards, bending his back, trying to keep behind others. He reached the door, straightened up, and walked rapidly along the corridor to the front door.

Outside, he walked down the street as fast as possible, forcing himself not to run. He must not draw attention to himself. Along Commercial Street, then down Church Street, around the corner, and back into his house. Today no-one was out on the street.

He barred the door and stood for a moment with his back to it. Then, he walked along the narrow dark corridor, past the stairs, and into the kitchen.

Mary Ann sat there, elbows on the table.

'You've been up to something. I know you.'

George raised his hand, but she didn't flinch. She knew he would not, could not, strike her. She was the eldest and only living child out of five that had been born to George and Thomasine. She had grown up with death in the house; had been the one who comforted him as each little boy died. In his own strange way, he loved her.

He sat at the table. 'I have a story to tell you, Polly, and a great secret for you to keep.'

Chapter 12

The online meeting had been a tiresome, pointless waste of time. Recriminations, accusations, and arguments, ending in no resolution and no plan.

Henry Camberwell closed down his computer screen. Thank God he didn't have to put up with them in person. He would likely have killed one, if not more. A bunch of useless, greedy bastards. Especially the Russian. He was a thug. An immeasurably – although estimates hovered around fifty billion dollars - wealthy thug. But still, a thug, who had made his fortune by plundering the natural resources of his own country when communism had collapsed. Why the man wanted the vase Camberwell had no idea. It certainly wasn't for its aesthetic beauty. It was just avarice. Rich Russians, in Camberwell's opinion, had no class. Unlike himself, who came from a family with a historic, patriarchal, aristocratic name, and wealth. Not that the wealth had been passed down. All he had inherited was this magnificent house on the banks of the Thames at Chelsea, in which he now sat. The title he had bought through astute political contributions. No, his wealth was derived from his talents. Camberwell, like generations of his family before him, had been born without a conscience, which in his opinion was a good thing. Throughout his life, and as instructed by his grandfather, he had been willing to take advantage of every trend in human misery that had presented itself as a business opportunity.

This latest venture, under the guise of his business in fine arts, had come about unexpectedly. Personally, he had no interest in the vase, other than in its value to a collector. One of his agents had alerted him to the story in the Fathergill papers, and Henry had seen an opportunity. He put together a list of potential buyers, not one of whom he trusted, but all of whom were willing to make a bid, and to finance an investigation into its potential discovery, which would never become public.

There were three: The Russian, the American, and the British Lord.

Finding the vase, however, would take a little time, although he had explained to them he was confident he could discover its whereabouts. After all, the history was there if you looked long and deeply enough. His agents had scoured every piece of information they could find on anyone who might also be looking, that he would need to eliminate, once he had discovered what they knew. And they had come up with: Maze Investigations.

Henry hadn't known whether to laugh, cry, curse, or all three. His previous interaction with Maze had caused him to lose a great deal of money in what should have been a profitable joint venture in human trafficking, his first move into Wales. It had gone horribly wrong, eventually forcing him into getting rid of the so-called partner. Good riddance as far as he was concerned. Now, he had other contacts, other irons in the fire.

His phone rang. He recognised the number and answered, listened for a few minutes.

'I put my faith in you and you have let me down.'

The voice on the other end argued, but he shut it down.

'I don't want to hear your excuses. Put it right.'

More arguing.

'You heard. Put it right. Your father would not be proud of you, for this.'

He ended the call. He knew which of the informant's buttons to press, and he knew action would be taken. But, best to be sure. He picked up the phone again. It was answered on the first ring.

'All is not well in Wales. I have a job for you … Yes, the same area, but just a watching brief, this time. However, action may be required. If that becomes necessary I will inform you … No, do not make contact. Your instructions and fee will arrive in the usual manner.'

He ended the call and threw the phone back onto the couch. He thought for a few minutes, stood then put another log onto the blazing fire, which immediately sent a flurry of sparks up the chimney, followed by crackling flames. He had been tempted the previous winter to replace it with a gas substitute, to save getting dirt on his hands, but in the end, had not done so. Henry did not like anything that was a substitute. No matter how authentic someone had tried to make them, gas flames weren't real. He had explained this last night to the prostitute who had visited him, who had tried to pretend she was from a wealthy background, as she screwed him in front of the fire.

'Do not pretend with me,' he whispered to her, as he pulled her up by the hair and pushed her hand into the flames. 'This is real. You are fake. I shall not require your services again.'

After summoning his driver, he had pushed her sobbing and uncontrollably shaking into the car with instructions to drop her at the closest A&E and a clear warning of what would happen if she mentioned his name. He had shivered and gone to wash his hands, to remove the smuts of burnt wood chipping.

It had almost been a pleasant evening. Women were often a disappointment.

Chapter 13

Finch had been furious, but nothing shifted Maggie. 'We can't have two clients looking for the same thing. I am willing to keep you informed, Mr Finch. I will call you as soon as we find anything that may be relevant to your interest in Camberwell.'

The call had gone on for ten minutes, at which point Maggie put the phone down.

'He's not for pacifying,' she reported to Nick and Zelah.

'Tough,' Zelah said. 'You've done your best. Now, we have to get on with our research. I must say, it gets odder by the minute.'

'We have to re-arrange our priorities, again,' Maggie said. 'Nick, what do you think.'

Nick was gazing out of the window.

'Nick,' she repeated. 'How should we proceed now?'

'He's thinking about Olivia,' Zelah said. 'Who was she talking to?'

Maggie shrugged. 'Could be anyone. She is a police officer; could have been her direct boss. Finch isn't, despite her being seconded to him. They can't have been too happy at us throwing her out.'

'There was something about her body language,' Nick mused. 'She was angry, but defensive at the same time.'

'Forget her,' Maggie said. 'We have work to do. Priorities.'

Nick snapped his head around. 'Yes, sorry. That was odd, the two ancestors being on the same transport ship. It could be just co-incidence. There were hundreds on each ship. They might never have seen each other. But the story of "treasure" on the Williams side of the family. That's no co-incidence.'

'Funny Anthony only found out about it now,' Zelah mused.

'Like he said, he was so certain it had come from the Evans ancestry he didn't look anywhere else. And remember, he only asked us to look for William George Evans. Once we had established he was just a thief and had no association with the Chartists, there was nowhere else to go.'

Nick walked over to his computer and sat, staring at the blank screen. 'The more I think about it, the more I'm liking the idea that William George Evans and George Evans were indeed the same person. I have to say, Olivia and Mischa could be right. I need to rule it in or out. That's my priority for the rest of today.' He opened up the computer and began a search.

'I'll get on with the Williams family tree,' Maggie said.

'I'll check out the multiple crime history of William Evan Williams, in Britain and Australia,' Zelah said. 'Let's go.'

**

After several quiet hours, Nick was the first to speak. 'You know what, I believe it's correct. William George Evans and George Evans were the same person. There is no baptism, marriage, or death and burial evidence for a man called George Evans who was forced onto the march and let go. There were quite a few men called Evans, but no plain George Evans. I found a reference to George Evans' examination at the Westgate in an extract of a book written in the late 1890s. It doesn't give his exact age, but says he was an older man, in his mid-fifties, which was the same age given for William George Evans at his trial.'

'Didn't his evidence say he'd taken the bread and beer for his family?' Maggie asked. 'Is there any reference in the 1841 census to a William George or a George?'

'Not in Newport. I've just found the daughter of William George Evans, Mary Ann who married Ebeneezer Phillips. She and Phillips had married the month before the census was taken, so no children. Ebeneezer was a miner, and they were living in Merthyr. With them was her mother, Thomasine Evans, who was recorded as a widow. I'm going to go down to Newport to get their marriage certificate, this afternoon, to be certain I have the right one. And my final piece of information: there is no recorded death of a William George Evans in England and Wales over the following forty years.'

'What about the baptism of Mary Ann?' Zelah asked. 'What's the name and address on the record?'

'She is the daughter of William George Evans, Labourer of Pillgwenlly, by his wife Thomasine Marley. Born in 1820 in Newport.'

'And what about the marriage of William George Evans and Thomasine Marley? Did you find that yet in the marriage records, probably at St Woolas? It should be in the online Monmouthshire records, with any luck.'

'No. Hang on a minute, I'll look now. The first son, Samuel, was baptised in 1817. Let me see …' There was silence for a couple of minutes, then he banged his fist on the table. 'Yes! The marriage is between George Evans – not William George - and Thomasine Ann Marley. It was in 1816, in Newport. Now, let me see if I can find his birth.'

Zelah and Maggie sat in silence. It took almost five minutes before Nick said, again, 'Yes! He was baptised William George Evans in 1781. The son of Samuel Evans. He would have called the first son after his father, and the second son after his wife's father. Then, the third son after himself. Exactly how they kept it. But, it's not enough.'

'Try all four sons,' Maggie said. 'See what the father's name is for each of them and the mother, if it was recorded and if the Monmouthshire records have them. If Mary Ann was the daughter of William George, the boys should all be the same.'

Nick turned back to his computer. It took him ten minutes before he turned around with a grin. 'I think this clinches it. Two of the boys were born to William George Evans and two to George Evans, with Thomasine Ann Marley the mother in all four cases. And there's a street named on one of them – High Street, Pillgwenlly.'

'I think it's enough to make a call,' Zelah said. 'Mary Ann's marriage certificate should be the final proof. There's one more you could try whilst you're there, Nick. See if you can find the death of Thomasine Marley Evans. See how she's described on the certificate. It shouldn't take too much time to trace the right one. I can't imagine there are a lot of women called Thomasine Evans in South Wales.'

Nick checked his watch. 'I'll give it an hour before I go down to the register office. I'll start with the census records, see if she's still with Mary Ann and Ebeneezer in 1851.' He checked again and found the family. 'Ebeneezer and Mary Ann are still in Merthyr in 1851,' he said. They had just one child, which seems odd. A girl, called Thomasine.'

'Well, that gives you a ten-year window to find a death for Thomasine Marley Evans, and it's likely to have been in Merthyr, which should narrow it down,' Zelah said.

'My turn next,' Maggie said. 'The family tree of William Evan Williams is straightforward. He was born in Newport, in 1810. As you discovered this morning, Nick, he married Roberta McHugh in Australia in 1847. They had one son, Timothy. Timothy married Judith Hartley in 1869 and their son was Jonathan Williams, Anthony's great grandfather. The only other piece of information I have is that William Evan was the son of Timothy, which probably isn't relevant in terms of what we're looking for, but it does confirm adherence to the naming conventions. What about you, Zelah?'

'Interesting. William Evan was definitely a "wrong 'un". His conviction for theft was in 1839 and it wasn't just theft. He attacked an old man and left him for dead. He was transported for seven years. Once he got to Australia, he must have kept his head down, although there are records of drunkenness. His ticket of leave was revoked, so he wasn't eligible for his Certificate of Freedom. He assaulted Roberta on more than one occasion, eventually killing her in a drunken attack in 1855 when little Timothy was six years old. He was hanged in 1855.'

'And he was on the same transport ship as William George Evans?' Maggie asked.

'Yes. I wonder if the fact they were both from Newport gave the men an introduction to each other?' Nick mused.

'I wonder if we can speak to Anthony's uncle Roger?' Maggie said. 'Perhaps he could tell us more about why he believes the story of the "treasure" came from the Williams and not the Evans family.'

'Good point. Send Anthony a message, see what he thinks.'

'Doing it. One more hour before we stop so Nick can go down to Newport.'

They turned back to their screens.

**

Almost exactly an hour later Nick raised his arms above his head, and stretched out his shoulders, saying, 'I think I have enough. There were two women called Thomasine Evans who died in Merthyr between 1841 and 1851. One was in 1844 and she was forty-nine years old. The second was in 1850 and she was fifty-nine. I'll get the death certificates for both.'

'I'm done for the day, on this.' Zelah said. 'I've got some traces going on the remaining seven Chartists who were transported. It looks like only John Frost came back. Of the other six, William Jones and Zephaniah Williams have easily discovered records due to their notoriety. That leaves four. Two died without marrying. Of the remaining two, they did marry and have children, but none of them are related to Anthony Bandon's Williams or Evans family. I've tracked down four generations of descendants, which I think is enough.'

'I agree,' said Maggie. I suggest we wait now for Nick to get the certs, then let us know if either of them is William George Evans' wife and if so, anything else useful.'

'I think I'll carry on at home,' Zelah said. 'I have a book to finish and I prefer no interruptions. Give me a call if anything useful turns up.'

Nick left shortly afterwards, leaving Maggie alone in the office. There wasn't much more she could do for now. Maybe some background information, so she began to look at internet sites with Newport history; not just of the Chartist uprising, but to pick up general information about life in the area at the time. After a quick lunch break, she resumed again, this time looking at maps and reading histories, both familial and general.

Nick's phone call came through at four. 'I had to wait a long time. They're busy down here. Anyway, we have something.'

'Excellent. What do we have?'

'It's the second Thomasine Evans, the one who died in 1850 when she was fifty-nine. Her death was informed by her daughter, Mary Ann Phillips. Her occupation: wife of George Evans, transported convict.'

'Wow!' Maggie said. 'That clinches it, doesn't it?'

'Yes, I believe so,' Nick replied, in an oddly subdued voice.

'I thought you'd be pleased, Nick. What's the matter?'

'Well, we can safely say now that there was just one George Evans, who was baptised William George but known as George. He was pressed into the march to Newport, but let off by the magistrate because a witness vouched for him that he wasn't a willing marcher. Then, a couple of months later, he's convicted of the theft of two candlesticks, by a man called John Pritchard, tried, convicted, and sentenced to transportation to Australia for seven years. And he never made it there. He died on the voyage.'

'That's good, isn't it, that we know all of this?'

'Yes and no. Whilst I was waiting I used my tablet to do some checking. The name John Pritchard was familiar. I thought I'd heard it before, but I couldn't think where. Anyway, I found him. John Pritchard was the name of the head servant of Mervyn Prosser. Maggie, I'm now theorising, that George Evans did steal the vase, as well as bread and beer, on the night of the march into Newport.'

'A possibility, I agree. What's bothering you, because something is?'

'What's bothering me is that, if I'm right, this puts us right back into the path of Henry Camberwell.'

Chapter 14

Newport 1839

Two weeks after the uprising the trials in Newport had picked up pace. There were appearances in front of the magistrates every day, with crowds gathering to observe.

George hadn't gone to spectate. He had heard that Mervyn Prosser had become an enthusiastic prosecutor of many captured Chartists and made frequent appearances at the courtroom and at the union workhouse, which still served as a gaol. He wanted to keep out of Prosser's way and not allow himself to be seen by Pritchard, who accompanied the coal master everywhere.

He was beginning to relax, thinking, that as soon as the trials of Frost, Williams, and Jones were done with in January, the soldiers would leave and the crowd would move on. He would then be free to plan how to release his treasure from its – in his opinion – excellently executed hiding place.

By the end of December, the weather had turned cold, freezing almost, but he had found some work on the construction that had begun on the new Town Dock that would link the canal bringing coal and iron from the valleys to the ships now coming into the town. The town itself was growing rapidly from the almost village George remembered from his boyhood; the village of Pillgwenlly practically joined the main town now, which meant plenty of work for men like George.

The pounding on the door came as he sat in the kitchen in front of the fire, with Mary Ann, warming his hands and discussing the start of his plan. Of course, he had had to tell her what had happened on the night of the uprising and how he had been let go. She was the only person he trusted with the secret.

He grumbled and walked to the door. As he opened it, half a dozen soldiers burst in. His first reaction, after the momentary shock, was anger.

'What the hell are you doing? You can't come into my house like this.' He was about to remonstrate further when he saw the man who followed them. His mouth dried up and his hands trembled. Pritchard.

'Good evening, Mr Evans. I believe you have something, let us say, that does not belong to you. We have a warrant from the magistrates to search your house.'

George breathed a sigh of relief and grinned at the man. 'Search all you like. I've nothing belonging to you or anyone else.' He leaned into Pritchard's face as he spoke the last few words, 'or anything I shouldn't have.'

Pritchard leaned back and winced at the rush of foul breath that had filled his nostrils. He signalled to the soldiers to begin to search.

Upstairs, they woke George's wife and turned her out of bed, and the same for the family of lodgers who slept in the front bedroom. They ran outside and waited, shivering, the young couple wrapping up their children as best they could against the freezing night air, not daring to ask what was happening.

Mary Anne had joined George in the passage leading to the front door. They had been there for five minutes, listening to the sound of banging and clattering as drawers were emptied, beds overturned and possessions scattered.

'You'll regret this,' George snarled at Pritchard as the man came back down the stairs, followed by the soldiers.

'I think not.' He turned to the soldier in charge. 'Arrest this man.'

George roared. 'What for? I've done nothing wrong.'

'You are a thief. You have stolen goods from a citizen of the town.'

'No, I haven't. What goods?'

Pritchard brought his hands, which had been behind his back, to the front and held up two silver candlesticks. With a sly smile, he said, 'And what are these?'

'I never took those! You brought them with you. Why are you doing this to me?' As he spoke two soldiers took his arms, pinned them behind his back, and marched him through the door into the street.

George began to scream for help. His wife followed them out, wringing her hands and crying. Mary Anne stood grim-faced in the doorway, beckoning the lodger family back into the house. She knew what had happened. This was Prosser's doing. She shut the front door and ran after the group.

When she reached them she grabbed Pritchard's sleeve. 'Sir, where are you taking my father? Please, he is a good man, he is not a thief.' She could both look and sound innocent and pitiful when she needed.

Pritchard shook her off. 'Your father will be taken to the gaol in Monmouth, where he will be examined and tried.'

Monmouth! How would she get there? It must be more than twenty miles. As they marched off into the distance, she knew she had to try. She probably only had days. There would be a way.

She returned home, calmed her mother, gathered up a few belongings and some food for her father, and set off for what would be a long walk.

Chapter 15

Given the potential re-entry of Henry Camberwell into the case, they had decided to convene another extended family get-together, to update everyone on their progress, and to decide on whether or not to continue. Michelle Quinn had opted out – again, sending Gerry along to speak on her behalf.

'What does that mean?' Zelah asked him, as they waited for the Rosscarbery group to join them by video link.

'I'm to give you her message – get out now before Camberwell comes looking for any of us,' he replied. 'That's not my opinion, but I promised I'd say that for her.'

'Fair enough,' Zelah said. 'Noted and ignored.'

Maggie called them all to attention as the Irish group appeared on the large screen on the wall.

'Welcome, everyone,' she began. 'We've made good progress in the last couple of days, or at least on the genealogy. What we have to discuss and decide this morning is: do we want to go further? I'm going to hand over to Nick, to sum up. Succinctly, please, Nick.'

He gave two short coughs, clearing his throat. 'Mischa, you were right in your suggestion that William George Evans and George Evans are the same person. The man was baptised William George, but it looks like he was known as George, as that name appears on some of the official documents, such as birth, marriage, and death certificates for children, for example. When he was taken for examination by the magistrates following the Newport rising, it was as George Evans. He was let go because he was able to prove he did not go willingly with them. He admitted to theft of food and drink, but nothing more. However, at the end of December, he was re-arrested and again charged with theft, this time of two silver candlesticks, accused by a man called John Pritchard. Turns out, Pritchard was the Steward at the estate of Mervyn Prosser.'

'What, the one who had the vase?' Gerry asked.

'The same. He was taken to Monmouth gaol this time. He was put on trial, found guilty on the evidence given, and sentenced to transportation. The ship on which he was transported left Southampton in February 1840. He should have arrived in Australia two months later, but he was taken ill and died onboard.'

'So, he wasn't the client's ancestor?' Stephen McCarthy Miller asked.

'No,' Nick replied. 'and this is where it gets quite fascinating.'

'Why have you stopped?' Zelah asked.

'Because Maggie did the next piece of research and she can take over from here.'

Maggie sat forward. 'The client's new information was that his family history joined the families of Williams and Evans with the marriage of his great grandparents. He followed the Evans line, in the belief that William George Evans was the Chartist and thief. However, it turns out other members of his family thought it was the Williams line, as the story of the whereabouts of a valuable precious object was first told by a Williams ancestor, a man called William Evan Williams. He was on the same convict transport as George – that's how we're now referring to him – and was also a thief and from Newport. Zelah has investigated his criminality and he was as nasty a piece of work as we've come across. I won't give you the whole story, but he ended up marrying in Australia and murdering his wife, for which he was hanged, but not before the wife produced a son and that son was the father of the male side of the Williams Evans marriage.'

For a few seconds, there was silence. 'That's an incredible co-incidence,' Stella said.

'They don't happen often, and normally we don't believe in them, in our line of work,' Zelah said, 'but this time it is just that – an incredible co-incidence. So, that's where we're at.'

Niall McCarthy Miller spoke up. 'I thought the client originally wanted you to find out if the story of a treasure of some kind was true, and find it?'

'Sort of,' Maggie said. 'He was certainly fixated on finding it. However, now that reality, in the shape of us having a good idea that the treasure is the Chinese vase, possibly stolen by George Evans on the night of the uprising, has moved on to include Sir Henry Camberwell, our client is – what can I say – somewhat taken aback.'

'Does he still want you to carry on?' Gerry asked.

'Not sure. We haven't discussed it at that level of detail. And before we go back to him, we wanted to get you together, because if we move into that detail, we inevitably move closer to Camberwell.'

'Do you actually know that George Evans stole the vase?' Stella asked.

'No, we don't, Stella. It's a strong possibility, but we don't have definitive proof. And if he did steal it, we have no idea at all what he did with it.'

'I don't understand,' Gerry Quinn said, in a low voice. 'I'm going to sound a bit stupid here …' he ignored a snort from Mischa, 'but what you're saying is, you don't know if he stole it and if he did, what he did with it, but he died anyway. But this other relative also told a story of having stolen something valuable …'

'Let me stop you there,' Nick interrupted. 'As far as we can tell, the other relative, William Evan Williams, didn't say he stole the vase. He said he knew the whereabouts of something extremely valuable, that was stolen. And this is my theory: both men were transported on the same ship. They were both from the same town. Both were transported for theft, but the items in each case were noted at their trials and both stole silver. I think one of them was responsible for the theft of the vase and I think it was George Evans. I think he told William Evan Williams as he was dying ...'

Zelah stood up. 'Stop there. There's absolutely no proof whatsoever of any of that.'

Nick nodded. 'Quite right. And that's why we're here. If we continue with the research, it is inevitably where we are going to go. If we are heading towards finding out what happened to that object, we will have to work on speculation.'

Maggie noted that his face had unconsciously grimaced when he described the vase as an "object", as if it was something dark and dirty. 'You don't want us to go on, Nick, I think.'

'Correct,' he said. 'But, it's not my decision. Camberwell is looking for the vase. If we look for it, we find him. I don't want that.'

Maggie sat and folded her arms. 'And we don't know what the client wants, because we haven't fed any of this back to him. I've been wondering if we could speak directly to his Williams relatives, that's his great uncle Malcolm and his uncle Roger, who told him he'd got the wrong side of the family.'

'I think he'll want us to continue,' Zelah said. 'Whatever it turns out to be, one of his ancestors knew of the existence and whereabouts of the vase. What I don't understand is, what he thinks he can do with it if we do find it. The vase was stolen from the British Museum back in 1838. And that's where it'll go back, should it ever be found.'

'Is there a reward?' Gerry asked.

'Not as yet,' Maggie said. 'I don't know who would pay it, if there is one.'

'Henry Camberwell?' Gerry asked again. 'He's the only one with enough money.'

'Finch believes that Camberwell is looking for it to sell it on,' Maggie said. 'I suppose he could pay a reward to whoever finds it. But I'm speculating, again, and I have no intention of finding out.'

'It'll be a lot of money,' Max Howell said from the back of the room.

'Very possibly,' Nick replied, then turned to Gerry. 'You aren't proposing we do a deal with Camberwell, are you?'

'No, of course not,' Gerry blustered. 'He got my dad killed. I'm just saying, like, someone might be tempted by that much money.'

'He's right,' Zelah said, deliberately not looking at Stephen McCarthy Miller. 'But only to a point. If Camberwell did offer a reward he couldn't do it publicly. He'd have to contact individuals privately and then only people who might know what we've found out so far. And if someone bites, then they'll be in big trouble, if they believe that Camberwell would genuinely make the offer. He'd kill them once they handed it over.'

'All of this is moot if the client decides to pull out,' Maggie said.

'No, if the client pulls out, Finch will come back to us.'

'Yes, Nick I suppose he will. So, I guess we have to decide, if the client is in, are we going to carry on? Everyone here gets a vote. Who wants us to carry on?

She glanced around the room as she put her hand into the air, surprised to see that, in addition to Nick sitting with his arms folded, Jack had also not indicated his agreement.

'That's eight for, two against.'

'Three,' Gerry intervened. 'My mother doesn't want us – me – to have anything to do with it.'

'OK. Three. That's still a majority in favour,' Zelah said. 'The next step – we get the client's input. If he's willing to carry on, we do.'

'But very carefully,' Maggie added. 'I've been thinking about Gerry's point, about the potential for Camberwell offering a reward. I am going to suggest we don't tell you all everything. Not that I don't trust all of you,' she added quickly at the sight of protest heading towards her from several directions. 'I think it's safer if you don't know.'

'Works for me,' Gerry said. 'I will want to know if there's any sign of Camberwell, though.'

'Of course,' Maggie replied. 'Same goes for all of you. Right, we should get back to work.'

The video call ended and Maggie began to shepherd others out of the house. She wanted to speak to Jack, in private.

Ten minutes later they had all gone, except Zelah. Nick decided to take Stella, Flora, and Max home, but did say he would return.

'Go,' Zelah said to Maggie. 'He went upstairs.'

**

Maggie found Jack in his room, sitting on his bed, eyes fixed somewhere in the distance, staring at nothing in particular.

'If it's too much for you, I will stop now,' she said, sitting next to him and taking his hand. He squeezed her fingers but didn't reply.

'I mean it. You are more important to me than anything on this earth. The job is just that – a job. I didn't sign up to put any of us in danger.'

He shook his head. 'I'm scared. I've never been before, but I am now. That man scares me.'

'Scares me, too.'

He turned to look at her. 'Do you believe you can stop what he does before he gets to one of us, mum?'

'If I said "yes" I'd be lying. I can only say, I hope so. And that I'm not going to risk any one of us. But I will say again – if you are that bothered, then we'll stop. Everyone will understand.'

'They'll blame me.'

'No, they'll blame me.' She took her hand away and put her arm around his waist. 'I can take it. Maze won't be affected. Nick doesn't want to do this. Secretly – Zelah doesn't want to either, really, but you know what she's like. She wants to stop Camberwell. But I also know, if she thinks it's too much for you, she won't hesitate in calling it off.'

He stood up. 'No, carry on. Just let me know what you're finding out. OK?'

'OK. Promise you'll tell me if it does get too much?'

He nodded. 'I'll come and help you. The sooner you get the info, the better. Then you can finish with the client.'

She smiled and they went down to the office together. He sat in the office with her and Zelah for the next hour until Nick returned and the four of them worked on. All the time, Maggie's stomach was clenching. She had been forced to admit to herself, and to her shame, that she had put the job before her child. She silently admitted that the sooner they saw the back of Anthony Bandon, the better she would feel.

Chapter 16
Newport 1839

Now that George Evans was safely locked up, Mervyn Prosser had a little breathing space to decide what to do next.

The more he considered his predicament, the greater he felt the threat from the knowledge that George Evans had about the vase and about the meeting with Fathergill, which the man must have overheard. He must know the item was not only valuable but stolen and even now was being sought by what Prosser thought of as high offices of state. The very idea brought him out in a cold sweat. He might be able to brush off accusations about himself, but if Evans was given the opportunity to bring Fathergill into it, he doubted that man would perjure himself if called upon to give evidence in court.

Evans had already been in jail for two days and his appearance in the dock was approaching. So far, he had said nothing, which should have re-assured Prosser, but in fact, made him more nervous. After several hours of deliberations, arguments with himself, and nightmare visions of discovery and humiliation, he summoned Pritchard.

The servant, shoulders rounded, hands clasped in front of his long dark coat, stood, waiting. It was never advisable to speak before Prosser had given forth.

'He has to go.'

'Sir?'

The man Evans. I cannot allow the possibility that he will be allowed even to speak in his own defence.'

'He will be allowed that, Sir.'

'Yes, yes. But you must ensure that no regard is given to anything he might say. I cannot afford to be involved. I have decided that what he stole from me is not negotiable. I must do without it.' Here Prosser twitched and shook his head. 'Whatever its value, it cannot be associated with me.'

This last sentence was spoken as if to himself. Pritchard didn't comment, but an interesting possibility arose in his mind.

'I see, Sir. So, how are we to achieve this end?'

Prosser rose and went to his desk, from which he produced a piece of paper, handing it to Pritchard. 'Take this to the Magistrates. It confirms the theft of the candlesticks. Then, visit Evans and give him to understand that an agreement can be reached. When is the trial?'

The day after tomorrow, Mr Prosser.'

Good. Speak to Evans the night before; tell him you will return in the morning to confirm the arrangement to have his case withdrawn. But, Pritchard, appear to drive a hard bargain.'

'You can count on me, Sir.'

'As soon as you have spoken to him, return here. He will wait for you the following morning. The trial will come as a surprise. He won't know what's happening until they convict him and send him off to that colony.' He paused and barked a laugh.

'What about the object he stole from you, Sir? Do you not want to know what he did with it?'

'No. He has probably sold it on already. I want nothing more to do with it. It's a cursed object.'

Pritchard raised his eyebrows but didn't respond. No need to let Prosser know what he was thinking.

The following afternoon Pritchard set off for Monmouth. Prosser felt that at last, he could put the whole unfortunate business out of his mind. He had been taken for a fool. That would never happen again. And he would ensure it would be some time before he saw Samuel Fathergill. No need to give that man the chance to ask questions, either.

He was satisfied. Now, he should get back to the business of prosecuting those damned Chartists.

Chapter 17

Nick was the first to interrupt the silence. He had been looking again at the ancestry of Anthony Bandon.

'I've found his actual ancestor,' he said in a quiet voice, without looking up from his screen.

Maggie, Zelah, and Jack spun around to face his back.

'Go on then,' Zelah said.

He turned his chair around. 'We were OK as far as James Evans, Anthony's three times great grandfather, but we couldn't find a father called William George Evans and we now know that's because he never reached Australia. Well, and I am embarrassed to admit this, I missed a piece of information the first time around. The situation in Australia was much the same as here. Civil registration began in the 1850s, although the date varied from state to state. For example, in Victoria … '

'Nick, this is interesting, but can you please get to the point?'

'Sorry, Zelah. Yes. Last year I worked backwards from the marriage of James Evans and Sarah Brown. Their daughter, Mary Jane, was registered as the child of these named parents and I also checked the marriage in the church records. That's where the mistake occurred. The marriage was between a James Evans and a Sarah Brown. But there was what I thought was an ink blot in front of the "James", and so did the transcriber. It wasn't. It was another name: Job. Job was the son of one William George Evans, but not the same one we are looking at. This William George was a free settler, a farmer from Norwich, who had married in England and taken his family out to Australia with help from the British Government.'

'They were paying passages even back then?' Maggie asked, surprised.

'Yes, and many who took up the offer were relatively well-off families who saw an opportunity. They were sheep farmers. Job, who must have been known as James, was their sixth child and Mary Jane was one of three children of James and Sarah. There's no evidence of the farmer's father, William George Evans ever returning to England. Nor Job James Evans.'

Zelah shook her head. 'Names,' she said. 'They can really mess you up. Can't blame yourself for not spotting a blob was actually a name, Nick,' she added, trying to lighten the atmosphere.

'I'll be happy to pass that on to Anthony,' Maggie said. 'Doesn't that mean that your theory about the meeting of the two convicts on the transport ship becomes a stronger possibility?'

'Maybe.' He turned back to his computer.

Maggie turned to Jack. 'How are you getting on?'

'Cool. I've got a good tree going for George Evans in Wales. His daughter Mary Ann who married Ebeneezer Phillips had three children. There were two boys as well as a daughter, Thomasine who was born in 1843. Then came the two boys, George and David, but they both died in childhood. I'm going to look for what happened to the daughter, Thomasine Phillips, who might have stayed in Merthyr.'

'Well done,' Maggie said, glancing over at Nick's back. 'I know it's not directly relevant at the moment, but you may find something that could become pertinent further down the line of descent. Zelah, how're you getting on?'

'I've finished the final draft of the latest storybook, so if there's anything any of you want help with, throw it over.'

Jack stood up. 'I have to get ready for work. Could you take over from me, Zelah?'

She nodded and he left the room. Zelah gave Maggie a quizzical look, the response to which was a flat palm moving side to side like a seesaw, indicating fifty-fifty followed by a shrug.

'I'm leaving now,' Nick said suddenly, standing up.

Maggie accompanied him to the door. 'All is not well with you, my friend.'

He shook his head. 'I don't like this.'

She put a hand on his arm. 'Look, you can back out. We understand. None of us will object.'

'No, we're a team. But, only up to a point,' and he turned and walked away to his car.

Back in the office, Maggie said to Zelah, 'This isn't fun. We're supposed to enjoy what we do. Anyway, I'm going to call Finch, give him an update, such as it is.'

**

Maggie gave Bob an update on their progress over dinner.

'Finch isn't happy, but we're nowhere close to finding out anything about the theft of the vase. I've told him we may never find out. Honestly, Bob, I'm not sure I want to pursue this much further,' she said. 'This afternoon in the office was tense. None of our usual banter. I don't know what to do next.'

'How much more is there you can do?'

'We can trace the ancestors of the convict George Evans who died on the ship, see if they know anything about the story.' She paused tapping her knife on the table. 'Nick's right. If we go further, it has to be into the story of the theft from Prosser. Was it George

Evans, and if so, what did he do with it? When Anthony Bandon first came to us he wanted us to help him find out that information. Now his house has been broken into and his passport stolen with the man in London taking his name, I'm not so sure he'll maintain his enthusiasm. I'm going to email him first thing in the morning, with the update about his real Evans ancestor, which is a dead end on the "treasure" story, which then reverts to his Williams family. We've discussed speaking to his great uncle Malcolm and his uncle Roger if he will allow us. Beyond that, if there's nothing more to be gained, I think we're done with this. Camberwell will have to look elsewhere for help.'

'I'm thinking that won't upset you too much?'

'No, and yes. We all want to see Camberwell stopped. But not if it brings him closer to us. I can't see another way forward.'

'Sleep on it,' Bob replied. 'I'll have a chat with Jack when he gets home. Is Alice OK?'

She's the only one happy about their current situation. She's loving being at the flat in Cardiff. She doesn't have to catch buses and she and Matthew can study together. I spoke to his mother earlier and she said Alice is being a model guest. Complimented me on having such a pleasant, tidy daughter. I almost choked at the "tidy" bit!'

Bob laughed. 'You brought her up well enough to respect other people's space.'

'But not mine, or her own. Never mind, I'm relieved she's OK. Let's switch off from work for the rest of the evening.'

'Fine with me. We'll find something to watch on TV. No police box sets.'

**

Zelah arrived bright and enthusiastic the following morning and immediately took up the research that Jack had started on the lines of descent of George Evans.

'You've changed your tune,' Maggie said as she wandered into the office, yawning, with a cup of coffee.

'I thought about it overnight,' said Zelah as she set up several online research sites. 'As long as Anthony Bandon is happy to continue paying us, we should do the best we can for him.' She stopped and sat back. 'But if he isn't, and in that scenario, if Finch wants to take over, what are we going to say?'

'Let's wait and see what Anthony says. I'm going to email him this morning to let him know about his real Evans ancestor and also tell him that we're still looking at the descendants of George Evans, even though we know he's no longer a relative of Anthony's. Plus, I'll ask him if we can speak to Malcolm and Roger.'

'OK. I guess until we have his response, we just keep on keeping on.' Zelah turned back to her computer screen and began to search amongst the various sites. 'What are you going to do this morning, after you've messaged Mr Bandon?'

'I'm going to take another look at the Fathergill papers, in case there's any clue I've missed. I also have a couple of books to read about the Newport uprising, that should arrive this morning. I want to read more about Prosser.'

'So, you're still thinking about the theft?'

Maggie sighed. 'Yes, I suppose I am. I hate knowing something is out there that we can't reach. It's like having an itch in your head. I want to ignore it, but I can't.'

Zelah grinned. 'Me too.'

The doorbell rang. Maggie went to answer and came back in with a package. 'My books. I'm going to settle down here and read and make notes.'

Two hours later, as Maggie stood up to head to the kitchen for more coffee; Zelah slapped her hand on the desk. 'Got them!'

'Sorry, got who?'

'The descendants of George Evans. They're in North Wales.'

'That was quick.'

'They've had an unfortunate ongoing problem in their families, of children dying young. Interesting that in each case, it's the daughter who survives. In three generations all of the sons have died before they reached the age of five.'

'That's awful, Zelah.'

'Yes, but it's made them much easier to research down to the present day. There are three generations still alive. There's a Richard Wilson, who's ninety-five and in a home in a place called Deganwy, near Conwy. He has a son called Hugh, born in 1952, who also has a son, called Michael, born in 1982. Michael is a prolific poster on all sorts of social media, hence finding the names of his dad and grandfather.'

'Do we know where they live?'

'Not yet, but I'm going to send Michael a message. He hasn't posted anything for the last week or so, which is rather unusual for him, and – oh, my God.'

'What?' Maggie said, stopping in the door and turning around.

'I've just checked his pictures. I think we've just found the identity of the dead man in the hotel in London. It's Hugh Wilson, Michael's dad.'

Chapter 18

Maggie walked back across the room and leaned over Zelah's shoulder.

'Yep, that's him, isn't it? Damn. What do we do now?'

'Two things. We need to tell Finch. And we wait to see if I get a response from Michael to my request.'

'If you do?'

Zelah turned around. 'I suggest we go up to North Wales to meet with Michael.'

'After we tell Finch. The family has to be informed officially.'

'I suppose so,' Zelah replied.

'Whatever Hugh Wilson's reason for being in that hotel, with my business card, his family is going to be devastated to hear that he's dead. I'm going to call Finch now.'

Maggie left the room, leaving Zelah frowning in front of her screen. Two minutes later a ping announced a message. She checked it – a response from Michael Wilson. He had accepted her request. She sat for a few minutes wondering what to do. Should she begin to ask him questions? No. Not until she at least heard what Maggie had to say. As she waited there was another ping. Michael Wilson wanted to have a personal conversation. She hit the "agree" button and waited.

Two more minutes and a message arrived, from Michael Wilson.

You are Maze Investigations. Where is my father?

'Oh, shit,' Zelah muttered as Maggie returned. 'I've spoken with Finch. He's just checking out Hugh Wilson, then he'll have the local force go to the house and … Zelah, what's up?'

He accepted my request right away, then asked me for a personal convo, which I accepted. Look.'

She leaned back from the screen and Maggie saw the message. 'Oh no! I'll have to call Finch again.'

She dialled the number immediately and gave Finch the information. Even without the speaker on, Zelah could hear the instruction to have no further interaction with the Wilson family. 'Is that clear, Mrs Gilbert?'

'Yes, of course it is. Under no circumstances would we interfere in such a situation. We'll just not reply, but I hope you can get someone there quickly to let them know Hugh Wilson is dead.'

Zelah was waving her arms. 'Ask him who's going to speak to them to find out why the man had your business card.'

Maggie shook her head. 'Not yet,' she mouthed.

The call ended.

'So what do we do now?' Zelah asked.

'Nothing at all. We know, most probably, that the man in the hotel, Hugh Wilson, was given my card by Henry Camberwell. We need to give it time until the family is informed about his death before we even think about contacting them, a couple of weeks at least.'

Zelah nodded. 'Well, apart from speaking to Anthony Bandon's uncles in Australia, I can't see there's much more we can do on this one.'

'Agreed. Much to everyone's relief, I suspect. It's not like we don't have enough other work to be going on with.'

'I'll call Nick and let him know so he can tell Stella and Max. You can speak to Mischa and the boys in Ireland and Gerry Quinn.

I'll tell Jack as soon as he wakes up. Then, I'm going to carry on reading. I still want to know about Prosser.'

'That itch not stopped giving you trouble?'

Maggie nodded. 'We shouldn't let it go entirely, not yet. It will just be on the back burner for the next few weeks until we have something to work with. If there's anything.'

'There will be. Finch won't let Camberwell go and the dreaded Olivia desperately wants to find the vase.'

'We'll see. Right, phone calls, coffee, cake and carry on with other work.'

Nick expressed his relief that Maze wasn't going to play any further part in the discovery of the vase – his interpretation of the news, which Maggie didn't agree with, but she didn't push him too hard. Zelah said the same of Mischa, Niall, and Stephen. And when Maggie told Jack, he too was pleased.

'Looks like we're the only ones who think there's more to come,' she said to Zelah over coffee and cake. They were sitting outside overlooking the garden, as the weather had had a burst of spring activity and warmed up several degrees.

'What if there is more and it's just the two of us?' Zelah asked. 'Are you willing to carry on? I am. And, strangely, so is Gerry Quinn. His grudge against Camberwell is strong and not going to go away any time soon.'

'Don't ask me to commit just yet,' Maggie replied, as her phone rang.

'Hello, Mr Finch. Is there some news? I'm with Zelah, so I'm going to put you on speaker.'

'The local police have been to see the Wilson family. Naturally, they are very upset. Mrs Wilson will be travelling down to London tomorrow to identify her husband. Once that's done, the body

118

can be released back to North Wales, as there are no suspicious circumstances around his death.'

'Other than why he was in London with Maggie's business card bearing the fingerprints of Henry Camberwell,' Zelah said.

'Are you going to ask her about my business card tomorrow?'

'I can't discuss that,' Finch replied.

Zelah went to retort but Maggie shook her head.

'Why not? He had my contact details. How do I know someone else won't take over where Hugh Wilson left off? This is not fair to me personally, not as part of my job, but for me and my family's safety, given the involvement of Henry Camberwell.'

'I'll let you know if there's anything pertinent to you, personally,' he replied, emphasising the "personally", 'but for now, Maze Investigations is not involved and will not be informed further. Good day, Mrs Gilbert.'

'Well, if he thinks we're just going to quietly back off-' Zelah spluttered.

'I can't think of a better way to ensure we don't,' Maggie finished her sentence. 'But still, nothing we can do for the time being.'

'No, I agree with that.'

'Then let's carry on with what we have.'

**

Maggie was reading in the kitchen over lunch when Zelah called her to come into the office, there was something she needed to see.

'He's been in touch again.'

'Who has?' Maggie asked.

'Michael Wilson. Look.'

The message was stark and simple. *Police have told us my father is dead, of a heart attack. My mother going to London tonight. I want to speak to you in person. Can you come to North Wales now?*

'This is the message I sent back,' Zelah said. *Very sorry for your loss. Perhaps we should wait a while until your mother is back.*

'Now his response.' *No, tomorrow, please. This can't wait.*

Maggie sat on the chair next to Zelah, biting her bottom lip. 'This has to be something to do with Camberwell,' she said.

'Or, something to do with the family story,' Zelah replied. 'I say we should go. He's clear he doesn't want his mother involved. We need to find out why.'

Maggie sat back in the chair, running her fingers through her hair, frowning. 'I don't know, Zelah. Finch was very clear about us not being involved with the Wilson family.'

'Look, we haven't chased this, not really. He's the one pushing us.'

'Why do you want to go, Zelah? You were the one who didn't want anything to do with Camberwell. We were at least two steps removed from him. If we go to meet this man, we'll bring ourselves a step closer. Think about it. This Michael Wilson may be the one reporting back to Camberwell, who'll then know that we're still on the hunt.'

Zelah nodded slowly. 'Maybe, maybe not. What's bothering me is: if Camberwell didn't know anything about the family history of the Evans family, how did he find Hugh Wilson and why did he give him your business card?'

Maggie paused, thinking of the various permutations. She scowled and twitched, as Zelah sat, watching and waiting.

She turned to Zelah with a stunned expression. 'He knows what we've been doing. He must have used another company and given them the details we found, and they came up with George Evans' line of descent.'

'More than that, I think. He has someone on the inside, someone who's been with us, and is giving him everything we find out. Think about how long it took me to find the Evans line down to Michael Wilson. A couple of hours. Any decent genealogist could have done the same, with the right information. But only with that information.'

'So, someone close to us has been informing Camberwell? Is that what you're saying?'

'That's exactly what I'm saying. Now, before you go off trying to work out who, don't bother. For now, it doesn't matter. But we're only going to find out if we take that step closer and that's why I'm for going up to North Wales, to meet Michael Wilson. Someone is betraying us.'

Maggie nodded. 'Yes. But we can't tell anyone else why we're going.'

'Agreed. I'll invent a call from a new client, someone who wants to meet urgently with us. I'll say it's, um, let me think, I'll say the meeting is in Chester.'

'Why not just say we're going to North Wales?'

'Because we can't rule anyone out, and Finch knows that's where the Wilson family lives.'

'Finch?' Maggie said.

'No-one is ruled out, right now,' Zelah replied. 'We'll have to stay overnight. There's a smart hotel on the estuary in Deganwy. I'll book us a couple of rooms there and I'll message Michael Wilson to meet us there tomorrow morning.' She looked at Maggie's increasingly horrified expression. 'Maggie, I don't for a minute think it's anyone really close.'

'Exactly, me neither. That's why I hate to deceive them all.'

'It has to be done. Right, pack an overnight bag. I'll get online and reserve the rooms. I keep an overnight emergency bag in my car. We can go in an hour after we let people know we'll be away overnight.'

Maggie nodded. 'I remember from the previous case it's about a 4-hour drive.'

'We'll be there early evening. Let's get started.'

Maggie left Zelah in the office and went upstairs to put some clothes and toiletries into a bag. Forty minutes later, they left the house.

**

'So what did Bob say?'

What do you mean?' Maggie asked, staring out of the front windscreen.

'When you told him where we're going and why? Did you think I wouldn't guess?'

Maggie grinned. 'He said to be careful, meet Michael Wilson in a public place, and give away as little as possible.'

'And to keep him posted at regular intervals?'

Maggie didn't reply.

'So where are we going to meet the man?' Maggie asked.

'The hotel has a deck where they serve morning coffee, right on the Aberconwy estuary. I've asked him to meet us there at ten thirty. Gives us time for breakfast, and for you to use the pool and gym if that's what you want to do.'

'Might as well make the most of it,' Maggie replied.

'We'll let him do the talking,' Zelah said. 'He's asked for this meeting.'

'What if he mentions Henry Camberwell?'

'Pretend we have no idea who he's talking about.'

'Not sure that will get us far, but, let's make sure we have a backup position.'

For the rest of the journey, in between periods of silence, they discussed possible scenarios and their responses to whatever Michael Wilson might say. After which neither asked the other what they had been thinking about.

They arrived at the hotel at seven. Zelah had booked two rooms, each with balcony looking directly onto the estuary. The tide was out but beginning to race in, towards a narrow neck where a road bridge ran across to Conwy and the world heritage site that was Conwy Castle standing on the banks. After settling in Maggie made herself a cup of tea and sat at the table and chairs, looking out over the view.

At the end of the estuary to her right, was the Irish sea, where two opposite spurs of land marked the boundary between sea and estuary. Directly ahead, yachts bobbed on the sparkling rushing water as it filled up the basin, and on the opposite bank, was a marina next to the small harbour and walls of the ancient town of Conwy. To her left, at the end of the roadway, was the magnificent castle. It was enchanting. She resolved she and Bob would come back to spend time here at their leisure. But for now, she had an hour before meeting Zelah for dinner, after which she was going to retire into what looked like a comfortable king-size bed.

**

The following morning, as they breakfasted they went over the scenarios they had discussed at length on the journey and over dinner. Afterwards, they went out onto the deck and waited. And waited. They were about to give up just before eleven, when a man came through the glass doors, out of breath. He looked around.

Zelah called out, 'Michael Wilson?'

'Sorry I'm late. I had to take a call from my mother.'

For a man probably in his mid-thirties, he looked younger. He had straw-coloured blond hair and green eyes, smooth skin, and a torso that spoke of hours in a gym. He also had a soft tan, which was smooth enough to have come from a machine rather than the sun, or a bottle. He took the third seat at the table and held out a manicured hand on which he wore a gold signet ring. Zelah took it, gave a short shake, and said: 'So, why are we here?'

He looked somewhat taken aback. 'We are very sorry about your father, Mr Wilson,' Maggie said, scowling at Zelah.

'Please, call me Michael. It was a terrible shock. You know it was a heart attack?'

'Yes.'

'We didn't know he had a problem. He kept himself fit. He was a keen cyclist.'

'It can happen to anyone, I guess,' Maggie said, 'without warning. Are you sure you want to be speaking to us? We came, of course, at your request but we'll understand if it becomes too much for you.'

Michael Wilson shook his head. 'There's something I need to know from you, urgently?'

Guessing it was something about the family story, Maggie said, 'Please ask. We'll do whatever we can to help.'

'How well do know Sir Henry Camberwell?'

Chapter 19
Monmouth Gaol, 1840

George couldn't understand why he had been taken so quickly to Monmouth. The majority of the prisoners taken for trial following the uprising had been tried in Newport. Why had he been whisked away here, and now, after two days, still with no explanation? He had tried asking, but had received a beating and told to shut his mouth.

The answer came the following day, with a visitor. Pritchard.

'Well, George Evans. Surprised to see me, I expect.'

George said nothing. He was filthy, cold, and hungry. Also angry.

'What you want from me? You put those candlesticks under my bed. I'll tell them in the courtroom, what you did.'

'You expect to be believed? Look at you. You were seen running from Mr Prosser's house, with food and beer taken from his kitchen. Seen by myself and two other witnesses who will testify. And when Mr Prosser returned to his house, he found his candlesticks missing.'

'No, he didn't,' George replied. He gave Pritchard a sly look. 'But he did find something else missing, didn't he?'

'He will of course take no part in your trial. But he has a letter ready to go to the examining judges, describing in detail the property stolen from him and his recommendation that you be treated to the full severity of the law for such an audacious theft.'

George understood what he was being offered.

'Unless?'

'There is another matter we could discuss.'

George whispered through the iron bars, 'Indeed we could. And what would be in it for me, to have such a discussion with you?'

'I am certain you do not want to stay in this place any longer than is necessary. Matters … shall we say, could be arranged to our mutual satisfaction.'

'That's all well and good, but I don't trust you, Mr Pritchard.'

'Nor I you, Mr Evans.'

'Seems we have nothing further to say to each other, then, Mr Pritchard.' George turned away and walked back into his corner of the cell.

'Give my proposition some consideration. I shall return in the morning. Perhaps after another night, you may feel more inclined?'

George ignored him and Pritchard called for the constable to lead him out. It was almost dark outside and George had had nothing to eat, bar a few stale crusts, for two miserable days, having had no time to take money with him to buy food from the gaolers. He slumped down onto the floor, thinking. He knew Pritchard would be back in the morning. He would insist on the provision of food and beer, first and foremost. But could he trust Pritchard to keep to his word to let him be freed if he gave up his secret? Of course, he knew Prosser was behind the visit. He could imagine Prosser's horror on returning home, to find the vase no longer in its hiding place. Unfortunate he had run into the crowd of marchers, damn them! He could easily have outrun the two older men and could probably have found a way to give Pritchard a knock on the head to allow himself to escape. How was he going to get out of this?

He pulled his coat around his shoulders as tightly as possible and put his head down to try to sleep, despite the gnawing hunger pains, when a shout from the gaoler raised his head.

'Evans! You got yerself another visitor.'

He looked up, seeing Mary Anne standing uncertainly at the end of the corridor. He stood and ran to the bars. She ran to meet him.

'I brought you some bread and pie,' she began, pushing the food through. 'I had to give some of it to that pig out there, to let me in to see you, father.'

'What else you got, girl?'

She emptied the contents of the basket, more bread and pie, a small flask of beer, and a woollen smock. 'Taken me two days to get here, it has.'

'You're a good girl.' He had been tearing lumps off the bread with his teeth, but now he faltered. 'I'm in right trouble, this time.'

'They said you'll go to the court tomorrow.'

'I didn't steal them candlesticks, you know that.'

'I do, father, but I also know what you did take.'

'They want it back. I haven't agreed anything yet, and I don't trust that bastard, Pritchard. He's offering me a deal to get out of here, but if I tell him where it is, how do I know he'll keep his side?'

'How about you offer to take them to where it is?'

'Because he can have me thrown back in here any time he likes. No, I need something more. Something to hold him back.'

'You have the knowledge.'

'What?'

'You were there when those men talked about it. You know their names. If you were to tell someone, secret like what they really want, and who had it, might that hold them back?'

George rubbed his stubbled chin. 'Could do. Could do. I'll have to think who I should speak to.'

'I thought about it on my way here. If you were to say there was something you left behind, telling the whole story and if you don't come back, the person who has that something would tell about it …'

'Blackmail?'

'Yes, father.'

'You're a good girl. You have somewhere to stay the night?'

'I'll find somewhere.'

'Good, somewhere close by. Come back in the morning. Pritchard is due here first thing. You get here before him. I'll have our offer ready by then. You can confirm it for him.'

She nodded and left him alone. After he had finished the food, keeping a piece of bread by with some beer for the morning, he hunkered down to think through his plan. By the time dawn came, he was ready. Pritchard was in for a nasty surprise.

**

As light appeared over the mountains Mary Anne arrived back and waited outside the prison. The guard let her in and she waited with her father, who told her of his plan.

'But don't you forget, girl. If anything should go wrong, you'll be the one with the secret. Remember where we put it.'

'Can't hardly forget, can I? she laughed. 'His lordship. A good joke.'

His toothless face lit up in a huge smile as he pulled at his mutton chop whiskers. 'Good girl. We'll wait for Pritchard now.'

An hour later, there was still no sign of the servant.

'Lazy so and so,' George muttered. He called out to the guard. 'Is there no other visitor for me?'

The guard shook his head. Another hour and George began to seriously worry. 'Where is he? He said matters could be arranged.'

A constable arrived at the cells and called out names. 'Evans, George; Masters, William; Lewis, John.'

These were the men sharing George's cell. 'You're to be taken to the court.'

George gasped in horror as Mary Anne was pushed aside. She grabbed at the constable's coat and received an elbow in the face, but clung on. 'Where are you taking him? He's to be set free, there's to be an arrangement.'

The constable took no notice. He cuffed the men together then dragged them out of the gaol and up into the courtroom. Mary Anne ran up and found a court officer, a sergeant. 'Sir, my father was promised a visit, from a man called Pritchard. He is to explain it was all a mistake and my father is to be released.'

'The man who was here last night?'

'Yes, sir, the same one.'

'He's gone. He left a message as he left here. He has returned to Newport.'

**

An hour later, it was all over. George Evans had been found guilty and sentenced to transportation to the colonies of Her Majesty in Van Diemen's land, Australia, for seven years. For the theft of two candlesticks valued at five pounds each. A letter from the lawyer Mervyn Prosser had condemned the actions of George Evans, emphasising his role in the theft and his lies at his first trial in Newport some weeks before. And his attempted beating of two of Prosser's brave servants who had given chase. George had protested his innocence, claiming that he had knowledge of a great secret that Prosser wanted no-one should know. The Magistrates laughed as he was led away.

Mary Anne was allowed five minutes with him before he was removed to the transport that would take him to the waiting prison hulk at Chepstow, from where he would be transferred to Portsmouth and the ship that would take him, and a hundred other prisoners, to Van Diemen's land.

She could barely speak through her tears. 'They have betrayed you, father.'

'Prosser must have seen he couldn't deal with me, in case anyone found out the true nature of what I took. So, he has ensured I'll be as far away as possible. Go back to your mother girl. Look after her. You're the only one who knows where it is. God rot it. Wish I'd never seen the thing. It's cursed, right enough.'

'It had best stay where it is,' she whispered.

'No, get it back, if you can. Perhaps you can deal with Prosser. Get money for yourself and your mother.'

Then, two guards dragged him away.

Mary Anne made her way back to Newport, to give her mother the news that George wasn't coming home, ever again. Thomasine Evans took the news well enough. They had lodgers. They would have to find more. She could move in with Mary Anne. That gave them another room and there was always a family in need. She wasn't sorry to see the back of the man who had beaten her almost every day, drunk and sober. And she could take in laundry. Wouldn't be the first time.

**

Six months later, after a short courtship, Mary Anne Evans married Ebeneezer Phillips, a young miner from Merthyr Tydfil, where they went to live, taking her mother with them.

They were married in the church of St Paul, in Commercial Street in Newport, where George Evans had hidden as he ran from the crowds and the constables chasing the escaping marchers.

Mary Anne only returned to Newport on the occasional day trip, with her husband. She thought many times about her father's treasure and often wondered what had happened to him, but knew they would never find out, or hear from him again. She hoped he'd found some kind of decent life.

From time to time she thought about whether she should have attempted to retrieve the object from its hiding place but knew that would now be impossible. Best left to rot. She agreed with her father's final words. *It's cursed, right enough*. She eventually told the story to her only surviving child, before she died, but not the location nor the clue. She didn't want to pass on the curse. Best left where it was. Best forgotten. Just a story, to regale her grandchildren and their grandchildren, on dark nights; a story of how their ancestor got his hands on a treasure beyond value but lost it.

Chapter 20

'Who?' Zelah asked, with her best poker face.

'Henry Camberwell, your client,' Michael Wilson said.

'We have no client of that name,' Zelah said. 'I assure you. Isn't that right, Maggie?'

Maggie nodded. It was the truth, not quite entirely, but …

Michael Wilson leaned back and folded his arms. 'Look, I don't know why you're saying this. I know you're working for him. My dad was supposed to meet up with you after he made contact.'

It was Maggie's turn. 'Michael, I will presume it was Camberwell or someone working for him who gave you this information. It's a lie. He is not, has never been, and never will be our client. But,' she glanced over at Zelah, who tipped her head, 'we do know who he is. That's why we won't have anything to do with him. Look, are you able to tell us what's been happening, from your side?'

The man licked his lips, looking from Maggie's open, slightly smiling face to Zelah's intense stare, then back again.

'Fair enough. There's a story in my family, been handed down over generations-'

'We know,' Zelah interrupted. 'A fabled treasure, or something of the kind.'

'Let him speak, Zelah,' Maggie said.

'Thankyou. But, you're right, Mrs Trevear. My grandad, who's still alive – just – in a care home up on the hill behind us, used to talk about it sometimes, although I don't think he ever really took it seriously, but since my dad retired he's been enthusiastic about trying to find out whatever it was. We know it began with a man called William George Evans, my three times great grandfather. He was transported to Australia in 1840, for the theft of two candlesticks. Family tale is that he stole something else, that was never named, and hid it somewhere before he was caught with the candlesticks. The tale also says he was framed.'

He paused and took a drink from a large coffee that a waiter had placed on the table in front of him. 'My dad has scoured paperwork and stories for the last two years. He discovered that this ancestor didn't actually reach Australia, but died on the convict transport ship. Well, two weeks ago, dad was approached by a genealogy company who said they had been commissioned by a client of theirs to find out more about our family history and the story of the treasure.' He paused. 'Do you know anything about this … whatever it is?'

Zelah began to shake her head, but Maggie put a hand on her arm. 'We know there's supposed to be something. Please, continue, Michael.'

'Just a minute,' Zelah said. 'Another genealogy company?'

'A husband and wife called Ian and Moira Desmond.'

Zelah shouted 'Ha!' and banged her hand on the table, causing people sitting around them on the deck to turn to see where the noise had come from.

'You know them?' Michael Wilson asked.

'You bet,' Zelah said. 'Anyway, carry on.'

'The story they told us was that you are trying to find this "thing" and want to keep it, illegally. Their client – and they didn't name him – was determined to find it first. The Desmonds described him as an expert in fine arts and antiques. Anyway, they told dad that if he was to work with them he'd have to be incognito. They gave him a passport in the name of some Australian, I can't remember the name now, and sent him down to London with your business card. He was supposed to get in touch, pretending to be this person. Dad was very, very excited; thought he was James Bond. My mother and I were starting to get worried when we didn't hear from him after he checked into the hotel in Soho. Then yesterday, the police came. I told them the story of the Desmonds. They told me about the passport and asked me if I knew what happened to it as it seems to be missing. I had no idea.'

He stopped, swallowed, and shook his head.

Maggie leaned forward. 'Have you heard from the Desmonds in the past twenty-four hours?'

'No. I've been trying to get in touch with them, but they aren't answering the phone.'

'Doesn't surprise me,' Zelah said. 'Why did you give us the name Henry Camberwell?'

I worked out who their client was. It wasn't difficult from the clues they gave away and when I saw that you're a genealogy company, well, I assumed that someone had commissioned you, too, possibly this man Camberwell, playing both sides.' He turned to Zelah. 'Why did you react when you heard the name of the Desmonds?'

'I know of them, going back years.'

'Good or bad?'

'My personal experience – not good. But I'm not saying any more than that. Professional courtesy.'

Maggie was surprised. Zelah didn't usually hold back.

'But you have an opinion?' Michael asked.

Maggie grinned in the face of Zelah's pursed lips. 'She has an opinion and usually, she's not afraid to share it.'

'We'll discuss it later,' Zelah muttered to Maggie.

'Is that what you came here to talk to us about,' Maggie asked, 'Henry Camberwell?'

'I was hoping you might be able to tell me more.' He sat forward. 'I didn't like it, what the Desmonds proposed to dad, him going to London, impersonating some Australian guy, Anthony – something. Ah, is that your client?'

Maggie realised she must have reacted to the name and cursed herself. 'I can't discuss our clients,' she said. 'I'm still not sure what you want from us, Michael.'

'I want to know about Henry Camberwell. Moira Desmond, or was it, Ian, I can't remember, promised my dad a lot of money. He said this – what did he call it?' he paused and looked up, thinking. 'An artefact, that was it. She said it was invaluable and would be returned by the client to the British Museum.'

'Was it a very substantial sum?' Zelah asked.

'Yes,' Michael said, looking down at the table.

'Over a million?' Zelah pushed.

'Might have been,' Michael said, shuffling in his chair.

'Here's what we can tell you about Henry Camberwell,' Zelah said. 'You wouldn't have seen a penny of it.'

An expression of wide-eyed, open-mouthed shock hit Michael Wilson's face. 'Are you saying he's a crook? Wait, did he do something to my father?' He began to stand up.

Maggie put a hand on his arm. 'No, your father's death was entirely natural.'

He fell back into the seat. 'How do you know that?'

'He had my business card, remember. The police asked me how he came to have it. I couldn't answer that question. They told me he had died of natural causes.' It was a version of the truth. She hoped he wouldn't question the timeline more closely.

'I see. Well, I guess there's nothing more for us to discuss. Thank you for your time.' Now he stood.

'Michael, we really are very sorry for your loss. And I'm sorry there isn't anything more we can do for you.'

'Can I contact you again, if anything comes up?'

'Of course. You have our details.' She took a card from her pocket. 'Here's our office number.'

She watched him leave, then turned to Zelah. 'I'm not sure about him.'

'Me neither. I presume you picked up the issue that young man could have asked us about?'

'Of course. Hugh Wilson was given Anthony Bandon's passport, which wasn't found on him. So, if the Desmonds gave it to him, what happened to it? Someone took that passport from Hugh Wilson, either before or after he died.'

'Exactly. Plus several more. And I don't believe there's any way he could have worked out from clues given by the Desmonds that Henry Camberwell was their client. I don't like them, but they are professional and would never have done that. No, that young man knows a lot more than he's telling us.'

Chapter 21
At Sea, 1840

George began to feel unwell during an horrendous storm in the Bay of Biscay. He had never been to sea before, which was true of many of the convicts. The stench of seasickness was overwhelming and unavoidable throughout the ship.

Work schedules had been abandoned for the duration of the storm. The convicts were allowed onto the deck of the ship in shifts three times a day. On a few occasions, George had stood next to a younger man, whose accent he recognised.

'You a Newport man, then?'

'Who wants to know?'

'George Evans.'

The younger man looked suspiciously at him, grasping onto the rail as the ship raised to what looked like its full height, then fell into the trough of yet another twenty-foot wave. As the ship hit the depth and a great plume of water headed towards them George lost his grip and the young man reached out and grabbed him, just as the water hit them. George managed to find the rail again as the group of bedraggled men and women were ordered back down into the hold.

'William Evan Williams,' the young man whispered with a grin. 'You're in my debt, now, George Evans.'

Two days later they met again. The storm had settled but the sea was still dark and rough. They were both swabbing the same deck.

'Newport man, eh?' George said to Williams' back.

'Call me Evan.'

'Well, Evan, what's my payment to be?'

William Evan Williams puzzled for a moment, then turned around and grinned at George. 'Blanket,' he said. 'Mine's too thin.'

George shook his head and began a spate of coughing that didn't stop for several minutes. 'Not going to happen, son.'

'I'm not your son, old man. What else you got to give me?'

George was about to reply when dizziness hit him and he staggered. Evan moved forward to hold him up. 'Need the surgeon, old man.'

George shook his head again. 'No fear.'

For the next three days, George shivered uncontrollably. On the fourth day, he was unable to leave his bed and the surgeon was called. He was diagnosed with a fever, given some medicine that he spat out, and demanded rum. The surgeon laughed.

The following day he began to sweat and shiver at the same time. This time, the surgeon had him removed to the small medical facility. Whatever this was, if it was infectious he didn't want to be blamed if it spread to others.

The conditions were a little better in the medical facility, but George didn't improve. On the sixth day, he asked to see Evan Williams and this was approved.

'What's up, old man?'

'I believe I am dying, Evan.'

'Not you. You're tough and strong. You'll make it.'

'No. My bones ache right through me.' He pulled the young man close. 'I see visions. My wife is calling me. I believe my time has come.'

Evan pulled back. He wasn't sure why George had asked to see him, but whatever it was, he didn't want to be contaminated by George's illness. He went to stand but George grabbed his sleeve and pulled him down again.

'I have a secret. Someone must know. I had the means to great wealth.' He stopped and coughed again, this time bringing up phlegm and blood. Some of it hit Evan's sleeve and he pulled back in disgust but wanted to hear more. He thought the old man might be delirious, but if there was something to be had ...

'What you talking about, old man?'

'I was in a house, two rich men talking, one showed the other something he said was priceless. They had to leave in a hurry, because of the marchers.' His voice was rasping now. 'I was in a cupboard, hiding ... got out, took it. But, the marchers got me. Hid it, His Lordship,' he grinned and coughed again. 'My daughter knows, but she won't touch it. Thinks it's cursed.' His fingers dug into Evan's arm. 'If you get back, take it. Remember, His Lordship at Newport. You're a Newport man.' His head fell back.

'I don't understand,' Evan said. 'What's His Lordship?' he asked, leaning over the shaking body.

'His fault, Lordship,' George mumbled. 'You'll find him.' His eyes closed.

Evan had been transported for seven years, for the theft of bread and a silver watch and for beating the old man from whom he'd stolen both. As he watched George pass into unconsciousness his thoughts were focused on a priceless object, somewhere in Newport. Evan was just twenty-four. He would be able to return to Wales in seven years, earlier possibly if he behaved himself. But what if the daughter had changed her mind and taken it? He shook his head. He wasn't sure what this meant, but it was a piece of information to be stored for the future. He had to survive these seven years. Who knew what would happen after that?

He left the compartment without bothering to look back at George. George's blanket was already gone from his bunk. There was nothing further that Evan could take immediately and he had already lost interest in the man.

William George Evans, aged fifty-five, died two days later of unexplained fever and was buried at sea. His family was not informed.

Chapter 22

After checking out of the hotel Maggie and Zelah decided they needed a walk and to find somewhere they could sit and discuss the meeting with Michael Wilson and his unasked questions.

They took a five-minute drive across the Aberconwy estuary, past the castle perched on its banks, into the small medieval town of Conwy, and parked in the High Street, then headed down to the quay. The tide coming in from the Irish sea pushed lapping water up against the edges of the harbour wall. There were a few visitors strolling along towards the castle and children trying to catch crabs in the clear water with a line and bucket.

They sat on a bench halfway along the quay with an ice cream each, watched by a couple of seagulls.

'Keep your ice cream close to you,' Zelah said to Maggie. 'Those bloody birds are lethal. They'll have it out of your hand in a second.'

'How do you know that?'

'There were signs on the wall where we walked through the gateway.'

Maggie looked out across the estuary, and up to the clear blue sky. 'Lovely place. I didn't know it was walled.' She watched a couple descend an open stone stairway in an exposed round tower where the thick, high medieval defensive wall reached the edge of the quay. 'I might ask Bob if we can bring the camper van up here in the summer. He'll be all over that castle.'

'World heritage site,' Zelah said. 'Right, the Wilson family. Your thoughts?'

'Michael Wilson didn't show nearly enough interest in what we might know. He only wanted to know about Camberwell.'

'Agreed. Mind you, he's probably still in shock.'

'I'd like to know why he insisted we came here today, barely twenty-four hours after he found out about his father's death, and while his mother's in London,' Maggie mused, licking the now melting ice cream. 'Doesn't want her to know he's spoken to us?'

'Says to me he's as interested in pursuing the case as his father is … was.'

'Tell me about the Desmonds,' Maggie said.

'I have nothing good to say about them. About six or seven years ago, not long before we started Maze, I'd taken on a couple of clients, my first venture into the commercial world of genealogy. Fairly simple stuff. What I didn't know was that one of the clients had come to me because he was dissatisfied with the work the Desmonds had done. When Ian Desmond found out he called me and was disgustingly rude, accused me of underhand practice and of stealing their client. Then he put it about that I had done a poor job.'

'Nasty,' Maggie said. 'How good are they?'

'There have been complaints. They cut corners. But they are just the kind of people Camberwell would go to and, if they're involved, they'll cause us as much trouble as they can.'

'Just what we need,' Maggie grimaced. 'So, what do we do now?'

'You'll have to let Finch know that Hugh Wilson was given the passport by the Desmonds. We can't keep it to ourselves. If the wife has any sense, she'll have already told whoever accompanies her to the morgue.'

142

'Michael Wilson didn't demonstrate much interest in the "artefact", didn't even ask us if we knew what it was,' Zelah mused, 'which suggests to me that he already knows.'

'Let's find somewhere to have lunch, then get back home,' Maggie said, finishing off her ice cream and standing up. As they began to walk back up into the town Maggie's phone pinged and she stopped to check it.

'It's from Anthony. He says we're welcome to speak to Malcolm and Roger. Oh, and some more information has emerged.' She began to type a message. 'I'm telling him we're away today, but home tonight, so I'll set up the call for first thing tomorrow, evening for them.'

When Maggie had finished and put the phone away Zelah said, 'Should we tell him about the Wilsons?'

'My gut reaction to that is "no", but I can't tell you why. Let's leave it for now. We can discuss it on our way home.'

'On to the next stage, then,' Zelah said. 'We aren't any closer to finding out which of us gave the information to Camberwell, but at least we know he's working through the Desmonds and it wouldn't surprise me if they turn up in Newport any day now.'

For lunch, they chose a small café with a garden that looked up towards one of the many towers of Conwy Castle. An hour later they left the town and were home by early evening.

**

Zelah dropped Maggie at home before heading back to her flat. An unmanned police car sat outside the house. *They must be inside, whoever they are*, she thought as she walked briskly up the path, on edge, taking a deep breath to prepare herself, as she put her key into the lock.

Immediately she sensed something was wrong. Bob stood in the hallway, with a white-faced Jack on his shoulder.

'What's happened? Who is it?' she asked, clutching at Bob's sleeve. He didn't answer but led her into the office, where she saw a man she didn't recognise and a uniformed constable. Bob put his arm around her shoulder, but shook his head again, as the unknown man stepped forward.

'Mrs Gilbert, I'm Detective Inspector Tom Middleton from the Metropolitan Police. We'd like to interview you about the death of a man in a London hotel.'

'You mean Hugh Wilson?'

'That's correct. I would be grateful if you would accompany me to the Newport police station.'

'Why? Hugh Wilson died of a heart attack.' She glanced uneasily at Bob.

'It seems Mr Wilson did not die of a heart attack, as was originally believed. Now, if you will come with me,' he took a step towards her and she stepped back.

'I've just got back from a long trip and I'm tired. I don't know what I can do to help you, so if this could wait until the morning …'

'No, it can't wait. Are you unwilling to come with me? It would be better if you did.'

She looked at Bob again. 'What's going on, Bob?'

'I don't know, he won't tell me. But,' he stepped around to face her and put his hands on her shoulders. 'Go with them. I'm guessing, if you don't, this man may arrest you.'

Maggie felt like she'd been punched in the gut. She looked questioningly at him, saw the intensity in his eyes, and nodded. 'OK, I'll come with you, but if you're going to question me, I want a lawyer present with me.'

'If you believe you need one, for an informal chat,' Middleton said, a hint of annoyance in his voice.

'She's within her rights to ask, and I think it's a good idea. No chance of anything untoward happening at the informal chat, is there, with a lawyer present,' Bob said, glaring at the Inspector.

Maggie turned to Bob. 'Will you find one at this time of night?'

'Already done. She's on her way and she'll meet you there. I'll be there, too,'

The Inspector went to protest but Bob held up a hand. 'Of course, I can't be present, but it's my station and I've every right to be on the premises.'

With the constable on the other side, she was led from the house and put into the back of a waiting police car. As she was driven away, her last sight was of Jack in tears on the doorstep.

**

On arrival at the station, the Inspector led her into a room with a table and four chairs. A female police constable arrived and asked her if she would like a drink. She asked for tea, uncertain of what might turn up, given Bob's knowledge of the site catering, but was now so tired that anything hot would do.

When the constable returned with a plastic cup she said, 'Your lawyer has arrived. She'll be with you in a few minutes.' Still in a state of shock, Maggie realised that she hadn't asked any questions, even though she knew they probably wouldn't have been answered during the car journey. She had been thinking through everything she knew about Hugh Wilson, which was not much, apart from his basic life and death dates. She would have to talk about the meeting with Michael Wilson earlier in the day. But first, she needed to speak to the solicitor Bob had arranged. *Better be a bloody good one*, she thought, as she sipped the tea, which wasn't too bad.

The door was opened by the constable and a woman entered. Immediately Maggie's thoughts went to Zelah. The woman was short and wearing six-inch heels. Her hair was held up in a bun at the back of her head. She wore a black business suit and a white blouse and as she marched to the table, Maggie's impression was of a woman who took no prisoners. A Zelah clone.

She held out her hand, showing off blood-red nails. 'Norah Collins. Pleased to meet you. Detective Chief Inspector Pugh and Mrs Trevear have given me an update on the case and …'

'Zelah has spoken to you? Do you know her?'

Norah Collins smiled. 'I know her well. She and I go back a long way. Now, what have they told you so far?'

'Absolutely nothing,' Maggie said. 'I'd just returned from a trip to North Wales, where Zelah and I met with Michael Wilson.'

'The son?'

'Yes. He asked us to go and meet him.'

Norah frowned. 'You'd better give me a full brief on everything you know about the Wilsons and about the case you're involved in.'

Twenty minutes later Norah said, 'Right, I think we're ready. Let's see what they have to say, and remember, this is just an informal interview, although it will be recorded. If they go into territory I don't like, I'll butt in and stop it, OK?'

Maggie nodded and swallowed.

Norah put a hand on her arm. 'Don't worry. You haven't done anything wrong.' She stood, marched to the door, and flung it open. 'You can come in now,' she said to no-one in particular and returned to the chair next to Maggie.

Detective Inspector Middleton entered, accompanied by a woman he introduced as Detective Sergeant Michaela Westcott. They put files on the table in front of them and the Sergeant, having turned on the recording, began with the words Maggie had heard so many times on television programmes, 'You do not have to say anything, but …'

Maggie shook her head.

Middleton began. 'Mrs Gilbert, you were in London on the night of April 4th. Is that correct?'

'Yes, I already told this to John Finch. I stayed at the Victoria Palace Hotel. I arrived around seven o'clock at Paddington and made my way to the hotel, where I had dinner. The following morning I went to the London Metropolitan archives when they opened at ten and spent the day there. I had made a reservation. You have to do that for now, you can't just turn up, because of Covid. From there I went back to Paddington. I then caught a train home at around five that afternoon.'

'I am assuming you've verified those details, Inspector?' Norah Collins asked.

'Yes. Mrs Gilbert, from the time you left the archives building to reaching Paddington station, did you go anywhere else?'

'No. I went straight to the station. I was early, so I went into a café and had something to eat until it was time to board?'

'Which café?'

'Um,' she closed her eyes and shook her head. 'I'm not sure of the name, but it's the big one, at the back of the station, it's surrounded by shops.'

'What did you eat and drink?'

'A coffee and a small cake.'

147

'Did you keep a receipt?'

'I … I don't think so.'

'I see. So you can't prove you were in the café between four fifteen and five that afternoon.'

'Not unless they have CCTV,' Maggie said, glancing at Norah. 'But I was there.'

'My client says she was there,' Norah interrupted again.

Middleton opened the file and took out a plastic wallet containing Maggie's business card. 'This was found in the coat pocket of the dead man. Can you explain how it got there?'

She shook her head. 'No, again, I told John Finch I give dozens of cards out at each of the genealogy shows I visit. I don't expect to have to account for them afterwards.' She was beginning to feel rattled. Norah sensed it and said, 'A good enough answer, Inspector.'

'Anyway,' Maggie said, 'You'll also know that there were two fingerprints on the card, one unknown and the other belonging to Sir Henry Camberwell. Are you interviewing him?'

The Inspector didn't respond. He brought out another cardboard wallet and took out what looked like a black and white photograph, which he put in front of Maggie.

'Do you recognise the woman in this photograph?'

She leaned forward. 'It's not clear. I mean, it looks a bit like me.'

'This picture is taken from CCTV at the First Point hotel in Soho, where Mr Wilson was staying.'

'Can't be me, then,' Maggie said. 'I didn't know that hotel even existed.'

'The CCTV is from the afternoon of 5th April, when you said you were at Paddington Station, Mrs Gilbert. Are you sure it isn't you?'

'My client has answered your question.'

He nodded. 'This woman asked at the reception desk for a Mr Anthony Bandon, who had recently checked in from Australia. I believe Mr Bandon is known to you?'

'He's a client, but I've never met him and I thought he was in Australia. In fact, I now know he never left Australia and that his passport was stolen.' She leaned forward. 'So, that definitely cannot be me.'

'Earlier today you met with Michael Wilson, the son of Hugh Wilson. Is that correct?'

'Yes. He asked my colleague and I to travel to North Wales to meet him.'

'That's not what he is saying.'

Maggie turned to look at Norah and shrugged.

'Then you had better tell my client what Mr Wilson junior is saying.'

'He says you demanded the meeting and threatened him.'

'What!' Maggie started to rise out of her seat, but Norah pulled her back down.

'What am I supposed to have said?'

'You threatened him that he and his family would be financially penalised if they didn't give up the hunt for an artefact. The same one you are pursuing for Mr Bandon.'

'Not true,' Maggie said, gritting her teeth. 'He asked for the meeting. That's on record. Zelah Trevear did contact him, but he was the one who pursued the meeting. When we met with him this morning he asked us about Henry Camberwell. Zelah told him that if Camberwell had promised the Wilsons money, they'd likely never see a penny of it. And anyway, Camberwell seems to be working through another genealogy company, run by a couple called Desmond. Michael Wilson said his father got my business card from one of the Desmonds.'

The Inspector sat back, took a quick look at the sergeant, then said. 'I see. That's enough for now Mrs Gilbert. You can go, but I'll be continuing our enquiries.'

'Just a minute,' Maggie countered. 'I was told by John Finch that Hugh Wilson died of a heart attack. Is that not right?'

'Hugh Wilson died of a heart attack induced by forced administration of a drug. It happened on the afternoon of 5th April, at approximately the time you allege you were at Paddington Station waiting for a train.'

He closed the file. 'I am releasing you under further investigation. I will let you know if you will be required to attend a supplementary interview.'

After they left the room, Maggie's legs were shaking so much she collapsed back into her seat when she tried to stand.

'Take a few minutes,' Norah Collins said. 'Breathe. Now, it's clear to me they don't have enough to charge you. In my opinion, that picture isn't clear enough. However, they may try VIPER.'

'What's that?'

'It's an electronic identity parade. This woman at the hotel must have spoken to whoever was at the reception desk. They'll show pictures to that person and ask if they recognise any of them. One of those pictures will be you. The one they just showed you will be another.'

Maggie slumped down into the chair. 'I think I'm being set up.'

Norah reacted sharply. 'By whom?'

'Henry Camberwell, or the Desmonds. They're working for him, we're sure and Zelah has a history with the Desmonds, as we have with Camberwell.'

'I see. Come on, let's go. Chief Inspector Pugh and your son are waiting for you.'

Once they were clear of the station she gave Jack, then Bob, a tight hug.

'What's going on, mum?'

She shook her head. 'Let's get back home and I'll tell you about it.' She glanced at her watch. It was almost eleven. 'I'm exhausted.'

'You're being set up,' Bob said as they got into his car.

'I know,' Maggie replied, 'and I don't think we have long to sort it out before I'm arrested. This is Camberwell's doing.'

Bob nodded. 'Then a gathering of the clans is needed, asap.'

'I've already called Zelah,' Jack said. 'She's going to round everyone up in the morning.'

'Then let battle commence,' Maggie said. 'They aren't going to get away with this.'

Chapter 23

Tasmania, 1855

William Evan Williams cursed, spat on a patch of weedy grass, and sat down, wiping the sweat from his filthy forehead. This was not how he had planned it.

He had never been able to control his temper, which had been the cause of his punishment in the first place and which worsened with each tropical season. His suffering from the heat and rain had been the cause of him giving his wife such a beating that she lay unconscious for weeks. The gaol sentence he had received had put paid to any possibility of a pardon, partial or full.

He had managed, after seven years, to obtain his ticket of leave and had had great plans to work for himself and become respectable. But the woman he had married had put paid to that. She had turned out to be a drunk. So, it wasn't his fault when she provoked him. At first, it was a slap, then a punch. When the child came she had seemed to settle down, but it hadn't lasted.

He had gone too far. She hadn't recovered from the final beating and he was now being hunted down for murder. He knew he'd get away with it, of course. He had the child with him and he presented the two of them as a family, who had lost their precious wife and mother and were now looking for work to survive. At six years of age, the child had an appealing look, with his white-blond hair and huge dark eyes. Of course, he had to deliver the occasional slap, which recently had been a punch, when the brat cried, which was too often now. He had warned young Timothy clearly enough that he was never to speak about his mother, or he would kill him.

This latest job, on a remote farm, had been well timed. The farm was run by an old woman, a widow, accompanied by her two unmarried daughters. She had taken him in, fed them, and offered him work because of the child. He regretted the punch. Not because of any compassion he felt, but because the woman might see the bruises. He planned to work his way further into their trust, then marry one of the daughters. However, neither had shown any interest in him, at all. As he sat, he pondered on what he could do to make himself more appealing. He knew his looks were good; he had often been told he had a kind, honest face, much to his secret amusement. His plan was to marry the elder daughter, get his hands on the family money and return to Wales, to find the "treasure", the secret that George Evans had shared with him before he died. The family didn't know he had no certificate of freedom, not even that he had been a transported convict. Evan had become obsessed with the thought of the treasure, developing a deep well of patience, knowing that, in the end, he would find it and live a fine life.

A noise in the distance disturbed his thoughts. A trail of dust led up to the house. Visitors. He stood, wary. The family hadn't seen anyone else in the month he had been at the farm. The daughters made the five-mile journey into town each week for supplies. The widow never accompanied them.

He began to walk slowly towards the house. He shouldn't be returning for several hours yet, but he was uneasy. Three horses were tethered on the rail in front of the veranda. There was no noise, no sound of the chatter of welcome, just the screeching of the damned strange birds that inhabited the countryside. The feeling in his gut rumbled harder. Something was wrong. He had to get away. As he turned a voice called out to him.

'Mr Williams, won't you come inside, please.'

The widow. He smiled and shook his head. 'I just wanted to check on Timothy, he seemed unsettled this morning, but if you tell me he's well, I'll leave it and go back to work.'

'Timothy seems well, but would be pleased to see you.'

'You have visitors, Mrs McCarthy?'

'A few friends from town. Do come in and meet them.'

She was smiling, but he saw that her hands were clasped inside her apron, and her mouth twitched as she gave a rapid glance behind.

It was enough. He turned away again and began to run. As he did so, three men burst out of the house. He ran until his lungs were bursting, but one of them had jumped on a horse and was ahead of him in seconds. The man jumped down and pinned Evan to the ground.

'William Evan Williams, you are under arrest for the murder of Roberta McHugh Williams. You'll be coming with us.'

The remaining men dragged him to his feet, binding his hands behind his back, then tied the rope to the back of one of the horses.

'What about my son?' he yelled as the rope pulled him away.

'He'll be staying with Mrs McCarthy. Means you won't be able to beat him again like you did his mother.'

He glanced back and saw the three women standing on the veranda. One of the daughters had her arms around Timothy and he was hugging her in return.

Little bastard, William thought. *Must have given me away*.

The rope jerked his arms and he was forced to turn his head forward, to see the direction in which they were taking him.

**

Three weeks later the trial concluded. William Evan Williams had been found guilty of the murder of Roberta McHugh Williams and was sentenced to hang.

He had wept, pleaded repentance, and asked for mercy, but nothing had changed the mind of the presiding judge. To reprieve a former convict who had already served a gaol sentence would send the wrong message to others. Wrongdoers were to be harshly punished, especially convict wrongdoers.

On the eve of his execution, William had asked to see his son. His gaolers had agreed. After all, they were father and son. Timothy was brought to the gaol.

The terrified child tried to pull away from the embrace of the man who had so often threatened him with horrific punishments – sometimes carried out – and even death.

As he hugged a reluctant Timothy to him, William whispered the story of the "treasure", trying to instil in the boy the importance of returning to the mother country to find this fabulous thing – whatever it was.

**

Timothy was returned to the McCarthy women, who loved him and brought him up as their own son.

But, he never forgot the story his father told him. The mother country meant nothing to Timothy. He had been born in Australia. He was its citizen and took great pride in that.

However, on his deathbed, he told his son Jonathan the story. Jonathan didn't take much notice, but he also didn't forget.

The story became the family myth, to be laughed over and not taken seriously for several more generations until it reached Anthony Bandon, the 3xgreat grandson of the thief and murderer, William Evan Williams - who decided there might be something in it, albeit he had started with the wrong ancestors.

Chapter 24

At nine the following morning the office was full. All were seated except Zelah, who paced up and down the room, with a face like thunder.

Maggie hadn't been sure if she could face meeting them all so soon. Her initial reaction of rage from the previous evening had dissolved into upset and fear. She was aware that she had been the flag carrier for pursuing the research when Nick and Jack wanted to have nothing further to do with it. Although everyone else had agreed with her, she nevertheless felt a burden of guilt.

She was the last to enter the room. Bob, who had accompanied her downstairs, had put off his journey to work. When she asked why he had seemed uncaring of any consequences when he told her he was staying at home but, they had known each other long enough for her to perceive there was more to it. She didn't ask. He'd tell her if there was something she needed to know.

As she walked in Jack stood and ran to her, giving her a breath-crushing hug, as the chatter died and everyone turned to look at her.

'I'm OK,' she began as he let her go and she moved to a vacant chair. 'I'm worried, of course I am, but I know I'm being set up. Whoever is doing this, we'll have to find out. Zelah, please sit down. I don't think I can concentrate with you parading up and down. You look like a tiger behind a barrier eyeing up lunch on the other side of the glass.' It was a weak attempt at humour, but the best she could manage.

Zelah paused, drew in a deep breath, then sat in the closest chair.

'Maggie, what's happened is shocking, but can you please fill us all in on what happened yesterday and last night? It will help if we hear it from you.' The quiet, measured tone of Niall McCarthy Miller coming from the speakers around the room helped Maggie concentrate her thoughts.

'Yes, of course. I'll start with how Zelah's research led to the Desmonds and when and how we received the message – that Zelah received – from Michael Wilson and I'll try to remember as much as possible from there. Zelah, up to the point we separated yesterday evening, please chip in if I get something wrong, or miss anything out.'

She laid it out in detail for them. Zelah added the occasional piece of detail and one correction to the timeline, but otherwise confirmed Maggie's story as accurate. When she had finished there was silence and much contemplation.

'Questions, anyone?'

'These Desmonds,' Gerry Quinn began, 'Do you think he's right, they are working for Camberwell?'

'Michael Wilson says he figured it out but, no, we have no direct proof they are.'

'But do you think he's right? Is that what your gut is saying?' Gerry persisted.

'Yes, I do. They wouldn't be involved without a client and who else is there who has any interest in finding the vase?' Maggie replied.

'Well, that's a question, isn't it?' Nick said. 'We haven't considered that there might be someone else. Once Fathergill's diary was published, there might be other hunters who recognised what he was talking about and are on the trail too.'

'True,' Zelah conceded, 'but they wouldn't have had the information about George Evans' theft of the vase on the night of the uprising. Remember, he was subsequently convicted for the theft of two candlesticks. My guess is that Mervyn Prosser decided he couldn't work with George, even if that meant giving up the vase, but he couldn't risk being associated with a "hot" item.'

'Is there anyone else who could have known about the theft, apart from George Evans' family and this Australian family going back to William Evan Williams?'

'No,' Maggie replied. 'There was no-one else, if we've traced the story well enough and …'

Nick put a hand up. 'There is someone else who knew.'

All heads turned towards him. 'Prosser didn't get his own hands dirty. In the trial, in fact in both trials, of George Evans, there was one consistent character.'

'Of course,' Maggie said. 'The servant, John Pritchard. We haven't considered him.'

'The Monmouth court records confirm he led the soldiers to the home of George Evans where the candlesticks belonging to Prosser were discovered. What if he planted them? If Prosser wanted George in a place where he couldn't argue, then where better than Monmouth gaol. We should try to find out if Pritchard visited George Evans whilst he was waiting for his trial.'

'Nick, will such records still exist? Did they record visitors?' Max asked.

'I don't know. Some gaols did, some didn't. Only one way to find out. But if we find evidence that Pritchard did visit George, then that's another line of enquiry.'

'Well, it will give me something to do,' Maggie said. 'And Anthony Bandon has agreed we can speak to his great uncle Malcolm and uncle Roger.'

'I can help,' Nick said.

Maggie stood up. 'No. At this point, I want as few of you as possible to be involved. Zelah will work with me. If we need help, we'll ask you, but for now, of course, I'll keep you all informed of what happens to me, but please, keep out of the research. You can't be seen to have any involvement. Nick, I will be asking you for ideas, if that's OK.'

He nodded. 'Of course. I'll always be here to talk to. In the meantime, I'll pick up the slack on other cases.'

'Are you sure you can manage this with just the two of you?' Mischa asked. 'Seems to me there's a lot to do.'

'We'll have to,' Maggie replied. 'Please keep yourselves safe over there.'

She hit the button to end the call. 'Thanks for coming, everyone. Please see yourselves out. Bob, a word.'

She walked out into the kitchen and he followed.

'Why aren't you going to work? You have an important drug case on and …'

'Let me stop you there. The case is gone. It's shut down. My Super has suggested I take some time off.'

'Because of me?'

'Yes. She won't suspend me, of course, but she doesn't want me around the station for the next week or so. I can see her point. Means I can be here, though, to help you. And she knows I'll get news of anything that happens, regarding you.'

She sat down. 'I'm sorry.'

'Not your fault. You're being set up. I can be useful. I have contacts.'

'Don't do anything you shouldn't, please.'

'I won't get caught. I'm owed some favours. Time to call them in.' He pulled up a chair, sat next to her, and took her hand. 'We're going to find whoever's done this. They won't get away with it.' He leaned forward and hugged her as Zelah joined them.

'They've all gone except Jack.'

Bob stood. 'I'll go speak to him.'

Maggie nodded. For a moment she couldn't speak. Zelah took Bob's vacated chair.

'He's right, we'll find them. But you have to stay strong.'

Maggie shook her head. 'We've been through some difficult stuff, haven't we, but nothing like this, not for me.'

Zelah took her hand and squeezed her fingers. 'Whoever it is, they'll be sorry they messed with us. Now, I'm going to find the Desmonds.'

'Is that wise, Zelah?'

Probably not,' she replied, with an evil grin. 'Why don't you get on with setting up the call with Anthony's relatives.' She glanced at her watch. 'Too late for today. How about tomorrow morning, eight our time. That'll be six in the evening for them. Let me know.'

'Shall we ask Nick to be on the call?'

'Let's give him the choice.'

**

After some hesitation, Nick decided he would join them. 'I want to keep in touch with this; like you said, I may be able to offer some insights.'

'Thanks, Nick. You know how much we value your insights.'

As she waited for Zelah and Nick the next morning, she went back over the thoughts that had troubled and frightened her throughout the night. She didn't know how far Camberwell, or the Desmonds if it was them, would go to ruin her. Could she end up being charged with murder? It was a possibility. Behind the scenes both Zelah and Nick and, of course, Bob would be working furiously to discover as much as possible. That all three had her back was a comfort, but she was no longer convinced that even between them, they could keep her from further harm. Not that she would ever say that to any of them.

Neither Zelah nor Nick said much when they arrived. Zelah gave her arm a squeeze and Nick nodded and smiled.

They were ready when Maggie started the call, and three faces appeared on the screen.

'Good evening, gentlemen,' she began, and made the introductions, which were reciprocated and pleasantries exchanged. She had decided not to tell Anthony Bandon about her encounter with the police.

'Anthony, you said some new information had come to light. And we have some news to share with you. Shall we begin there?'

She began with the Williams and Evans family trees, sharing the screen with them for each family.

'Well, I'll be damned,' said Roger Evans. 'So our Evans ancestors came here by choice. Well, that puts our credit down a notch.' The other two men laughed. Bob, who had joined them, frowned and opened his mouth to ask why, but Maggie shook her head and mouthed *I'll explain later*.

'Well, you already know about the Williams side,' Maggie said, 'which I'm sorry to say is not a good story.'

She proceeded to confirm the information about William Evan Williams, and his misdemeanours that ended in the killing of his wife. All of which left them silent.

'We did know, but it's still shocking to hear the detail,' Malcolm Evans said, in a reedy voice. 'Don't think we'll be talking much about that.'

'Sorry to have to confirm such awful news,' Maggie said. 'Yes. William Evan Williams was a murderer, which came at the end of a long line of offences. That's the problem with family history. Sometimes you discover something you wish you hadn't known.'

'Where does that leave us with the family story?' Anthony asked.

'That's an interesting one,' Maggie replied. 'We were right about George Evans, who was the thief, being transported on the same prison ship as William Evan Williams. George died on the journey. My colleague Nick, here, believes that William got the story from George. That's how it came into your family. William didn't steal the artefact, but he was told about the theft and – we think – given some information about where it might have been hidden.'

'That we can confirm,' Roger Evans said. 'We've been helping Malcolm here go through his old paperwork. He's been checking his will, yet again, and as we were trying to recover an earlier draft we found something written by his grandfather, who was Evan's son, Timothy.'

'Maggie sat up. 'Is this what you want to share with us?'

'Certainly is,' Malcolm said, handing it over to Anthony with a trembling hand. 'You read it, Tony boy.'

Anthony took the piece of paper. From what they could see, it was an old, crumbling piece of paper that had yellowed with age. 'This is what I was going to tell you about. It's a first draft of

Timothy Williams' will, written in 1918. Most of it is irrelevant here. But this is the interesting part. It says:

"Finally, to my son, Jonathan, and his heirs, I leave this information, given to me by my father William Evan Williams, the day before his death in 1855. He was given the location of a valuable object by his friend George Evans, who died when they were both unfairly brought to this country. It belonged to George Evans and if found, he declared it should be my property. The location is in Wales, in Britain. It is the fault of His Lordship." That's it. This paragraph didn't appear in the final draft of the will. I don't know why not.'

After a few moments' silence, Anthony said, 'Do you have any idea what it means?'

Maggie, Zelah, and Nick looked at each other and shook their heads.

'No idea, Anthony. Now, I need to tell you more. You aren't the only person interested in discovering the whereabouts of this artefact.'

She told them about the discovery of the true identity of Hugh Wilson and their visit to Michael Wilson, but without mentioning Henry Camberwell or the Desmonds.

'So, this was the man who had my passport?'

'Yes, Anthony.'

'Does anyone know where it is now?'

'No, it hasn't turned up, but that's a matter for the police. The main question we have for you is: do you want us to carry on? We've found out all we can about your family ancestry, for both the Williams and Evans lines.'

'I've not asked this question so far, but do you know what this "treasure" is?'

'Yes,' Maggie replied. 'We believe that it was an artefact stolen originally from the British museum in 1838, which ended up in the hands of a man in South Wales. Somehow, George Evans got his hands on it, but he ran into the Chartists on the march and was forced to hide it. He was tried as a Chartist but was able to prove he was pressed, so he was let off. But then, a couple of weeks later, he was re-arrested for the theft of two candlesticks. He claimed he was set up, but was convicted and transported.'

'You still haven't said what the thing is.'

'It's a vase, Chinese, and very rare. Also, valuable.'

'If it still exists,' Nick interrupted.

'Why would it not exist?'

'Well, that depends on where George Evans hid it,' Nick said. 'It was delicate. It could have been broken, or just fallen to pieces by now, dust to dust, and so on. It was made around the mid-1700s, so was already almost a hundred years old when it was stolen from the British Museum. It was known to be a very fragile piece, so it's unlikely it will have survived.'

Maggie and Zelah gave him a quizzical look. Although they realised it could be a possibility, Nick hadn't sounded serious on the only occasion he had suggested it.

'If it has, though, what would it be worth? A million dollars?'

'Probably more,' Maggie said. 'But, ultimately it's the property of the British Museum. You couldn't claim ownership, whatever the will says.'

'Well, I don't suppose we have any need to carry on, do we?' Anthony looked around at his uncles, who nodded. 'Thanks for what you've done. At least we have the truth about our Evans ancestors. I can try to find out more about them. But, if you do carry on and find the thing, do let us know.'

'You still need to take care, Anthony. Someone out there has your passport and they took it for a reason.'

'We will. And I'd still like to be kept informed about anything further that involves my family.'

The call ended and the investigators sat back.

'Do you honestly think it's gone?' Maggie asked Nick.

He shrugged. 'I've no idea, but it's possible. As I said, it depends on where George hid it. The clue means nothing, for now. But, we're the only people who have it.'

'And the next question is: what are we going to do with it?'

'That's the only question, Zelah,' Maggie replied.

Chapter 25

Henry Camberwell was becoming more annoyed as each day passed without any progress in discovering the whereabouts of the Chinese vase.

He had re-read the Fathergill papers to see if he had missed anything, any clue that might give impetus to the search, but again he threw the file down. There was nothing. Fathergill had advised Prosser to get rid of it. That was all. No hidden hints.

He began to go over the options, yet again.

One: Prosser had got rid of it. Destroyed it or sold it on. And if that was the case, there was certainly nothing remaining in writing as to who was the buyer.

Two: Anthony Bandon already had the vase. This he dismissed. The search made of Bandon's property had revealed nothing. As instructed, they had taken Bandon's passport, but nothing further. He needed the passport for another plan forming in his mind.

Three: Anthony Bandon knew its hiding place. He had discovered Bandon the previous year after Bandon had put messages online about Maze Investigations not being able to help him in his search for the "treasure" of an ancestor, who had been a Chartist. Henry Camberwell was always interested in anything described as a "treasure" and couldn't believe his luck when Maze Investigations came into the picture. He had not been able to follow up, due to having to turn his attention to another of his enterprises' thanks to their interference. He had discovered that Bandon had gone back to Maze with new information. He had thought he was poised to know what that was, having put out several feelers, two of which had bitten. So far, so good. But neither of these had been able to give him the detail he needed.

Four: Anthony Bandon did not know where it was, but had given Maze new information which he now needed. Urgently. His backers were becoming impatient. If he couldn't give them some sign that the search was reaching fruition he would have yet another problem on his hands. He had taken their money and invested it in a most promising venture, which also had not reached fruition, but would in a week or so when the cargo container reached England.

Back to the Desmonds. With the information he had gleaned, about William George Evans, he had instructed them to follow it up. They had come back with the current family, the Wilsons, in North Wales. An approach to them had been enthusiastically received. The father, Hugh, already knew about the "treasure" and was delighted to be the person to take on the persona of Anthony Bandon and head to the London hotel. It was unfortunate that he had lost his nerve. Fortunately, one of his contacts was able to retrieve the situation.

He was pondering whether or not he should make a direct approach to Maze, and to which member of the team, when his phone rang. He checked the number and tutted, but answered.

'What do you want? Do you have news for me?'

'The Gilbert woman has been questioned, informally for now. There wasn't enough evidence to go further, but the police are still looking.'

'Excellent. You have the passport?'

'It was delivered to me.'

'Then these are my instructions.'

After he finished the call Henry Camberwell sat back and poured himself a glass of whisky. This should give Maze an even bigger headache. He took and savoured another sip, then put the glass down. Two more calls, then he needed to speak to his Desmond contact.

Chapter 26

After everyone except Zelah had gone, Maggie sat down at her desk, determined to get on with the next piece of research, but couldn't help overhearing a conversation starting in the kitchen between Zelah and someone who was shouting back. After a few minutes, Zelah reappeared in the office.

'That went well,' she said, plonking herself down on the settee. 'Ian Desmond,' she said in response to Maggie's frown. 'He's officially disgusted that I should even think he had anything to do with the death of a man in a hotel in London. But, there was a slight pause when I asked about Moira.'

'What does that mean?'

'Moira is the stronger of the two. I believe Ian has some scruples, not many but some. Moira wouldn't recognise a scruple if it bit her on the leg. She'd just kick it off and carry on.'

'And?'

'And, Moira wouldn't care about anything Henry Camberwell might have done in the past if there's a big fat fee on offer. Nor would she care about anything she had to do to earn the fee. And – and I think I'm right about this – it was Moira, not Ian, who tried to put me out of business before we set up Maze.'

Maggie sat back. 'Zelah, this is all well and good, but I don't understand why you want to have anything to do with the Desmonds.'

'If they're working for Camberwell, which Ian wouldn't confirm but gave away because he's incapable of holding up under pressure, they now know that they're in my sights. So, any move they make, there's a likelihood we'll find out. That should keep Moira in check.'

Maggie raised an eyebrow. 'Is this about Maze or revenge?'

Zelah grinned. 'Both.'

'I'm going to start looking at the line of descent of John Pritchard,' Maggie said, shaking her head.

**

Just before midday she stopped, yawned, and stretched.

'Getting anywhere?' Zelah asked.

'Sort of. I've found Pritchard on the 1841 census. He was living in Newport and still working as a servant for Prosser. He calls himself Estate Manager.'

'Perhaps he was. The house stands in extensive grounds, or it did back then.'

'Whatever, but I've also found that Prosser died the following year. I've sent for the death certificate by express, to see if there was anything dodgy about his death. He was about forty-five or six when he died, which is still quite young, even in those times, for a man who could afford to look after himself.'

'What happened to the estate?'

'I haven't found that out, yet. I was wondering if that's something Nick could pursue. Prosser doesn't appear to have had children.'

'Give him a call.'

As Maggie called Nick, Zelah's phone rang and she walked into the kitchen to take the call. When she came back, Maggie said, 'Nick's going to take a quick look online, but thinks he'll have to either go to the library or the archives, to find out more. He did a quick check and in 1851 a man called Horatio Watts was living there, with a wife and two children.'

Zelah had been frowning, but asked, 'Was Pritchard still there?'

'No, there was an Estate Manager, but a different one. I'll work on what happened to Pritchard. It's strange he wasn't kept on. Anyway, he had a wife and six children. I'll need to find out what I can about each of them.'

'That'll keep you busy.'

'Yes. So, what was your call about? You're looking snarky.'

'That was Moira Desmond on the phone. She's somewhat angry with me. Said we're trying to malign their reputation.'

'And you said?'

'They hadn't got one to malign. No, not really, don't look so annoyed. I told her I had no interest in her or her clients, but I do care very much about my friends and family, and that if anything happens to any one of them because of her association with Camberwell, I will make her life a living hell.'

'Oh, Zelah, really? And her response?'

'She laughed and I ended the call.'

'If she's the person you say she is, Moira Desmond won't give a damn about your threats.'

'Yes, but Ian will. She'll rant at him, tell him what I just threatened.'

Maggie turned back to her computer. 'I hope you haven't just given us another problem.'

**

172

By late afternoon Maggie was exhausted and having trouble reading her computer screen. Zelah had already left, not saying what she was planning to do next so Maggie didn't ask.

'Time to stop when you're squinting that close to the screen,' Bob said. He had been in and out of the office all afternoon.

'I know.'

'Found anything interesting?'

'I've managed to track down several lines of the Pritchard children. My worry is there's going to be so many of them three or four generations on, I'll have far too many to find out what they know. And I haven't even begun to think about how I could approach them. How about you? What have you been up to?'

She'd noted that Bob had been on phone calls throughout the afternoon.

'Just putting out some feelers. See what's going on with anyone showing an interest in your "treasure".'

'Find anything?'

'Not yet. Too soon. I've put it out there. Need to wait now to see what comes back.'

Anything from work?' She gave him a knowing look.

'Nothing. All quiet there. As far as – someone – can tell, no more investigation going on in Newport. Must still be at the London end.'

Maggie nodded. 'I've had enough for today. How about we have some dinner, watch a film, and have an early night.'

'I'll start cooking. Anything in particular?'

'No. Hot food on a plate will be fine.' She paused for a moment. 'Bob, I haven't asked, but how are your talks with Jack going? I know you've been discussing all of this,' she swept her arm around the computers and the research notes on the whiteboard, 'with him.'

'He's upset and worried. You being taken to the station really got to him. I've told him we all have your back and there are other people out there watching out for you, too.'

She knew that he meant his colleagues and his contacts. She stood and hugged him. 'Thankyou. It means a lot, you know that.'

'Come on, let's talk some more. But nothing about this case. We can discuss the state of the country.'

'Not sure that's a good idea, either,' Maggie muttered. 'But, I'll give it a go.'

**

The following morning a call from Zelah confirmed Maggie's worst fears.

'I'm meeting Moira Desmond this afternoon. They're based in Hay-on-Wye. You want to come along?'

'Is this sensible, Zelah?'

'Two things. One: I don't care much about sensible right now. Two: we're meeting in a café, not at their office, so they can't murder me.'

'Why are you asking me if I want to come with you?'

'Safety in numbers.'

'That's a joke, isn't it?'

'Maybe. Anyway, are you coming or not?'

'Yes.'

'Good. Pick you up at two. Meeting's at half three.'

'Can we leave an hour before that, at one?'

'Why?'

'So I can have a quick look around the bookshops. I've found some gems there on previous visits.'

Zelah sighed and ended the call.

It took just over an hour to reach the town of Hay-on-Wye. At Maggie's request, Zelah had taken a route that led them past Llanthony Priory, one of Maggie's favourite quiet places. Today, with even fewer tourists than usual, the narrow single-track road was deserted. They stopped for a few minutes at the top of the pass, to take in the three-sixty view of the hills and mountains stretching for miles, down to the town itself.

'I don't think I'll ever tire of this,' Maggie said, as Zelah shivered in the colder air that ruffled the wool of the sheep grazing next to them on the unfenced trackway.

'I'm tired already. And cold. Can we go now?'

'Just a moment's peace and beauty in the midst of the current chaos that is my life,' Maggie replied with a smile. She turned slowly to draw in the view, then nodded and returned to the car.

They reached the town fifteen minutes later and went to find a café.

Few people wandered in and out of the myriad and variety of bookshops that allowed Hay to call itself the book capital of the world. After warming up with a hot chocolate and a cake, she left Zelah to pull out her I-pad to work on a report – the owner not minding in the least the prospect of someone ordering more food and drinks for another hour, Zelah being the only customer – and walked out into the main street to choose a bookshop.

This was the worst part – having to choose. Some shops specialised, others had random collections of fiction and non-fiction of all kinds.

After asking a few of the owners and managers if they had anything on Welsh family history, she eventually, after a few tries, found a shop that had a whole section so she dived in.

An hour later, with a call from Zelah prompting her to get a move on, she staggered out of the shop with two bags full of books covering both general and personal genealogy and family histories in the counties of Monmouthshire and Glamorgan, plus one she couldn't resist about a family in Brecon.

'You never know when these will come in useful,' she told Zelah as they returned briefly to the car to deposit the books before walking to the nominated café close to the Desmond office.

'If you keep doing this you'll have to move house, just to accommodate the library you're building up,' Zelah said. 'Come on, it's about five minutes away, but we don't want to keep Moira waiting.'

As they made their way towards the far end of the street past the bookshops, the souvenir shops, and the cafés, Maggie noticed that Zelah was wearing some of her most expensive jewellery. It hadn't struck her earlier as Zelah always dressed well no matter where they were going, or not going. She often wore a suit to the office. Today had begun with a trench coat over the suit and a pair of low-heeled shoes. When they had taken the books back to the car she had discarded the heavy coat and replaced it with one Maggie hadn't seen before, a light beige wrap-over with a collar and cuffs of heavy fur. She had also changed her shoes. As Zelah set off down the street two women they passed gave her interested glances, the way you might look at someone you recognised but weren't sure why. Maggie realised it was the coat.

'Please tell me that's not real fur,' she muttered.

Zelah didn't reply.

'Cashmere?' Maggie prompted.

Zelah nodded.

'And the shoes?'

The black shoes, with the high heels that Zelah was seldom seen without, clicked on the pavement as they walked. The jewelled pins in her hair glittered in the wind and she wore just two rings, both clearly diamond, as were her earrings. Maggie knew that even if the fur was not real, the diamonds were.

Zelah still said nothing.

'Is this supposed to impress or intimidate?'

'Hopefully, both,' said Zelah as they reached the end of the street and turned right uphill. 'There it is.'

The door of a small café opened and as a couple came out, Zelah held the door and marched in. The room was an old-fashioned tearoom, with lace cloths on the tables, several of which were occupied. There were two waitresses in black uniform, with white frilly pinafores and caps, moving around and between the customers. The walls were covered with portraits of the royal family, mostly in their youth with the children still young and innocent.

Zelah snorted and was about to say something cutting when she spotted a couple sitting at a corner table well away from the other customers. She marched over to them.

The man stood. He was a little over six feet tall, with the beginning of a paunch and thinning nondescript brown hair. 'Hello, Zelah. Long time no see.' He held out his hand but the woman next to him, who had not stood, pulled his elbow back.

'We aren't here for pleasantries,' she muttered, scowling at Zelah and, Maggie thought, looking enviously at the coat. *Well, that's working*, Maggie thought. They both sat. Moira Desmond's face was long and pinched, but with a wary look in her dark brown eyes. Her black hair was short and well cut, but she shot another envious look at Zelah's diamond-pinned coiffure as she unconsciously patted her own head.

'You weren't supposed to bring anyone with you,' Moira Desmond began, without looking at Maggie.

'Wasn't I?' Zelah said in a voice that feigned surprise.

'I was clear enough. Just you,' the woman snapped.

'Didn't hear that instruction,' Zelah replied. 'But let me introduce you to my …'

'I know who she is,' Moira snapped again, still not looking.

'Oh, just carry on like I'm not here,' Maggie said. She turned to Ian Desmond. 'I'm Maggie Gilbert,' she said, holding out her hand across the table. He was still standing, awkwardly. 'Do sit down.'

Ian Desmond blushed, sat down on his chair, and stared at his coffee cup. Maggie withdrew her hand. 'Do we get a drink?' she said to no-one in particular. When no-one answered she stood up, shook her head, and walked over to one of the waitresses.

When she returned, Zelah said, 'Hope you didn't bother ordering anything for me. We aren't going to be here long enough.'

'Actually, I did, but never mind.' She went to speak again, but changed her mind and sat back, folding her arms as she stared around at the pictures that adorned the walls.

'You asked for this meeting,' Moira Desmond said to Zelah. 'What do you want?'

'Nothing,' Zelah asked. 'That's the point. We're doing well enough with our client and don't need anything from you. So, why are you interfering in our business?'

'I don't know what you mean,' Moira Desmond replied. 'We have a legitimate interest in following up a claim by our client that he has an entitlement to a family possession. We're trying to track it down.'

178

As she spoke she turned her head for a fraction of a second away from Zelah and towards Maggie. There was something that struck Maggie, perhaps in the pursed lips, or the narrowing of the eyes, something she thought she recognised.

'Have we met before, Moira?'

'Mrs Desmond to you.'

'Whatever. I have a feeling I know you from somewhere.'

'We've never met.' Moira turned back to Zelah. 'If I – we – find that you've been illegally advising a client of yours that the artefact is theirs, then we will not hesitate to bring in a lawyer and –'

'Hold it right there,' Zelah said, leaning forwards. Moira did the same until they were just inches apart. 'The artefact was stolen, twice. First from the British Museum, then from the man who bought it illegally, by your client's ancestor. If it's still in one piece and found, we will return it to the British Museum. And, the law is already involved, plus your client is dead.' She paused and sat back, as a waitress brought coffee in two delicate china cups, put them on the table, and hesitated for a moment, glancing at each side of the table. 'Anything else I can get you?'

'No, go away,' Moira said. The waitress took a few steps backwards, scowled, and turned to the service counter.

Zelah pushed the coffee away. 'Unless you are now taking up the case on behalf of Wilson Junior, I would say there's nothing left in this for you. Unless, of course, Hugh Wilson never was your client.' She stared at Moira.

The stare was returned unblinking. 'I have no idea what you're talking about.'

'Moira, we've had some experience of Henry Camberwell. My advice – strong advice – is that you get out of this now. For your own health and safety.'

Ian Desmond, who had not looked up from his coffee, which he had been stirring slowly throughout the exchange, now looked at Maggie and said 'Who?'

Maggie wasn't sure what to say. Surely they couldn't think she and Zelah wouldn't have found out about Camberwell's involvement. She peered at him for a few seconds, at the expression of surprise on his face. He glanced quickly at Moira, then back at her. The surprise was still there.

'Oh, wow,' she said, sitting forward. 'You don't know do you?'

Moira leapt up. 'This meeting is over. You,' she pointed at Zelah, 'keep out of my – our – way.'

'Or what?' Zelah replied, sitting back, with what Maggie saw was her smug grin. 'I suggest you tell Ian what's really going on. Come on Maggie, time for us to leave.'

'Just a minute. Mrs Desmond, are you sure we haven't met before? I'm having a "Deja Vue" moment.'

'Quite sure,' Moira Desmond snapped. 'Ian, we have work to do.' She stood and put on her coat, giving Zelah's coat, which Zelah had thrown over the back of her chair, the evil eye.

Ian Desmond didn't move.

'Ian?'

'Carry on, Moira. I'll be with you shortly.' He folded his arms and sat back in his chair. Moira Desmond was caught off balance. She didn't want to be seen to follow an order, but she had threatened Zelah and the threat would look weak if she now stayed. She chose.

'I'm going.' To Zelah, 'I don't expect to have to speak to you again. I've made our position clear.'

At the door, she took one final look back at Ian, who didn't look at her.

'So, who is Henry Camberwell,' he said to Maggie.

'On the surface, a dealer in fine arts and antiques. Below the surface, well, like the iceberg, very much hidden and all of it bad. He's been clever enough not to get caught, yet. He's without scruples. We believe he had someone killed last year.'

Ian blanched. 'Why do you think Moira knows him?'

'Because Michael Wilson worked out that Camberwell was involved. I'm not sure how, though. But he assumed that you and Moira are working with, or for Camberwell.'

'As far as I'm concerned our client, Hugh Wilson came to us. It was a shock when he died, but I understood it was from natural causes.'

Maggie wasn't sure if she should say more but decided caution was not appropriate. 'It may be that he didn't. Die of natural causes, that is.'

Ian's eyes widened.

'We have to go,' Zelah said, now standing. She put on her coat. 'Be careful, Ian. Sir Henry Camberwell is dangerous, as is your wife,' she added.

This time Maggie stood and called over the waitress. She went to pay, but Ian Desmond said, 'Leave it to me. Thanks for coming up. I have a lot to think about.'

Zelah and Maggie left him sitting at the table, frowning, but making no attempt to move. As they walked back towards the car, Maggie said, 'Poor Ian Desmond. Do you think he actually didn't know?'

Zelah shrugged. 'Looks that way. I've never taken him for a fool before, but maybe Moira has gone rogue.'

'She's incredibly jealous of you, isn't she?' Maggie said. 'If she'd been in possession of a pair of scissors she'd have cut your coat to shreds. I could see her imagining doing it.'

'I think she always has been. Moira believes she's been hard done by.'

'By whom?'

'By the world,' Zelah replied as they reached the car. 'She's a spiteful, resentful woman. I pity Ian right now. Let's get back, see how Nick's got on.'

'What was the real purpose of that meeting? What did you expect to learn?' Maggie asked, 'because I can't see that we found out anything we didn't already know. Was it just a shot across the bows?'

'That, and more. Moira is in much deeper than I expected. We'll need to add her to the list of people to be wary of. God knows how much Camberwell has promised her.'

'There's something about her. It's bothering me. I know her from somewhere. I just can't think where.'

'If it's important, it will come to you.'

Maggie sat back and closed her eyes, then nodded off for the remainder of the journey. It was a puzzle, but she had more important matters to think about. Like, was she about to be arrested?

Chapter 27
South Wales, 1841

Mervyn Prosser's sudden death in February 1842 came as a great shock across the South Wales mining and iron communities, but to none more so than John Pritchard.

The widow Prosser had asked him to remain at his post but informed him that she intended to sell the property and return to her family in Bristol. She could give him no guarantees that the new owner would retain his services. So, Pritchard, his wife, and their six children remained in their small cottage on the edge of the property next to the canal whilst Mrs Prosser and her lawyer looked for a quick sale.

Since the trial of George Evans, not a word had been spoken between the two men on the subject of the missing "treasure". Pritchard had tried once to raise the subject and was brutally put down by his employer, who made a none too subtle threat to Pritchard's job, which made it clear to Pritchard that Prosser never wanted to hear about any aspect of the affair ever again. George Evans was safely out of the country and in all likelihood would never return. It was as if the episode had never happened.

Without telling Prosser, Pritchard had made it his business to find out about anyone who had visited George Evans in Monmouth gaol and discovered that the daughter, Mary Ann Evans, had travelled from Newport to Monmouth on the day before her father's trial. Further enquiries had elicited that Evans and his daughter were close. Hence, his certainty that Mary Ann would know something about George's exploits on the night of the uprising and march. If he had told anyone what he had done with the "treasure" it would be her, not the slovenly, quivering wife he had questioned on the day he had led the raid on George's house and planted the candlesticks.

Then, within six months of Mervyn Prosser's death, just when Pritchard thought it would be safe to go back to the Evans house to speak to the girl, and possibly issue a threat in the name of Prosser, the family was gone. The girl had married and left the town, taking her mother with her. When questioned, none of the neighbours knew where they had gone. He was certain at least one of them did know, but they weren't going to tell him.

It took him a further two months to find the family. Mary Ann Evans, now Mrs Ebeneezer Phillips, he found living in Merthyr Tydfil. After two days of watching, she was at last alone in the house she shared with her husband and mother. He waited behind the wall of the yard in which the privy stood until she came out with an armful of washing.

'Good morning, Mrs Phillips.'

The girl jumped, spun her head in the direction of the wall, and exclaimed as Pritchard slowly walked into the ungated entrance, recognising him at once, and turned to run back into the house.

'No point, Mary Ann. No point. I've found you and I'm not going away until you give me what I'm here for.'

Mary Ann decided to brazen it out. 'You'll get nothing from me. I know what you did.'

'Now who do you think is going to believe you? I can name you as an accessory any time I like. Who will the magistrate believe? The faithful servant of the well-known and respected Mr Prosser, who had spent his own time looking for the woman who assisted the man who stole Mr Prosser's valuable property? Or the daughter of the convict?'

Her hands shook, but she hid them beneath the washing. 'And might not the magistrate ask why you didn't name the woman at the time?'

'Indeed he might. But, I'm willing to take the risk. Are you?

She pressed her lips together. 'What do you want, you snake?'

He smiled, slowly. 'That's better. That your father trusted you, I have on good authority. Therefore, he will have told you what it was he really stole, and where it is now.'

Mary Ann fought with conflicting thoughts. She wanted to be rid of this man and his threats, without her mother and Ebeneezer knowing, but she couldn't give up what her father had told her. Perhaps, she could give him part of the story, convince him it was all she knew.

'My father said to ask His Lordship. That's what he told me. He wasn't expecting to be transported. We were supposed to go to His Lordship to retrieve it. He never told me where that was. There was no need. It's your fault he got taken away without me being able to speak to him again.'

'Come now, I can't believe that.'

'Believe what you like, you evil bastard. You never came back, like you promised him. So, he was taken away without being able to speak to anyone he trusted. Serves you right.'

She turned back to her washing line and continued to jab pegs into the shirts and underwear.

Pritchard was in a quandary. Could she be telling the truth? There was honesty in her story of his non-return, and George Evans had been taken away immediately. But, what did it mean? *Ask His Lordship.*

He walked up behind her and grabbed her hair, pulling it hard as her head whipped back onto his shoulder.

He whispered into her ear as she cried out in pain. 'You had better be telling me the truth, Mary Ann. I will be watching you, now. If you ever return to Newport, I'll be there, waiting for you.'.

'Whatever the thing is, I don't want none of it,' she yelped. 'If you can find it, you can have it. It's almost ruined my family. My Da is gone. Leave me alone.'

He let her go with a push and laughed as she stumbled and dropped her washing onto the mud. He stepped forward, pulled her up, and slapped her face so hard she screamed.

'Remember what I've said.'

He turned and walked slowly out of the yard and disappeared into the maze of streets.

Mary Ann slowly pulled herself up, rubbing her stinging face. She would have to tell her mother and Eb that she fell, hit her face on the rubble in the yard. Then, she smiled. Of course, she knew exactly where *it* was. But she would never tell anyone outside the family. That had been her promise to her father, a solemn word, never to be broken.

She was telling the truth when she said she didn't want it. Despite his faults, she had loved her father and that man had taken him from them, all for nothing, as it turned out. For a moment, her head filled with a raging blaze of hatred for Pritchard. She wished everything bad to come to him and his family. Enough. It was done. One day, she might tell her children, but for the immediate future, the secret was hers, and hers alone.

**

Back in Newport, Pritchard sat in front of his fire and pondered over what Mary Ann Phillips had told him. *Ask His Lordship*. Meaningless. Obviously, some kind of joke on the part of George Evans. The only official "Lordship" in the immediate area was Viscount Tredegar and although he was well known and often visited the town, Pritchard dismissed any possibility that he could have anything to do with the likes of George Evans.

Perhaps it was a nickname for one of Evans' associates? That was a much more likely option. He would begin his search again in Pillgwenlly, visit the houses, and interrogate the people who knew the man.

A further two months passed before a clue arose. Nothing had come out of his enquiries, threats, and interrogations of the people of High Street. But, he had heard in one of the local pubs, of a man in Cardiff, a well-known fence of stolen property, sometimes referred to as "His Majesty", a man called Henry Adams. He hunted the man down and found him in one of the poorest areas of the town, around Whitmore Lane, where it was hardly safe to walk in the daytime, never mind at night.

Before setting out from Newport Pritchard, having told his wife he would be away for a few days on business for Mr Prosser, had told his eldest son, Albert, a boy of fourteen, what he was really doing.

'Just in case anything should happen to me in that place,' he said, knowing that where he was going would be dangerous.

The boy nodded and swallowed. 'I'll look after Ma while you're away, but please come back,' the boy begged.

Pritchard nodded, ruffling the boy's dark hair. 'They won't hurt me. I am a man of reputation and knowledge.'

The following day, he found Henry Adams in a dark, dirty room where men sat drinking beer and spirits in The Noah's Ark, a notorious public house on the side of the canal, amongst the many brothels that defined Whitmore Lane. Pritchard, already more nervous than he had anticipated, despite being armed with a knife and the small pistol he had acquired but not yet having had the opportunity to learn how to use, was intimidated by the silence and the threatening glances in his direction. No camaraderie here. "His Majesty", Adams, sat in a corner alone. Pritchard joined him, telling him what he wanted, offering to share the proceeds of a sale. The man laughed.

'Never heard of any George Evans.'

'Come now, there's a fortune in this, for both of us.'

'You're wasting your time. Now, get out of here, while you're still in one piece.'

The man's size and threatening tone, plus a gesture of a slit throat were enough. Despite the feel of the gun in his pocket, Pritchard shot up out of his seat and left the pub.

As he stumbled through the maze of streets towards the Newport road where he had found a small but respectable Inn for his overnight accommodation before taking the coach back to Newport, Pritchard, heart in his mouth at every sound of scuffling nearby and yells and screams in the distance, knew that he would have to think again as soon as he reached home. In the meantime, he just needed to get away from this place. He should have taken the advice he was given and never come near this hell hole. He took the gun out and stared at it.

Stopping suddenly, thinking he had heard a step behind him, he turned around. No-one was there. He quickened his pace. Suddenly, two men jumped out of a doorway in front of him. He stopped abruptly. They were engaged in a fight, striking out and swearing, one flashing a knife, so intent on their battle they didn't notice him. As they rolled into the gutter he took his chance and ran past to the end of the street, where he stopped and calmed his breathing. He was just a few hundred yards away from the Newport road and the Inn.

He took one deep breath and turned to walk away. An arm caught him, spinning him around and knocking the pistol out of his hand. He caught the quick flash of a knife, as one of the fighting men hit him on the head and threw him to the ground. He had a few seconds to look up into the face of Henry Adams as the knife came down and across his throat.

**

Mervyn Prosser expressed great sorrow to Mrs Pritchard on the loss of her husband and promised to do all he could to help find the perpetrator. However, he needed a manager for his estate and he had already hired a new man, with a family. Therefore, Mrs Pritchard and her six children would have to leave the cottage. He would take on the eldest boy, Albert, as a servant, at a fair wage. It was the least he could do. For the next in line, a thirteen-year-old girl, he found a situation as a live-in servant at a local house.

Having nowhere to go, Mrs Pritchard and her remaining four children went to the workhouse, where she contracted the disease known as phthisis, and died nine months later, shortly after the death of the youngest. The remaining three children stayed in the workhouse. Two years later Albert, who had done well as a servant and had saved some small amount of money, found a job in an iron foundry in Dowlais. He took his brothers and sisters to live with him.

He had never forgotten what his father told him before he left, but he put little store in it. He married, had three children of his own, and before his death, told the story to the eldest son. The story continued down the line for a further four generations of Pritchards. By this time it was no longer "ask his Lordship", but had become "the Lord knows where it is now," which one of the living holders of the secret took as a homily, rather than a clue, but nevertheless, remained interested. Very interested.

Chapter 28

Nick was waiting for Maggie and Zelah on their return. He looked as gloomy as they felt.

'I couldn't help myself,' he said. 'It's worse being on the outside. I had to get back in and help out, so I've been tracking down the descendants of the Pritchard children or trying to. I picked up the activity from the log.'

'Thank you,' Maggie said. 'I was beginning to struggle. How many do you have so far?' Maggie asked as she took off her coat and shoes and sat down next to his desk, whilst Zelah went to the kitchen.

'There were six Pritchard children, from the eldest, Albert, who was sixteen when his father died. According to the 1841 census he continued to work for Prosser. Then a girl called Hannah, who went into service. The last one was a baby called Emily, who died shortly after Mrs Pritchard and the four remaining children went into the workhouse.'

'Why did they go there, Nick?'

'It's an interesting story. Pritchard died in mid-December 1841, in Cardiff, close to the Whitmore Lane area, one of the worst, most lawless, violent areas of the town at the time. He'd had his throat cut in what seemed like a robbery.'

'Seemed?' Zelah said, coming in with a tray of coffee and biscuits. 'Suggests more to it, Nick.'

'Well,' he replied, pouring himself a drink and taking a handful of biscuits, 'The Police report says that's what it was, but I don't understand what he was doing there. So, I did some checking and I found a newspaper report saying he'd been seen in the Noah's Ark, drinking with a man called Adams. It turns out Adams was a well-known fence.'

'Could he have been looking for the vase?' Maggie said, crunching absent-mindedly on a custard cream.

'That would be my guess,' Nick replied. 'He must have been trying to find out either if Prosser had already sold it, was working on his own account, or was asking if Adams would be interested in buying it.'

'The former,' Zelah said. 'Prosser would never have risked anyone associated with him being in the public company of a fence. He would have sent for Adams, or arranged to meet him somewhere away from his usual haunts.'

Nick nodded. 'Taking that thought through a logical progression, Prosser had given up on the idea of getting the vase back, which confirms the theory that George Evans didn't give it up to Pritchard at the gaol, either before or after his conviction. So, Pritchard was working alone. Perhaps he decided that, even if Prosser had decided to cut his losses, there was no reason he shouldn't have a go at discovering its whereabouts.'

'What happened to Prosser?' Maggie asked.

'He died two years later.'

'Childless, wasn't it?'

'Right,' Nick replied. 'Which leaves us now with the strong possibility that John Pritchard was trying to find out what George Evans might have done with the vase. Remember, there was a period of three or four weeks between the Chartist trial at which George was set free and his re-arrest, organised by Pritchard acting for Prosser. Pritchard went to Monmouth gaol on the day before

George's trial for theft, but didn't appear as a witness; he had already given a written statement to the court. So why go to the gaol?'

'Trying to do a last-minute deal with George? Offering him freedom if he told Pritchard where the vase was hidden, or what he had done with it? But that didn't happen. George was convicted,' Zelah said.

Nick sat back and pressed the fingers of each hand against his temple. 'There's something I've missed. Give me time, please.'

He sat in silence, eyes closed, elbows on the desk, fingers digging into the sides of his head, muttering under his breath. Maggie took another custard cream and squeezed her eyes shut, trying to recall yet again when she might have met Moira Desmond. Zelah looked at them and grinned.

'Looks like a meditation session. Ohmmmmm.'

'Shut up,' Maggie muttered.

'I'll get on with something productive, then,' Zelah said.

It took five minutes until Nick slapped one hand on the table. 'Got it!' He spun around in his chair and Maggie opened her eyes, not ready to admit that she had fallen asleep.

'Henry Adams, the fence. He was known as "The King" and "His Majesty".'

'But not "His Lordship", who's fault it's supposed to have been,' Zelah replied.

'No, but whoever told Pritchard the clue could only have got it from George Adams or a member of his family. Maybe he just searched around and came up with Adams, and thought that the soubriquet was close enough.'

Maggie nodded. 'Possible. But that still doesn't tell us if he was acting on his own behalf or Prosser's.'

'Doesn't matter,' Nick said. 'As he never got back to Prosser, did he? What matters is whether or not he told anyone else the reason for his being in that area of Cardiff. The newspaper report says he had been seen drinking with Henry Adams. For me, it adds up.'

'We can't know if Pritchard told anyone else before he left home,' Maggie said.

'No, we can't,' Zelah agreed. 'But, we have to act on the basis that he might have done and find the descendants of his children. How many did you say there were, Nick?'

'Six. But one died in childhood and another in late infancy. That leaves four to trace. If they all made it to adulthood and married, that's going to be a lot of descendants.'

Maggie nodded and yawned. 'I've already found quite a lot, but there's plenty more. Something to get on with tomorrow.'

'No,' Zelah said. 'Tomorrow's Saturday and we all need a break. Let's leave it over the weekend. It can wait.'

'Not sure I can,' Maggie said.

'Why don't you just try to chill over the weekend,' Zelah said. 'Whatever's bugging you about Moira Desmond might come back to you.'

'What's that?' Nick asked. 'You haven't told me about your meeting with Ian and Moira.'

'I'll get off,' Zelah said. 'Maggie, can you give him an update? I'll see you both on Monday.'

When Zelah had gone Maggie gave Nick a quick summary of the meeting.

'Did you have the impression they're involved directly with Camberwell?'

Maggie sat back. 'Moira became agitated when Zelah mentioned his name, but what surprised me, was that Ian looked astonished. As if he was hearing the name for the first time.'

'Odd,' Nick agreed. 'Right, I'll head off too. I guess, if you're right, there's going to be an interesting discussion occurring in the Desmond house, right now.'

Chapter 29

Is this convenient?
  No.
  When? It's important
  One hour. I will assume you have good news
  No

Henry Camberwell smiled politely and turned the phone face down on the restaurant table. The food was excellent but he had hardly tasted it. The company was too sour.

'Problem, Sir Henry?'

'No problem. Just something to be arranged.'

'I hope this will not affect our venture?' The words, spoken with a strong accent through the glitter of the gold teeth – which made Henry wince – had the usual hint of menace.

'No, Mr Dmitriev, nothing to do with our venture.'

'So, you have made no progress, Sir Henry.'

'Not so, not so. Progress has been made and we are close, now.'

'And you are still convinced the object exists, are you not?'

'Indeed I am, Mr Dmitriev.' Henry Camberwell sat back, controlling his breathing. He needed to get away from this cut-price hoodlum, without showing his regret at having ever thought it was a good idea to include him in the venture. The Chinese magnate and the British lord were old customers of his other goods, and more realistic.

The Russian stood, snapped his fingers and a waiter approached with his fur-collared coat. Henry bit his lip to stop from wincing at the ostentatious display of wealth. The man had no class.

Outside the restaurant, they said their farewells, with the Russian insisting on daily updates. Henry could only agree. There was no point trying to explain how delicate an operation this was.

In the taxi, he took out his phone and texted.

Ten minutes. Call me.

As the taxi deposited him on the pavement outside his Chelsea home, his phone rang as he reached the door.

'Well?'

'There's a problem. I think she's cottoned on. I could see her staring in a puzzled kind of way.'

Henry sighed. 'Deal with it.'

'I will. As it happens I have a plan.'

Henry listened for a few minutes, his smile growing.

'Excellent. Go ahead. I expect news soon.'

The call ended as he reached his study, where he immediately took another call and his concentration went to another subject. A shipment was due in from Europe. He couldn't afford for it to have any problems at the port. He sighed. Calls to be made. People to bribe. People to threaten. Life went on. He would have to work out soon how to deal with Dmitriev. The man had become an exasperating nuisance, with his gold teeth and threats. His man on the ground in Newport had had little to report for days. Time to set him onto another job back in London.

Chapter 30

Maggie wasn't sleeping well. There had been nothing further from the police, but the lack of information and action was becoming more of a worry than a comfort. After another night of out-of-control dreams, she couldn't bear it any longer and got out of bed just before six on Saturday morning, leaving Bob snoring gently.

In the kitchen she made a pot of coffee and sat at the table drinking it, hands cupped around the mug, wondering if she could distract herself with some non-genealogical activity. Gardening, maybe. It was that time of spring when the garden was about to become demanding.

No. It just wasn't going to work. She wondered if Zelah and Nick were awake or asleep. Nick had said that Flora was now sleeping almost through the night. Zelah was an early riser. She was contemplating making a call when her phone rang. To her surprise and worry, it was Alice.

'Hi, Mum.'

'Hi. Are you OK? It's very early.' Alice wasn't known for being out of bed much before midday at weekends.

'I'm fine. But, I've changed my mind, if that's OK. I'd like to come home for the weekend.'

'Of course, but what's happened?'

'Honestly, nothing. Matthew and his mum are lovely but, I'm just a bit homesick, after all. I'd like to see you and Jack and Bob.

'Of course. I'll come and pick you up. It'll be lovely to have you here.'

'Thanks, mum. About nine, if that's OK?'

'I'll be there. You must tell Sarah.'

'She's usually up around eight. I'll tell her. She'll be fine with it.'

Maggie ended the call. Six thirty. This wasn't like Alice at all. Maybe it was just homesickness, but she was concerned.

Bob appeared. 'Who was that? I heard the phone ringing.'

'Sorry. Alice. She's coming back for the weekend.'

'Something wrong?'

'She says not. But I'm going to get her.'

'Not like her,' he said, pouring a steaming mug of coffee, adding sugar and milk as he moved around the kitchen.

'That's what I think. I'm worried, now. It seemed to be going so well.'

He stood behind her and put his hands on her shoulders. 'You'll figure it out, the two of you. Whatever it is, it can be fixed.'

She took his hand and squeezed it. 'I know,' then turned away, frowning, trying not to speculate on what might be coming.

**

Alice was already waiting in the car park with Matthew and his mother as Maggie drove in. As they exchanged greetings and put Alice's suitcase into the trunk, Maggie indicated to Sarah that she wanted a quick chat.

'Has something happened? Have they fallen out?'

Sarah gave her a surprised look, eyebrows raised. 'Maggie, this isn't about Matthew or me. It's about you.'

For a second Maggie didn't know what to say. Then she got it. 'Jack. He told her.'

Sarah nodded. 'She's so worried about you. I think she just needs to see for herself that you're OK and in one piece. Are you?'

Maggie nodded. 'I am worried, but I'm OK, so far. I don't know what's coming next, though.'

Sarah squeezed her arm. 'We'll do whatever you need. Just ask.'

'I will. Thank you. I do mean that. Now, we'll get on our way and I'll try to reassure her that I'm not about to be hauled off to jail.'

'Is that the truth?'

'It's the hopeful truth.'

Alice and Matthew finished their whispered conversation and Alice went around to the passenger seat. 'See you Sunday, mate.'

Matthew nodded and put an arm around his mother's shoulder, as Maggie and Alice drove away.

**

At first, their conversation was light. 'Who's around this weekend, mum?'

'Just us. No work. We're taking the weekend off. So, you, me, Jack, and Bob, who is also not working this weekend.'

'Who's also not working at all.'

'OK. Let's cut to the chase. How much did Jack tell you.'

'I know that there's a picture of you taken from a CCTV at a hotel in London, where a man died. And the police think you may have had something to do with his death.' Alice shifted in her seat, turning her head to Maggie.

'Before you ask, it wasn't me. Wait a minute.' She paused as they reached a busy junction taking them up towards the motorway. As soon as they were on the straight motorway lane she said, 'I agree it looked like me. But I wasn't at that hotel.'

'Can you tell me the whole story?'

Maggie thought for a moment. Her daughter was sixteen. Still a child, but way beyond childhood. 'Yes, I'll tell you everything, but when we reach home. It's going to be warm, so we can sit out in the garden and I'll give you the works. It's an interesting case, apart from my problem.'

'Why didn't you tell me yourself? I'm not a child.'

'I have to keep reminding myself of that. To me, you and Jack will always be children and it's my job to protect you. Every parent thinks like that.'

'But we're adults now. You should respect that.'

Maggie sighed. There was some truth there, but also a great deal of naivety about the world, still to be learnt. But at what cost?

**

Bob was waiting when they reached the house, just before ten, with a tray of croissants, jam, butter, toast, orange juice, and coffee. To Maggie's surprise, Jack was with him.

'I turfed him out of bed,' Bob said as they carried trays into the conservatory and folded back the doors, letting sunlight and warm air fill the room. 'Thought he might want to be here, given Alice is here because of him.'

Jack looked sheepishly at Maggie, but she gave him a small shake of her head, accompanied by a grin.

'I thought she should know,' he said.

'Just don't say anything about being an adult and having no need of my motherly protective instincts.'

He smiled back.

Carrying the final tray, Maggie paused by the door, watching them, chatting to each other, joking and laughing. She caught a memory of when he had once called his sister the "mini-witch". How they had changed.

She sat down and as they helped themselves to breakfast she began the story, of the initial request from Anthony Bandon, how the "treasure" was probably the invaluable Chinese vase, the unexplained death of Hugh Wilson, the meeting with Michael Wilson, and yesterday with the Desmonds.

'Are you any closer to finding it?' Alice mumbled through a mouthful of croissant crumbs.

'No, but we have the only clue. *The fault of His Lordship*. We still have no idea what it means.'

A quick conversation with Bob had decided her on two things. One: she wasn't going to share that they suspected someone in their trusted circle was not to be trusted. Two: the involvement of Henry Camberwell.

'What about those Desmond people? Do they have the clue?'

'Not as far as we could tell, Al, but we didn't say anything about there being one. Didn't want to give them so much as a hint.'

'Had you come across them before?'

'I must have done because I thought I recognised Moira Desmond from somewhere. I asked her if we had met before, and she said not. But, I think it must have been at one of the shows that we used to attend before Covid. They would probably have been at one of them at the same time.'

Alice was now on her phone. 'I've found a picture of them, on their website. She's got a long nose.'

Maggie laughed. 'Yes, she has. Maybe that's the feature I remember of her.'

'Apart from that, if you alter the nose and the hair colour …' Alice stopped and fiddled with the phone for a few minutes. 'There,' she said, turning the phone around to show an enlarged photograph. 'With a different nose and darker hair, she looks a bit like you.'

As Maggie looked at it, she drew in a sharp breath. 'Alice, could you put sunglasses on this picture?'

'Sure.'

She fiddled again, then turned the photo back to Maggie, whose mouth dropped open.

'What?' Alice said, as both Jack and Bob sat forward.

'I think that's the woman in the photograph the police showed me. It was Moira Desmond.'

Chapter 31

'What do I do now?' Maggie said to Bob. 'Should I call that Inspector, tell him about this?'

'Yes, definitely. Did he give you a number?'

'No.'

'I'll get him on the phone. Give me a minute.' He had left his phone in the house and walked back in to retrieve it from the kitchen table.

'Good job I came back,' Alice said. 'You wouldn't have figured this out by yourself.'

Don't be smug, Al', Jack said. 'This is serious business.'

'I'm not being smug. She wouldn't have.'

'*She* is still here, thank you.'

'Sorry, mum. Here's Bob.'

He was already on the phone. 'He wants me to send through the picture. He can look at the website for himself. Alice, can you please send it to me and I'll pass it on.'

When that was done, they sat in silence for a few moments.

'What now?' Jack asked.

'We wait,' Bob replied.

'Will they tell you what they're going to do, with this Moira Desmond woman?'

'No,' Bob said. 'Not right away.'

'That's not fair,' Alice grumbled.

'Spoken like a true adult,' Maggie said.

'Don't get snarky,' Bob said. 'Alice, it's a great catch, and will probably take the heat off your mother for a while. They'll interview Moira Desmond, I know for a fact. I might be able to find out what she has to say.'

'Please try,' Maggie said, taking his hand. 'This should make it easier, but it doesn't.'

**

Maggie decided not to tell Zelah and Nick about Moira Desmond. They had agreed to a weekend off and, despite longing to let them know, she held back. There was nothing they could do and it was likely to set them on edge. The particular decider was, that knowing Zelah, she would either call or even drive up to visit the Desmonds to confront Moira.

Instead, she sat in her garden, drinking coffee, trying to read a novel but, occasionally, unable to sit she wandered in and out of various rooms, accompanied everywhere she went by Alice.

'How about we talk about the case,' Alice asked, after Maggie returned from the bathroom, having forbidden her daughter to accompany her. 'It's not doing work, exactly, is it?'

It was tempting. She weighed it up.

Bob had gone next door to visit their neighbours, George and Mary. George had been out of hospital for some weeks, having recovered from a near-death experience with Covid. He was still weak and unable to leave the house. Bob was using his enforced leave to visit more often. He told George stories about past police raids and highly exciting cases which, according to Mary, whispered over the fence to Maggie, were more like the plots of a well-known TV series, being unlikely bucolic occurrences for South Wales' industrial towns and cities. However, George lapped it all up and couldn't wait for the next visit, so Mary bit back her grin and listened with a show of amazement, grateful to Bob for the pleasure he was giving George. She'd just have to be careful what George watched on TV box sets for the next few months.

'I'm thinking about the clue,' Alice went on, dragging Maggie's attention back from whatever was going on in next door's living room. '*His Lordship's fault.* It's odd, isn't it.'

'Yes. But, it may have changed as it was handed down through the generations. That can happen, just one word different can alter the whole meaning.'

'OK, like Whispering Gallery. So, which word do you think could change?'

'Honestly, Al, I haven't given it too much thought yet.' She told Alice the story of John Pritchard and the fence known as *The King* and *His Majesty*.'

'That tells me it must have been close if that was what the man thought at the time. So, maybe it's something to do with the fault.'

'That's a good notion.'

Alice jumped up. 'I'm going to check the Thesaurus on my phone.'

She came back five minutes later, peering at the screen. 'There are loads of words. Fault as in mistake, fault as in causing earthquakes. The closest I could see is a fault being a blemish. Might it be something to do with a monument that had been defaced? Or could it be to do with the Chartists, someone called His Lordship who met George Evans on the journey, someone he thought he could trust?'

'George Evans was in the crowd overnight close to the cathedral and at the Westgate Hotel. Maybe. Read up about it, if you like. I've a shelf-load of books.'

Alice set off and came back with an armful of books which, Maggie realised, would keep her occupied for the rest of the afternoon.

A couple of hours later, Alice closed the fifth book through which she had rifled. 'Nope. Can't find anything like a clue. Are there a lot of statues in Newport?'

'There are some now, but I don't think there would have been many, if any, at the time.'

'How about we go for a walk, down through the town from the Westgate towards where George lived? Some of the buildings might have been there, as well as the Westgate, in 1839.'

'My recollection of the town is that most of what was there was either destroyed or rebuilt as the town grew bigger and became more industrialised. But, I don't mind, if you want to give it a go. Shall we try in the morning?'

**

At ten on Sunday morning a somewhat sleepy Maggie and an enthusiastic Alice stood outside the Westgate Hotel, staring up at the facade.

'It's supposed to be beautiful inside,' Maggie said. 'Pity we can't go in. The bullet holes are just behind the door.'

'Will it be repaired?'

'Apparently, yes. Some work's been done already. Right, let's go.'

They began a slow walk down the now pedestrianised Commercial Street. There were few major chain stores now, just a bookshop, and stationers, one or two clothes brands, and many charity stores.

'I used to walk this street every day when I was in school,' Maggie said. 'Newport has suffered.' They passed a small street leading down towards the river. 'There's a shopping precinct down there and the library.' She shook her head. 'This main street used to be so dynamic.'

Alice was looking up. 'I see what you mean about the buildings. The architecture is quite amazing, isn't it,' she said, pointing at the fourth and fifth storeys of buildings from the late nineteenth and early twentieth century that had retained their original features.

'So many people never look up,' Maggie said. 'Still, there's very little, if anything, left before about 1850. I looked at the 1843 tithe map last night. Where we are now,' she pointed to the top of a steep street leading up to Stow Hill 'At the top of this hill, that's where the Chartists marched down to the Westgate. Thousands of them. To the left, behind these buildings, there was farmland. And once we cross further down into Commercial street, that was all farmland too, on either side. So hard to imagine.'

They had reached St Paul's church, now closed and slowly decaying.

'Apparently, this was the only church in Newport when it was built, apart from St Woolos.'

Alice peered through the locked gates. 'It doesn't have a graveyard. Where did they bury people?'

'I don't know. St Woolos, probably. There were almost certainly other graveyards. You know, if George Evans ran home after the march he would have run down this street and headed down to Pill, which was practically a separate village, in 1839.'

'Maybe he stopped to catch his breath,' Alice said. 'He might have stood here, like us.'

Maggie smiled. 'Indeed he might. As you say, it's unusual for a church like this not to have its own graveyard. I'll check it out when we're back.'

They walked on, across the main road to Cardiff and continued down towards the former village of Pillgwenlly.

'This is where the Irish families came, starting around the 1830s, but in huge numbers after the famine. A lot of them were labourers, or worked at the docks. Like your gran's family.'

The street had seen many changes in the community, from the Irish to the Italians and Spanish of the early twentieth century, now to the Bangladeshi and Yemeni communities and the asylum seekers running from the horrors of war and destruction in their own countries.

'It's always been big on community here. My grandmother used to walk me up to the fishmonger every Friday morning. It was always a big treat to stay with her,' Maggie said, seeing both present and past.

'Where did George Evans live?'

'High Street. Which is now St Michael's Street. It was just a small street of houses then, surrounded by fields and marshland. The docks were still being built.'

'I'm guessing it was poor?'

'Unbelievably so. A report commissioned in the 1840s, I think, said the sanitation was woeful, due to the houses being built on low-lying marshy land. And, like, one privy for eight people and open sewers. The death rate must have been shocking and the infant mortality rate doesn't bear thinking about.'

They walked in silence as far as the old Dock gate, then turned and began to walk back again.

'We're lucky, aren't we?' Alice remarked.

Maggie gave her a quick hug. 'Never forget that.'

**

After a lazy late lunch, Maggie checked up on St Paul's church. It had never had a graveyard. She checked out a few names of people who had died in 1839 and found that they were buried either at St Woolos church if they were sufficiently well-to-do to buy a plot, or they were interred individually or in communal graves in two other graveyards in the town, both of which had been abandoned when they filled up and began to overflow.

'Listen to this,' she called to Alice. 'I've been checking on the graveyards like those we talked about this morning. I can't find a reference online to the name of any particular one, apart from St Woolos, but there must have been some. This account refers to "burial places" which were so close to the drinking water source that the smell was vile and the water became fouled with leakage from the rotting corpses.'

Alice pulled a face of revulsion. 'That's disgusting. Didn't it make people ill?'

'Very. Outbreaks of typhoid fever and cholera. The drinking water was filtered through sewage.

The municipal cemetery, St Woolos, didn't open until 1856.'

'At least they had a proper burial place,' Alice said. 'Would they still have been buried in piles?'

'Yes. It was a matter of cost. Do you remember the cemetery? We went there to visit the grave of my great grandmother, Alice.'

'Of course, I do. It's huge. I remember some huge monument things, and a couple of little buildings.'

'They're called mausoleums. They often bury a family together over time, in one of those. If you're interested, we can go visit a couple of really interesting cemeteries in the summer. Highgate in London is amazing, but the best one is Pere LaChaise in Paris. Lots of famous people buried there and some amazing monuments.'

'London and Paris. That would make for a good summer,' Alice said, grinning. 'I'm in.'

'Not quite what I meant but, why not?' Maggie replied. 'I'll think about it.'

'That's what you used to say when I wanted something I was never going to get.'

'True. But now you're grown up, I mean I will certainly think about it.'

'Excellent. Right, I'm going to pack my bag. Can we leave at five? We can have an hour in the garden before we set off.'

Maggie closed down the computer and they walked arm in arm into the garden, joining Bob and Jack, plus Max who was visiting before heading over to see Nick.

'How's Stella?' Maggie asked. 'And Flora, of course.'

'Both fine. You do know they're with Stella's mother until we sort this out?' Max replied.

'Yes. You must be missing them, Max.'

'I'll live, and it's safer for them, right now.'

'Are you joining us in the morning?' Maggie asked.

'Yes. I'd like to hear what progress you've made.'

**

Maggie and Alice left at five to drive to Cardiff, where Matthew and Sarah were waiting for her.

'All good,' Maggie said to Sarah, as Alice took her bag out of the trunk and Matthew carried it towards the lift that would take them to their top-floor apartment. 'She's satisfied that I'm OK.'

'Are you, really?' Sarah asked.

'Much better, since I recognised the woman in the photo that the police thought was me.'

'Have you heard anything more?'

'No, but I'm hoping for an update in the morning. I'll be pressing for one.'

'Good luck,' Sarah said, squeezing Maggie's arm. 'Alice is fine with us, you know.'

Maggie nodded, shouted goodbye to Alice, and drove home. She spent the journey thinking over what they would be saying to the group gathering in the morning. Both Finch and Abbott would be present, plus the extended family from Ireland, who had decided to join in person, this time. They had arrived during the afternoon and were staying with Zelah for a couple of days.

Zelah and Nick were arriving an hour ahead of time, to plan how they were going to handle the meeting, knowing that one of them was not to be trusted. It was going to be a delicate balancing act.

The following morning, Nick arrived at eight, but not Zelah. The Irish group had hired a car to be independent of Zelah, so that wasn't the reason for her lateness. Unusual for her, Maggie thought. Zelah was a stickler for punctuality.

When she eventually arrived, just before eight-thirty, Maggie had started to feel concerned. Zelah's rush into the house, and her stern expression, told Maggie something was wrong.

'What?' Maggie said, as they sat at the conference table.

'A problem.' Zelah bit her lip. 'Look, I had to make a decision about something urgent. It happened this morning and I couldn't wait to speak to you both.'

Nick rolled his eyes.

'Don't,' Zelah snapped.

'Then you'd better tell us what you've done,' Maggie said.

'I had a call this morning from Ian Desmond. Moira has been in an accident. She's in a coma in Neville Hall hospital in Abergavenny.'

'Oh, that's terrible,' Maggie said. 'I didn't like her, but you don't wish that on anyone. But, what's the decision you had to make?'

Zelah took a deep breath. 'Ian was distraught. He told me he knew nothing about Henry Camberwell. It seems that Moira has been speaking to Camberwell behind his back. He got the story from her before she stormed out of the house. He thought the client was Hugh Wilson. Moira told him Camberwell wants the vase and is prepared to do anything necessary to get it.'

'We know that,' Nick said. 'And?'

'Ian wants to work with us, to find the vase and if it's still in one piece, to return it to the British Museum. He's disgusted with what Moira was doing. But, he now blames himself for her rushing off in a fury and crashing her car. She may not survive.'

Maggie sat back and folded her arms. 'You said yes, didn't you.'

Zelah nodded. 'I've known Ian for a long time and I've also known for as long that Moira was the driving force behind the business, in particular the dodgy parts. And, she was the one who tried to take me down. Ian let her do it. He's a weak man, but he does have some principles. He's offered us access to the file she built up, but kept from him.'

Maggie turned to Nick. 'What do you think?'

'I don't know what to say,' Nick muttered.

'Look, I had to think quickly. I told him we were meeting this morning and he's on his way –' before she could say any more, Nick threw his hands in the air.

'So we don't have a choice, do we?' he shouted.

'Yes, you do. I told him that I would speak to you both and you both have to agree. Not just one of you, for a majority, both of you. If you both say no, that's easy. If one of you says no and the other yes, that means he can't join us. Up to you.' She sat back.

'What does he have in the file?' Maggie asked. 'Is it worth our while to let him in? We already have someone we believe is passing information over to Camberwell. How do we know this isn't an elaborate trick?'

'I telephoned the hospital, someone I know. They confirmed that Moira is in Intensive Care and the prognosis isn't good.'

A few minutes of silence followed.

'Sorry, but you have to decide. It's almost nine and we haven't worked out what we're saying to the group.'

'Lucky I made some notes, isn't it?' Nick said, sliding a piece of paper to each of them, so harshly that Maggie had to grab at hers to stop it flying off the table.

Reading the notes gave them a few minutes' respite. 'This looks good, Nick. Thank you,' said Maggie. Zelah nodded in agreement.

'I'm sorry to put this on you without any notice.'

'You could have told him to wait until after the meeting,' Nick said accusingly.

'I could, but then we wouldn't have been able to have his input, which might be important.'

Maggie nodded slowly. 'I'm OK with it, for now. But Zelah, I'm not prepared to go any further than this meeting.'

'Understood. I agree. Nick?'

He nodded. 'I'm cross, Zelah. I don't like being ambushed. I just hope what he has to say is worthwhile.'

'We'll be kind to him, under the circumstances,' Maggie said. 'The man could be about to lose his wife, and after arguing with her. That's a terrible memory to carry for the rest of his life. What time will he be here?'

'About nine-thirty,' Zelah replied, 'And …'

The doorbell rang.

'I'll go,' Maggie said.

As she was greeting people, Bob joined Zelah and Nick.

'Wow, the temperature in here is chilly,' Bob remarked, looking from Zelah to Nick. 'Something happened?'

Nick nodded but didn't speak.

Maggie called to Bob, who joined her in the hall, where she was standing with Finch and Abbott, both of whom were unsmiling.

'Bob, would you take our visitors into the sitting room, until the rest of the family has arrived?'

He didn't ask, but led them in and began some small talk as Maggie went back to the front door and welcomed the Irish contingent. Zelah rushed out to greet them, giving Maggie time to return to the office to have a quick word with Nick.

'Thanks for the notes. As far as I'm concerned, Ian Desmond isn't to be trusted any more than the rest of them. Nick, can you watch him, plus Abbot and Costello? And I think we should keep an eye on Gerry Quinn.'

'Agreed,' he replied in a whisper. 'You and Zelah do the talking. I'm fine with being in the background. By the way, where's Max?'

'He stayed here last night. I'll go give them a shout. He and Jack wanted to join us this morning. Oh, here they are.'

Jack and Max had wandered down the stairs and introductions were going on in the hallway.'

Jack saw Maggie. 'Time for breakfast, or a coffee?'

'Quickly,' she replied. 'Speedy. I'm about to get everyone together. We're expecting one more.'

She shook her head as he started to ask, so he and Max headed to the kitchen, followed by Maggie, who began to take flasks and cups through to the office.

'We need to start,' she said to the crowd still standing in the hall. 'Sorry to rush you, but we have something to share, about an additional guest, before we start in earnest.' Gerry Quinn had joined them and was standing awkwardly, hovering from foot to foot, trying to catch his sister's eye. She had not yet acknowledged his presence, although Zelah had told her that he would be part of the group.

In the office, she put the tray on the table, then went to call Bob, Abbott, and Finch.

When all ten were seated around the table and one additional chair had been brought in, Zelah undertook the explanation about Ian Desmond and why he would be joining them.

'I thought he was the opposition,' Max said.

'Normally, yes. But these are not normal circumstances,' Zelah replied. 'He says he has useful input he's prepared to share and any help is welcome.'

'But do you trust him?' Max persevered.

Zelah paused.

'We're giving him the benefit of the doubt, for now,' Maggie said. 'In truth, not sure.'

The doorbell rang. Maggie went to answer and for a minute or so the group waited as the sound of low voices from the hallway, undistinguishable, loudened as Maggie returned with Ian Desmond in tow.

Zelah stood up. The man Maggie had met just a few days before had looked at least healthy, and somewhat cynical. The man entering the room now was a wreck. His shoulders drooped, his hair was greasy, unkempt, and standing up in places, as if he had run his hands through it so many times it had fixed itself in spikes. The reddened, swollen eyes and grey face told them this man hadn't slept for more than a day. He stopped on the threshold, looking around.

'Lot of people here,' he muttered.

'This is a family issue, as well as a professional job,' Maggie replied. She indicated the empty chair, but he continued to stand, his arms hanging loosely at his sides.

Zelah walked over to him, guided him to the chair, sat him down, and poured coffee for him. He nodded thanks.

'I know you've come straight from the hospital. How's Moira?'

Ian looked up at her, then slowly shook his head. 'They want me to agree to turn off the life support. I can't do it, not yet.'

She put a hand on his shoulder. 'Ian, I am so sorry. We didn't always like each other much, but this is … I don't know what to say.'

He gave her a feeble smile. 'I want to help solve this case.'

'Then let's get on with it,' Zelah replied, returning to her seat. 'Ian, do you feel able to add your contribution?'

He nodded.

'Over to you, Maggie.'

Maggie began an update, giving out the information as agreed on Nick's notes. There was one notable exception. With the news about Ian Desmond, she had forgotten to warn Bob and Jack. Bob caught on immediately, but not Jack.

'I thought there was more to the clue,' he began before Nick jumped in to talk over him.

'No, that's it, according to Anthony Bandon. You're muddled up with something else. There's been so much information, I'm not surprised. Sorry, Jack.'

Jack scowled and was about to speak again, when Bob, next to him, stepped on his foot. Jack took the hint, sat back with folded arms, and pressed his lips together, but not before taking a look at Maggie, who stared at him.

'Easily done,' she said. 'when we're working on multiple cases. Right, moving on.'

She took up the story again, ending with the visit to Ian and Moira. Here, she paused. They had planned to be forthright about the relationship with the Desmonds, but that wasn't possible, now. 'Ian, perhaps this is a good time for you to tell us what's been happening from your point of view.'

Ian Desmond coughed, raised his coffee mug with a shaking hand, took a long sip as everyone watched him, returned the cup to the table, and coughed again.

'Our client, or I should say clients, were Hugh and Michael Wilson. They are the direct descendants of William George Evans, the man who originally stole the Chinese vase from Vernon Prosser. No information about a clue has been passed down the family, but there has always been a tale about something valuable, that Evans was cheated out of.'

'Does that mean that someone else took it from him?' Maggie asked.

'I don't think so. He was falsely accused of stealing two silver candlesticks from Prosser, who had him arrested, tried, and transported to Australia. He died on the journey, as you know. His family never heard from him again. His direct descendent was his daughter, Mary Ann, who it appears knew something, but wouldn't tell her family, including her children. She only said the object, whatever it was, was cursed.'

'Is that it?' Zelah asked.

'More or less,' Ian said.

'You're saying you didn't know that Henry Camberwell was behind Moira?' Mischa asked.

'No, I didn't. I was surprised when Zelah mentioned his name. Once you'd left Moira and I went home. We had a row – a stupendous row – and she told me that he was financing the enquiry. I was outraged and told her it had to stop. That's when she ran out.' He stopped, his voice had broken down.

'What comes next?' Niall McCarthy Miller asked, anxious to divert Mischa, who was frowning. 'What about the woman who visited Hugh Wilson in London, just before he died?'

A quick look passed between Maggie and John Finch, who gave the briefest shake of his head.

'No news, yet.' She had asked Bob to inform Finch and Abbott that she now believed the woman to be Moira and they now understood that this wasn't going to be brought up in front of Ian Desmond.

'As to what comes next, we've decided we'll go back to the beginning, re-read everything, re-start some searches.'

'It may be,' Zelah intervened, 'that we just aren't able to find a resolution as to what happened to that vase. I don't see there's much else we can do on the family history, but we'll give it one more go. Maggie is going to brief Anthony Bandon as soon as we're done here.'

Ian Desmond stood. 'I need to get back to the hospital.' He swayed and put his hands on the table to steady himself. 'I'll read Moira's notes again when I'm back home and let you know if anything jumps out at me. If you'll excuse me.' He paused and shook his head. 'I'm not sure we'll ever find that vase.'

Zelah went with him to the door.

When she returned there were individual hushed conversations around the table.

'That's all for now. Thanks, everyone. Mischa, you, Niall, and Stephen come with me. We'll go back to my flat.' She began to usher them out of the room. Mischa shrugged at Niall but didn't argue.

Finch and Abbott also stood. He walked to Maggie and said in a low voice. 'Investigations are continuing. You can rest easy, for now.' Then he and Abbott left them, she with a scowl at Maggie.

Gerry Quinn followed Zelah out, hoping to catch a word with Mischa, which left Maggie and Nick, with Bob, Jack, and Max.

Nick gave Maggie a quick stare, then said to Max, 'Let's go refresh this coffee.'

'OK, what's going on that I don't know,' Jack exclaimed, as soon as the door closed.

'Sorry I had to kick you,' Bob said.

'Yeh, well, I suppose you had a reason. What is it?'

'Sit down,' Maggie said, in a voice that didn't brook argument. He sat.

'Within the group of ten, eleven now with Ian Desmond, someone is passing information to Henry Camberwell. We don't know who it is, but we aren't putting everything out on the table. We need to keep the family informed, because of the risk, but Zelah deliberately downplayed it. I intended to tell you before we started, but the news of Moira Desmond's accident and Zelah being late prevented me from speaking to you.'

Jack's eyes had widened as she spoke. 'Who do you think it is?'

'We don't know. The circle of trust is me, you, Bob, Zelah, Nick, and Stella. Plus Alice. I talked to her about it yesterday.'

He fell back in his chair. 'What's the real plan?'

'We're going to work on the second part of the phrase in the will: his fault. See if we can come up with some ideas as to what it might mean. And Nick and I are researching the descendants of John Pritchard. Might come to nothing, but we have to check everything. And I was telling the truth when I said we're going to re-read everything.'

'What about **you**, Mum?'

'Finch just told me that I'm OK for now. Police are checking into Moira's whereabouts around the time Hugh Wilson died, so they aren't coming for me, immediately.'

Jack nodded. 'And I can't say any of this to Max?'

'Sorry, no. It's hard for Nick, too. And Jack, I'm sorry but I can't have him staying here, not until we resolve this.'

'You can't think it's him,' Jack protested. 'Not after how he helped you.' He turned to Bob, 'surely not?'

'We can't afford to second guess anyone,' Bob said. 'He's your friend, and I believe, for what it's worth, that it's not him. But, for your mother's sake …'

'I get it,' Jack said. 'I don't like it, but I get it.' He stood up. 'I'll get him away from here now. I'll tell him some story about you being nervous.'

'Make me sound as paranoid as you like,' she said, smiling.

Nick and Max returned with another tray of coffee. Jack immediately told Max he was leaving, suggesting they go to Max's flat for an afternoon of computer gaming before they went to work. Max agreed.

As soon as they were gone, Nick sat down with a huff. 'This is beyond hard. It's exhausting. First I have to send Stella and Flora away, and now I'm keeping secrets from my son.'

'Not for long, Nick.' She was about to say more when her phone rang. She checked it and frowned. 'Odd,' then answered it.

'Hey, Al. Everything OK?'

'Absolutely fine. I have a personal study time. Who's with you?'

'Just Bob and Nick.'

'Put me on speaker. Matthew is with me.'

Maggie did so, with a worried glance. 'Right, they can hear you. What's up?'

'Matthew's dad was here last night. I talked to him about the case. Was that OK?'

'I don't think he's likely to tell anyone he shouldn't,' Maggie said. 'He's had enough practice.'

'Right. We were discussing the information in the Australian will. Matthew's dad went quiet for a bit. Then he said something, and I think he's got a point.'

'What did he say? About His Lordship?'

'Yes, and no. It's more about it being His Lordship's fault.'

Alice, don't drag this out. What did he say?'

'He suggested that the original word wasn't "fault". He suggested it might have been "vault". What do you think? *His Lordship's vault.* Does that mean anything to you?'

'It means Matthew's dad is a genius!' Maggie said, looking across to Bob and Nick, who were both grinning and nodding. 'I'm about to speak to Anthony in Australia. I'll ask him to have his uncle take another look. Alice, tell Matthew's dad many thanks. He may well have just propelled us forward.'

'Will do. We're off now. Study time over. Let us know, will you, if anything comes of it.'

The call ended and Maggie turned to Nick with a questioning look.

'Excellent notion,' he said. 'Call Anthony now.'

They sat around the table as Maggie set up the call. Anthony Bandon had been waiting, together with his uncle Roger.

She took him through the events of the past couple of days, leading up to Alice's phone call. 'Is it a possibility, Anthony? Could you ask Malcolm to take another look?'

'He's gone to bed already, but as soon as he's awake, we'll get onto it. This is exciting, isn't it?'

She smiled and told him to call as soon as he had the answer.

Nick was already at his computer. Before she could speak he had called up details of the Morgan family. 'I'll start with the most obvious one,' he said. 'The first Lord Tredegar. He was alive at the time of the uprising, so makes it unlikely. So, I'll rule him out.'

Maggie and Bob talked quietly in the background as Nick tapped away on his keyboard, leaning into his screen.

'What did Finch have to say?' she asked him.

'Nothing much. He knew about your call to Inspector Middleton, that you think Moira Desmond was the woman, not you, but he wouldn't say much more.'

'Did you tell him anything that didn't come out in that meeting?'

'No. He can wait until it's clear that it was Moira Desmond, not you. Although that's going to be difficult – ' he paused as Nick spun around.

'The Morgans had a vault in St Basil's church in Bassaleg, on the outskirts of Newport. It was originally inside the church but was moved outside in 1917. It's now somewhere in the church grounds.'

'We should go and take a look,' Maggie said, standing up. 'Now.'

Chapter 32

'Count me out,' Nick said. 'I'd prefer to carry on tracing the descendants of John Pritchard. I'm not sure why, but I suspect I may find someone we already know.'

Maggie stopped. 'Really?'

'Yes. Makes sense. If it was important enough for Pritchard to enter dangerous territory in his search for the vase, then he may well have told a family member where he was going. You started on his son, Albert, on Friday. He had three children, two of whom survived to adulthood, or at least until they were sixteen and eighteen. That's where I'll pick up now.'

'I'll come with you,' Bob said. 'I know that church. The graveyard is huge.'

Twenty minutes later, having parked outside the ancient church, they walked through the lychgate into what was an impressively large cemetery on two layers.

'The lower layer has more recent graves, from the last century and this one,' Bob said, as they walked down the path towards the church entrance. The gravestones and monuments were spread out on both sides, asymmetrically as usual in an old cemetery, both in the open and underneath old trees. The grass had recently been mowed and the smell was sweet, sharp, and summery.

'You're unusually knowledgeable,' Maggie said, gazing around. 'Is this a new hobby?'

'No, I once chased a couple of lads around here, who'd been trying to steal from the church. After we nabbed them, I took a walk around.'

'What's the oldest grave?' she asked. This had been a favourite game in her childhood.

'No idea,' Bob replied, 'I was looking more at the monuments, over there.' He pointed to a few tall, upright carved stone constructions. 'I remember they date around 1800.'

'The church is older than that,' Maggie said. 'Right, I suggest we start close and move outwards. I'm expecting it will be substantial and close to the building.'

She found the monument ten minutes later, at the back of the church, and called Bob to come and look at it.

'That's quite something,' he said, squatting down to read the inscription on the raised plinth. '*Beneath this stone are laid to rest those members of the family of Morgan of Tredegar, whose names are recorded above*.'

Maggie stood back to photograph the whole. It consisted of a low single bar iron rail enclosing two upright crosses in marble, each about ten feet high, and each on a plinth, bearing the Tredegar coat of arms. In between was a raised marble stone, darkened with age, around two feet high, with names engraved in two rows. She moved forward and counted them.

'Twenty in all, including two infants. The oldest dates from 1797. She's the wife of Sir Charles Morgan. The first Lord Tredegar is there, look, in the centre of the closest row. But he didn't die until 1843, so he can't be the Lordship in the clue of 1840. He would have been a Lord, but he wasn't dead and the vault would have been closed.'

She stood, frowning.

'There's a sign on the front gates of the church. It's locked up for now. They're not back to services yet, but if you want some information there's a phone number.'

'Let's try it.'

They walked back around to the front of the church and found a bench. Maggie dialled the number. It was answered immediately by a churchwarden who explained that they took it in turns to answer calls. She clarified what they were looking for.

'I know the internal vault was moved outside in 1917, but I'm not aware of anything other than remains being found with it. But, if you can wait five minutes, one of our members is a historian who knows everything there is to know about St Basil's history. I can call her, see if she might be aware of something.'

Maggie thanked him and said they would wait.

It was a sunny day and they sat back to enjoy the warmth and peace.

'Lovely spot,' she murmured. 'I do love an old graveyard.'

'Want to have a wander around?'

'Once we've had the call back, perhaps, although I do want to get back asap, to see if Nick's found anything useful.'

Her phone rang.

'Hello, Mrs Gilbert. Michael Stone here. I've spoken to Jenny, our history expert. She has all of the papers from that time and she's read up on the removal and re-interment of the remains. She says there was nothing recovered with the remains. So sorry, we can't help you.'

'Thank you anyway, Michael. At least we can rule out this line of enquiry.'

'Good luck with your quest. Do let us know if you find what you're looking for. It sounds intriguing.'

227

She ended the call with a sigh. 'Dead end.'

'Never mind,' Bob said. 'It was worth a try. Do you want to have a wander round?'

'No, not today. But I see there's a pub next door and I remember it used to have a reputation for good food. Perhaps we can come back when this is over, have a nice lunch followed by a walk around the graveyard?'

'Still does good food,' Bob said, laughing.

'Are you laughing at me?'

'If anyone else heard you say that a lunch and a nose around a graveyard was any way to spend a Sunday afternoon, they'd move away from you, quickly.'

She punched his arm. 'Drive me home. Let's see what Nick has been up to.'

**

Nick was disappointed to hear that the Morgan vault was not the answer to their clue. 'Maybe it was "fault", after all.'

'We'll know more in the morning when Anthony gets back to us. Maybe in a couple of hours, even. If he sends through a message tonight before I go to bed, I'll text you. You had any luck with the Pritchards?'

'Nothing yet, but I've only had a couple of hours. So far I have twenty great-grandchildren of John Pritchard from three of his six children and I haven't reached the current live generations. Going to take up most of tomorrow, and it may lead to nothing.' He turned back to his computer.

'I'll join you,' Maggie said. 'Bob's going next door to visit George. I can put in a couple of hours.'

'Good. Can you take the fourth child, Mary Ellen? She was born in 1837. She's present on the 1841 and 1851 census returns. Probably won't be on the 1861, but I'll leave it to you.'

Maggie's search of the 1861 census didn't turn up Mary Ellen Pritchard, but as the girl would have been twenty-four years old, she had most likely married. She tried the various sites, but couldn't find the marriage of an Ellen Pritchard, nor a registered birth.

' Perhaps, as it was 1837, she was born before national registration started in July that year. Even if she was born after, in those early months a lot didn't register their children. How about the Monmouthshire marriages?' Nick said.

'My next try,' Maggie replied, re-loading the site. 'And, there she is. She's been recorded as Mary Ellen Pritchard, which was probably her birth name. I'll just check.' She paused, opened another tab, and re-loaded the Monmouthshire indexes, this time the baptisms. 'Yes, she was baptised Mary Ellen Pritchard in January 1837, to John and Louisa. In Malpas in Newport. That's her, isn't it?'

'Yes. Who did she marry?'

Maggie flipped to the marriages index. 'He was called Josiah Lewis. Same age, twenty-four. He was a servant, like her. They married in Langstone. I guess that's where they met, possibly even servants in the same household. Next, children. They should have been born sometime after 1861.'

After five minutes she said, 'I've only found one child, in 1862. A girl named Louisa, probably after her grandmother. I'll just check something else.'

She re-loaded the Monmouthshire indexes. After a few minutes of switching between them, she said, 'Oh dear. Mary Ellen

Pritchard Lewis died in 1862, a few days after baby Louisa was born. She's buried in St Woolos in Newport.'

'What about the baby?' Nick asked. 'Did she survive?'

Maggie flipped sites again. 'There's no record of her death or her burial. I suppose she might have been brought up by her father. Back to the census records, then, see if I can find Josiah Lewis and Louisa in 1871.'

Nick stretched and yawned. 'I'm leaving mine until tomorrow. Up to thirty-three descendants now. I'm not sure we'll get anything from this. It's too many.'

'OK. Well, I can't find anything on the 1871 census and honestly, Nick, is there any point in pursuing Mary Ellen's descendants? I mean, she was only three when her father died. How would she have known anything? She was in the workhouse with her mother in 1841, and if her mother didn't know anything …'

'You may be right. The most likely is the eldest, Albert. If John Pritchard didn't tell his wife why he was going to Cardiff, he might have told his eldest son. That's just speculation, though. Let me think about it tonight and we can pick it up again in the morning.'

'Fair enough. I'm tired, too. I'll –'

Her phone rang. 'It's Zelah.'

'Is Nick still there?'

'Yes,'

'Put me on speaker.'

'OK, we can both hear you now.'

'I just had a call from Ian Desmond. They stopped Moira's life support. She's dead.'

Maggie closed her eyes. 'Well, Ian predicted that. How is he?'

'Devastated. But he did ask if we've made any more progress.'

'We have, just a little, but we weren't planning to tell him.'

'Were you planning to tell me?' Zelah snapped.

'Don't be snarky with me, Zelah. Here's what happened after you left this morning.'

She told Zelah the story of Alice's phone call, followed by her and Bob's decision to go immediately to the church, the discovery of the vault and the phone call to the churchwarden, its outcome, and their recent return to the office.

'Not the vault, after all.'

'I still don't rule it out,' Nick said. 'Maggie has emailed Anthony Bandon to ask him to check with his uncles, to ask them to take another look, to check again which word it is. We're waiting on his reply.'

'Thanks for the update,' Zelah said.

Maggi went to speak, but Nick put a finger to his lips. 'You're welcome, Zelah. Are you enjoying having your family around? Nice for you.' His tone was as sarcastic as hers had been.

'Yes, all right. We're going out to dinner, but let me know if Anthony comes back to you tonight.'

'You'll be my first call,' Maggie said, hitting the button to cut Zelah off. 'Sometimes …' she began.

'She's as stressed as the rest of us,' Nick said. 'I'm leaving now. Can I be your second call, if you hear from Anthony this evening?'

'Go, now,' Maggie replied with a grin.

Chapter 33

Maggie awoke at six the following morning and went down to the office, knowing that more sleep was impossible.

She and Bob had spent the evening discussing what might happen now that Moira Desmond could no longer be questioned about her involvement with the Wilson family and Henry Camberwell.

'Will they carry on assuming it was me, not her, at the hotel when Hugh Wilson died?' she asked Bob.

'Not necessarily. If there's doubt, they'll go back to the hotel with a picture of Moira. They'll also be trying to establish if she was in London on or around the day he died.'

'They could just ask Ian.'

'But he may not have known that was where she was going, and if he did know, he still might not know that she was directly involved with Camberwell, not just the clients.'

'So should I call the Inspector – what was his name?'

'Tom Middleton.'

Yes, him. Should I be asking for an update?'

'Maybe give it until lunchtime tomorrow. He'll have found out by then Moira Desmond has died, and he'll have to consider when to speak to Ian. I don't think he'll get back to you at least until he's spoken to Ian and has more detail around Moira's involvement with Camberwell.'

Five hours until lunchtime, at least. She needed to fully occupy her mind, so pulling up her research on the baby Louisa Pritchard she began to look for her on census records. There was still nothing to be found in 1871, nor on the following three census returns, either for Josiah Lewis or for Louisa. Emigration was her next thought. She went through the sites with records. And there, in 1875, she found the arrival in Australia, of Josiah, a new wife, Margaret, and two children: Louisa now aged thirteen, and a baby, Edward, aged two. Experience and a gut feeling told her that it was unlikely that there was any point in further research of both Josiah and Louisa Pritchard.

She decided to try some of the descendants of Albert Pritchard, that Nick had found. Thirty-six, all Albert's grandchildren. It would need both of them on it, to make quick progress. She checked his charts. Albert had had three children, two of whom had reached adulthood. She got stuck in with the second of the two boys, Lewis Pritchard, born in 1846. He had had five children: Albert, Peter, Mari, Lewis Junior, and Mary, who between them had had eighteen children. This was going to be a long day.

By the time Nick arrived a few hours later, she had dealt with the first two, Albert and Peter, down to the present day, with no connections, or recognisable names.

'Anything from Anthony?'

'Not yet. I'm surprised. I thought he might be keen enough to get back to us right away. Must be a good reason for the delay. So, I'll start on the next boy, Lewis Junior.'

'Thanks for the help,' he replied. 'I'll work on Albert's elder son, John. He married Susan Waites in 1870. They had six children, four of whom reached adulthood.'

They both proceeded in concentrated silence for another couple of hours, until Bob joined them.

'Progress – any?'

'Nope,' Maggie replied. She turned to Nick. 'Let's take a quick break. I've come to a conclusion with Lewis Junior. There's nothing there, which only leaves his daughter, Mari. She married a John Peterson and had two daughters. Nothing promising, but I might as well see it through.'

The morning had turned warm, so they opened up the conservatory and sat with coffee and biscuits, breathing in the scents of early spring flowers wafting in from the garden. Maggie had closed her eyes for a few minutes when her phone rang. She checked it. Unidentified caller.

'Hello?'

'Mrs Gilbert?'

'Yes. Who's calling?'

'This is Tom Middleton.'

She sat bolt upright, signalled to Bob, and activated the speaker.

'I was going to call you myself. Do you have something to tell me?'

'I do, but I'd prefer to discuss it in person. I'm on my way to Newport. Please come to the station at two this afternoon.'

She frowned at Bob, who nodded his head and mouthed that she should agree.

'I suppose I can do that. I'll be bringing my solicitor.'

'That's your right, of course.'

'Should I be … never mind. Two o'clock it is.'

She ended the call.

'Should I be worried, Bob?'

He reached out and took her hand. 'Honestly, I don't know. I'll be coming with you. I can't join you, of course, but let's get hold of Norah Collins.'

He called her. Maggie waited. The call was quick.

'She'll be there. She'll meet you at one thirty, just to go over everything that's happened since she last saw you. I'd say, "try not to worry" but I know you will.'

'Of course I will. With Moira Desmond dead there's no-one to say it wasn't me if the hotel receptionist still insists it is.' She paused for a moment. 'Come on, Nick, let's get back to work. It'll take my mind off it all. And Bob, Jack will be down soon. Don't tell him, please.'

Bob nodded. 'I'll stay here. Let me know if there's anything I can do.'

As Maggie and Nick reached the office, Maggie saw an email waiting for her, from Anthony Bandon.

'Let's see what he has to say,' she said to Nick. She opened the email, skimmed through it, and turned to Nick, smiling.

'They've checked again, and given the document to a handwriting expert to be sure. The word is "vault", not "fault". Well done Alice and Matthew's dad. They're agog to know what this means.'

'If you want to reply, tell them we'll have to think it through. As we know it's not the Morgans of Tredegar, this opens up new possibilities.'

'Do you have something in mind?'

'Not at the moment. Or, maybe. Leave it with me for a while, OK?'

She nodded. 'I'll call Zelah and let her know. What are her plans for today?'

'The Irish group is going home this afternoon, so I guess she'll spend this morning with them, then join us later.'

'I'll call her now and tell her I'll be at the police station.'

'Why couldn't he just tell you over the phone?' Zelah demanded. 'There can't be any doubt now. That was Moira in the photo, not you.'

'There must be a reason he wants to speak to me,' Maggie replied, gritting her teeth. 'As soon as we're done, I'll call you. And, Anthony has just sent an email. He and his uncles had the document reviewed by a handwriting expert. The word is definitely "vault". Nick says that opens up new avenues of thought.'

'He's thinking about it?'

'That's what he does, Zelah. So, will we see you today?'

'Of course. The flight to Dublin is at one thirty from Cardiff. I'll go straight to the office from the airport and wait for you to come back.'

'If I come back,' Maggie said.

'Well of course you will,' Zelah snorted and ended the call.

Maggie shrugged. 'I know she's got my back, but …'

'She does. She still struggles with telling you how much she cares.'

'I know. Right. Let's get back to this research. The sooner we can rule it out, the more time we have to think about another vault.'

It would be another two hours before the revelation came.

Chapter 34

Whilst Maggie returned to work, Jack sauntered downstairs to find Bob in the conservatory.

'Nice of you to join us,' Bob said. 'Just in time for lunch.'

'Whatever. I didn't get home until three this morning.' He looked around. 'Where's Max?'

'I haven't seen him so far today. Wasn't he with you?'

'He left at two. It was my turn to supervise the cleaning and locking up. He said he was coming here.'

'Have you checked the spare bedroom?'

Jack grinned and walked out of the kitchen. A couple of minutes later he came back.

'No, not here. Must have changed his mind and gone to his flat. He's not answering his phone.'

'Probably asleep,' Bob replied.

'Yeh. Where's mum?'

'In the office. She and Nick are finishing off some research. Then we're going out later.' He paused for a moment. 'Do you want us to call in on Max?'

'Nah. He'll get back to me later.'

Bob was deciding whether or not to ask Nick if he knew Max's whereabouts. He was mildly annoyed at Jack for allowing Max to leave the bar where they worked, alone.

'How did he get home, Jack?'

'Dunno,' Jack said, rummaging in the fridge and bringing out a quart of milk. 'He said he was going to take a taxi.' He paused, the milk halfway to his mouth. 'I did tell him to wait for me, but he said he was tired. Said he'd be fine.' He put the carton down on the table. 'Shit. Do you think we should go check on him?'

'Yes,' Bob replied. 'Get dressed. I'll tell Maggie and Nick I'm giving you a lift into town.'

He came back a few minutes later as Jack ran down the stairs and they left together. Bob told Maggie he would meet her at the station, as there wouldn't be time to drop off Jack and come back. She said she would drive herself, but was mildly annoyed at Bob, as she wanted him to be with her from the time she left the house.

'I can take you,' Nick said. 'We'll come back to the research later.'

She hesitated, then said. 'Yes, please, Nick. I'm shakier than I thought. I'd prefer someone else drive me.'

They left the house an hour later. As they reached the station, she saw Bob waiting outside with Norah Collins, and jumped out of the car, as Nick drove off.

'Don't be cross with me,' he said as she approached.

'Why not,' she muttered as she went to walk past him.

'I took Jack down to Max's flat. Max didn't come back with Jack last night, which he was supposed to do. He went home, or so Jack thought.'

Maggie stopped dead. 'What does that mean? Did you find him?'

'No,' Bob said. 'He wasn't at the flat and his bed's not been slept in. I told Jack to go back to the club to check, so he didn't know I was meeting you here. Just as well Nick doesn't know, either.'

'Oh God,' Maggie muttered.

He took her hand. 'We'll find him. Are you OK to go on in with Norah? I arranged with Jack to meet up in an hour. I'm supposed to be checking out other bars.'

She nodded.

'Maggie, concentrate on yourself,' Norah said. 'We need to talk, then meet with Middleton. Let's get this over with. As soon as we're done, and we will be done, we can find out what's happened to Max.'

'Nick's going back to the house. I told him as you were here, you'd drive me home.'

'Norah's right. Concentrate on yourself. Let me worry about Max.' He turned and walked off.

Norah led Maggie into the station, where they were shown into an interview room and told Inspector Middleton was on his way.

'His train doesn't arrive for another ten minutes,' Norah said. 'Gives us time for you to bring me up to speed on what's happened with this woman Moira Desmond.'

Maggie filled her in, up to the message from Zelah yesterday evening that Moira had died.

'Inconvenient,' Norah said, then, 'Sorry. Not known for my tact. Right, we'll need to know what information they have from Ian Desmond and any other sources about Moira's whereabouts when Hugh Wilson died. I can throw enough doubt on the ID, regardless of whether or not the receptionist is sticking to his recognition of you and not her.'

'Do you think he might have been paid to say it was me?' Maggie asked.

'Possible, possible,' Norah replied, rummaging in the file. 'I can have someone check it out, depending on what Middleton

239

has to say. There's unlikely to be proof she had direct contact with Henry Camberwell. He's too slippery for that.'

Maggie nodded. 'I just want to get it over with. And I hope you're going to challenge him again on Michael Wilson's lies.'

'I am. However, if young Wilson was in cahoots with Moira Desmond, he may have heard about her accident. He's unlikely to know she's dead, though, not yet. The problem is …'

Maggie didn't find out what the problem was, as the door slammed open and Inspector Tom Middleton rushed into the room.

'Sorry to keep you waiting. Train running a few minutes late. Now, Mrs Gilbert, we have matters to discuss.'

'I will decide what my client discusses and does not discuss, Inspector. No Sergeant Westcott today?'

He gave Norah a brief nod, ignored her question, and spoke again to Maggie.

'You'll be aware by now that Moira Desmond died yesterday.'

She nodded.

'We've been reviewing the information you gave us. We spoke to Mr. Desmond – before his wife died – and he was not aware of her having been in London on 4th April. He thought she was in North Wales with Michael Wilson. When we spoke to Mr Wilson, he confirmed that she had not visited the family on that day. When pressed, he also reviewed his previous evidence about your visit. He was, apparently, in a state of shock about his father's death. He remembered that he had asked you to visit him. He had misinterpreted your words.'

'You mean, he admitted my client did not, in fact, threaten him,' Norah intervened.

Middleton nodded. 'That is correct.'

'Good, but for me, the important matter is the identification,' Maggie said.

Middleton bit his lip and Maggie noticed a thin smile flit across Norah's face.

'We have discovered that Mrs Desmond was in London on April 4th. And the receptionist, when presented with the … her photograph, could not be certain which of you it was. In fact, he isn't now sure it was either of you. He thinks it was someone younger.'

Maggie went to remonstrate, but Norah got in first.

'Then there's no case against my client, Inspector.'

'I didn't say that. Mrs Gilbert is still a person of interest in the murder of Hugh Wilson.'

'Have you checked the CCTV from Paddington Station yet?' Norah demanded.

'It's being checked now as a matter of urgency.'

Norah stood. 'In that case, we'll be going, unless you have any further business that would keep my client here.'

Middleton sat back and folded his arms. 'Mrs Gilbert, I hope you realise what a dangerous man Henry Camberwell is.'

'I do,' Maggie snapped. 'I believe he's behind this and I'm looking to you to do your job properly and prove me right.'

She and Norah marched out of the room and the station. Bob was waiting on the pavement.

'All good?'

'Almost,' Maggie replied. 'Moira Desmond was in London but the ID is still inconclusive. The receptionist is now saying it was a younger woman.'

'They'll find the CCTV,' Norah said. 'Don't worry. You have more important matters to worry about. I'll go now. Call me if or when you hear from Middleton again.' She turned on her high heels and marched off towards Cardiff Road.

'She's a scary woman,' Maggie said. 'I'm just glad she was on my side. What news of Max?'

'None,' Bob replied. 'Now, I'm worried. I've been talking to taxi companies. Nobody picked him up outside the bar. I've got Jez in there looking at CCTV from the streets around the bar.'

'Oh God,' Maggie muttered. 'We'll have to go back and tell Nick.'

'Jack's waiting for us.'

'This is not going to be easy.'

**

Apart from one comment, Jack was silent throughout the journey back to the house, after Bob told him the results of his enquiries.

'Stupid git,' he said as he jumped into the back seat of the car. 'He knew he wasn't supposed to go anywhere on his own.'

Despite relief at her change of circumstances, Maggie was dreading telling Nick that his son might be missing. From the start Nick had been against Maze's involvement, being concerned for his family's welfare, only reluctantly agreeing to continue their investigations. She was terrified he would blame her. She was right.

As soon as she told him, Nick leapt out of his chair. 'I knew this would happen. This is down to you and Zelah.' He hadn't shouted. He hadn't needed to. Maggie felt as if a sharp knife had sliced into her and the wound was deep.

'I'm going to tell Stella and Flora. Then, I'll be back and you,' he pointed at Bob, 'had better have some good news for me.'

242

As the front door slammed Maggie burst into tears. Bob let her sob on his shoulder for the next five minutes, until she ran out of energy.

'It's not your fault,' he said, taking hold of her forearms. 'Listen to me. The rest of us have kept ourselves safe.'

'You're saying it serves him right?' Jack shouted.

'No. I'm saying it was a misjudgement on his part, but that doesn't mean I blame him. The best thing I can do now is go back to the station and see if there's any result from the CCTV. OK?'

Maggie nodded. 'I'll call Zelah and let her know.'

Bob grabbed the car keys and ran out of the house. As he was leaving he saw Zelah's car turn the corner at the top of the cul-de-sac. He didn't bother to stop, just waved to her as he started the car and accelerated to the end of the road and out of sight, tyres squealing.

Zelah ran into the house, took one look at Maggie and Jack, and breathed, 'What's happened?'

'Max may be missing,' Jack growled. He told her the story.

'What's being done to find him?'

'Police are checking the CCTV in the area. Bob's gone back to the station. Nick's gone to tell Stella, then he'll be back.'

'He says this is down to you and me,' Maggie stuttered.

'Rubbish,' Zelah replied. 'It's no-one's fault. Not even Max's, that is if someone has taken him. And if that's what's happened, it can only be Camberwell.' She went to her computer and began to hammer the keys. For a few minutes, Maggie and Jack waited in silence, both concentrating and grimacing.

'Camberwell is in London. Do you want to go to confront him?'

'No,' Maggie exclaimed. 'If he has Max, then he'll use him as leverage. We should wait for Bob, and see if we hear from Camberwell. Zelah, how do you know he's in London?'

243

'He has his spies, I have mine. I've been having him watched since we began this search.'

Maggie jumped up. 'Why didn't you tell us?' she shouted.

'Because there's been nothing to tell, except that he's been out of his house three times, once to a meeting, once to lunch, and the third time to a charity event.'

'And?'

'The lunch was with a Russian oligarch, second division thug. He must be the person Finch talked about. Could be he's putting on the pressure.'

Maggie sat down. 'I thought he might have taken Max for leverage.'

'If he has, big mistake. But also, if he has, we need to get a move on finding out if this vase still exists. Where are we with the research?'

'I can't think about that now.' Maggie said turning to Jack.

It was Zelah's turn to jump up. She stood in front of Maggie, feet planted apart, hands on hips. 'It's the only thing to think about now. What else are you going to do whilst we wait? Pace around the kitchen, moaning. How will that help Max?'

The two women were glaring at each other.

'I need something to do,' Jack whispered. 'You two carry on your staring match, I'll just find the file and see where to go next.'

Zelah and Maggie looked away from each other.

'It's in the Bandon file,' Maggie muttered. 'I'll help.'

'We'll all do it,' Zelah said, giving Maggie a wry look. 'OK. Maggie, please give us a quick – very quick – update.'

'We're onto the Pritchard family. Nick was looking at the descendants of Albert Pritchard, who had two surviving sons. He's been working on the first, John. I've been checking out the other,

Lewis, who had five children. I've eliminated two of them. One died without children. Zelah, how about you look at Nick's file? I believe he got as far as another Albert Pritchard, who died in 1910. Jack, could you take Lewis Pritchard Junior? I'll work on the daughter, Mari. She had two children.' She had spoken in a low voice, almost a whisper.

Without any further discussion, they all began work and were soon absorbed in records. There was no further word from Bob, nor Nick.

It was an hour later when Maggie stood up.

'Both of you, stop what you're doing.'

They turned to face her.

'You've found something?' Zelah said.

Maggie nodded.

'Don't interrupt at any point as I tell you this.' Taking a deep breath, she squeezed her fists together. 'We've been completely fooled.'

'Just tell us, mum.'

'Yes.' She began slowly, controlling the rage that was taking over her body. 'Lewis Pritchard's daughter, Mari, married John Peterson in 1900. They had two daughters, Sarah and Amy. Amy has come to nothing. Sarah, the elder daughter, married James Griffiths, in 1925. They had two daughters, Susan and Sarah. This Sarah was born in 1930. In 1951 she married and subsequently had one child. The man she married was called...' she paused again, to take another lung full of air. 'He was called Henry Desmond. Their child was...'

This time, Zelah intervened. 'Ian Desmond. The direct descendant of John Pritchard. The bastard has been stringing us along.' She stood and began walking towards the door. 'I'm going to wring his neck.'

'No,' Maggie insisted. 'Not yet. Let's wait to see what he does next. Now that we know, we're ahead at last. Let's not lose that advantage.'

The fury drained from Zelah's face, replaced by a knowing, cunning look. 'You're right.'

She went to speak again, but Maggie's phone rang.

'It's Bob. There must be news.'

Chapter 35

'Before you ask, I've already spoken to Nick, so he knows what I'm about to tell you.'

Maggie's stomach clenched. 'Tell us, please.'

'There's no sugar coating this. Max waited outside the bar for about fifteen minutes. He had booked a taxi, but it had been held up, so he started to walk.'

Maggie groaned.

'As he walked up Stow Hill and reached the cathedral, a car came around the road and pulled up beside him. The window wound down and someone in the passenger seat spoke to him. Whatever they said, shocked him. He got into the back seat and the car sped off. That was the last place there was a camera until the motorway. The car is picked up along the motorway heading in the direction of Cardiff. It turns off at the old A48 road. After that, we lose it.'

'Can you identify the car?' Maggie asked.

'We know the make and model, but the number plate is fake.'

'Can you track his phone?'

'We've had more luck there. There's a signal as far as Castleton, then it disappears.'

'What does "disappears" mean?' Zelah asked.

'The phone has been turned off, so we don't know if he's somewhere in that area. We think he is because he would never have voluntarily turned off his phone. We suspect someone took it from him. Maggie, I'm back at work now, and I'm staying here. Are you OK with that?'

'Of course,' she said, as tears ran down her face. 'Find him, Bob. Please find him.'

'Doing our best.' The call ended.

Before anyone could speak the front door slammed and Nick appeared in the doorway.

'If you're going to yell at us, don't bother,' Zelah said. 'You can't make us feel any worse.'

They hadn't noticed someone was standing behind him. Stella appeared, walking past him into the room.

'No-one's blaming anyone,' she said, gently. 'No-one is to blame for this, except the people who've taken him. Has anyone tried to contact you?'

'No,' Maggie replied.

'Nor us,' Stella said, 'but we both have phones switched on. My feeling is there'll be a call. Max is leverage, so the sooner you all get your heads together and find that bloody vase, the better.'

'We have some news on that front,' Maggie said.

Nick, who hadn't moved or spoken, now jerked his head in her direction.

'What news?'

'We've been fooled. We've tracked down a direct descendant of John Pritchard. It's Ian Desmond.'

Nick exhaled a long breath and muttered, 'That bastard. Does Bob think he's involved in taking Max?'

'He didn't say, but I guess that's one of the lines they're working on.'

Maggie realised that Zelah had left the room. She walked through to the kitchen and found her staring out into the garden.

She didn't move, or turn her head, but said, 'I'm re-assessing what we believed about Moira. What if it was Ian who's been working with Camberwell?'

Maggie sat in one of the chairs. 'Given what we know, it could have been, but – '

'Exactly,' Zelah said. 'You've just realised, same as I did. It was Ian who told us Moira had been working with Camberwell. Michael Wilson never confirmed which of them it was had given him the hint about Camberwell. Now, I'm wondering if maybe Moira's accident – wasn't.'

'That's too much to believe. He killed his wife, to stop her finding out more about what he was doing, then turned off her life support, deliberately? That's, that's … I don't have words for it.'

'It's murder,' Zelah said, still in a flat voice.

Maggie put her head in her hands. 'I would have said the time has come to abandon this project, leave it to Camberwell and Desmond, but now, with Max missing,' she went to say more, but they both turned around as a great shout went up from the front of the house. Maggie jumped up and ran, Zelah behind her.

The group stood close together in the centre of the office, all hugging arms and faces leaning in. Jack leaned back, a huge grin on his face as he saw Maggie standing in the doorway, revealing, at the centre of the huddle, Max Howell.

'What?' she shouted, running into the room. 'Max, you're OK. Well, not quite, I can see.'

Max had been beaten. He had a black eye, so swollen it was closed up. His lips were also swollen. He held up a hand to show what were probably a couple of broken fingers, but he smiled.

'Not so bad,' he said. 'Could have been worse.' He staggered, and Nick caught him.

'Let's take him into the living room, it's more comfortable there.'

'He needs to go to hospital,' said Nick, but Max put up a hand.

'No, no hospital. They were careful not to hurt me too badly. Apart from one of these fingers, there's nothing else broken. Bruised and battered, but I'll get over that. Absolutely no hospital. I need to tell you all why not.'

'Take him into the living room,' Maggie repeated. 'I'll call Bob, let him know that Max is back.'

A few minutes later, she joined them.

'He's on his way. He says, can you wait with the explanation. He wants – and needs – to hear it from you directly.'

Max nodded. Stella had run to the kitchen for a glass of water, which Max gulped down, then said 'Got a beer?'

Jack brought him one, which he also gulped down.

They all sat in silence, as Max downed his beer. Jack had also helped himself to a can, sitting next to Max as they drank together.

'How long will it take Bob to get here?' Max asked.

'I think I heard his car pull up,' Maggie said.

A few seconds later Bob walked into the room, took a look at Max, and said, 'Do you need to go to hospital?'

Max shook his head. 'Someone can strap up the fingers for me. That's all the hospital's likely to do. The rest is just – pain. They were very careful,' he looked around the room, 'like I said.'

'Are you up to telling me what happened? Not here, at the station.'

'They said, "no police". But I told them about you, and that Maggie would probably have told you and you'd be out looking for me. When they heard that, they looked at each other, then one made a phone call, after that they brought me back to the end of the road here, with another instruction.'

'We were out looking for you. It's formal, so you should come in and make a statement.'

Max nodded. 'I don't think they care too much, as long as I deliver the message.'

'Just do that,' Bob said, 'then we'll go.'

'The message is that you have three days to find it. Then, arrangements will be made to hand it over.'

'Let's go,' Bob said.

'Just one more thing,' Zelah said. 'Max, you've been saying *they*. How many and did you know them?'

Max nodded. 'Three. I knew one of them. It was that man who came to the meeting here, the one whose wife had the accident. He's the one who picked me up in the car. He said Nick was in trouble and I had to go with him to the hospital, where Stella was waiting.'

'Ian Desmond,' Zelah muttered.

Bob led Max away. Nick insisting on accompanying his son. Although Max shook his head, Nick wouldn't be put off.

'We'll be as quick as possible,' Bob said. 'Nick, you'll be able to wait in the station.' He turned to Maggie. 'I'm going to suggest you all stay tonight. Max can come back here.'

She nodded. 'Please don't keep him too long. He needs rest and support.'

'I'm going to call Mischa and Gerry,' Zelah said. 'Any of them could be next.'

'Yes,' Maggie replied. 'Look, everyone, it's late, and it's been a tough day. Why don't we all have something to eat and try to relax until Max gets back? I don't think we should talk to him tonight. As we'll all be here in the morning, we can re-convene as early as Max is able, then decide on what we're going to do. Stella, do you want to bring the baby here, too?'

'Yes, I think so,' Stella replied. 'I'll feel better if she's here. I'll drive over to my mother's.'

'I'll drive you,' Zelah said.

'And I'll come, too. Safety in numbers,' Jack added.

'Where does that leave me?' Maggie said. 'Home alone?'

'Lock everything and put on the external alarms. Nothing will happen now. We've had our instructions. He'll leave us to get on with it.'

'Who?'

'Camberwell, of course,' Zelah replied. 'He's behind this, and he's getting desperate.'

'We'll talk about it later,' Maggie replied. 'Please be as quick as you can.'

'We'll be back within the hour,' Stella said.

Once they had gone, Maggie went back to the office. There had been no time to share any thoughts, but now that she had some breathing space, something was troubling her. Ian Desmond was definitely in league with Camberwell, that was irrefutable. But, before him, someone else had been passing information to Camberwell.

She sat down at her desk. There were just a few unchecked possibilities. Time to see what she could find out.

Chapter 36

Stella returned with Flora and immediately went to bed. By ten, Maggie was the only one still awake.

Her internet search had continued to check the descendants of John Pritchard. By the time she finally gave up and slept, just before three in the morning, there was just one line to go.

It felt as if she had only been asleep for five minutes when a strange sound awoke her. At first, she thought it was an animal that had become trapped somewhere in the garden, before she realised, with a smile, that Flora Howell was awake somewhere in the house and was demanding breakfast. Bob was still asleep. It was just after seven and she had slept for only four hours. She knew there was no more sleep to be had, as the events of the previous day crowded into her mind, together with the start of ideas of what they could do, given the ultimatum, delivered by Ian Desmond, originating, she was almost certain, from Henry Camberwell.

She lay in bed, thinking about Camberwell and what had forced him to reveal himself. *He must be in trouble*, she thought. *This man is usually so calm and superior. Why the sudden desperate action and demand? Maybe his backers had put pressure on him.* She decided to check out the Russian oligarch Zelah had described as "second division". If he was a thug then he'd have no compunction in crudely threatening Camberwell. Problem was, she hadn't asked his name. Time to wake Zelah up.

'I'm almost on my way. What?'

'I thought I'd be waking you up. I want to know the name of the Russian oligarch.'

'Um, just a minute. Let me think. It's Dmitriev. Alexander. Why?'

'I want to find out more about him, that's all. If you're right about Camberwell panicking, it'll be because someone nastier than him is forcing him into it. So, the more information we have, the better.'

'Yes, can't argue with that. I'll be there in half an hour.'

By the time Zelah arrived Maggie had found out more than she wanted to know about Alexander Dmitriev. Third-class oligarch and thug was more appropriate. He was worth around four billion dollars. He had been involved with the Russian mafia and jailed in his youth for grievous bodily harm, the details of which were stomach churning. No wonder Camberwell was worried. He was still attached to his fingers. Dmitriev was on his fourth wife and the celebrity photographs showed that the breasts got bigger as the age of the wife got smaller. The latest was twenty-two years old. Dmitriev was believed to be in his sixties. His photographs, as he either preened at cameras or shoved them out of his way, revealed menace, even when he was smiling. Yes, Camberwell was in trouble if he had crossed this man. Good.

Maggie had already greeted Stella, who was walking around with Flora on her shoulder but joined her in the office. Fed and content, the baby had just started to smile.

'I'd forgotten how lovely it is when their little face spontaneously lights up. This time of the morning, I get a scowl and a grumpy *go away*, or *what do you want.*'

'That's all to come,' Stella said. 'For now, she's my perfect little girl.'

'How's Nick?' Maggie ventured.

'Angry. Beyond angry. But not at you. He has an idea he wants to pursue this morning. I'm praying it's a good one.'

'They usually are,' Maggie replied.

'What will you be doing?'

'There's a couple of children, the final ancestors of John Pritchard, we can still check out. Zelah will be here any minute. Apart from that, I don't know.' She put down her coffee and folded her arms. 'The answer has to be in the clue. Somehow, there's something we haven't seen or understood.' She shook her head. 'If Nick has an idea about the meaning, then it's the best lead we have. There's Zelah's car pulling up now.'

Zelah joined them, a travel coffee mug in hand. 'Any progress?'

'The oligarch's a thug, but I'd say third class, not second.'

'That all?'

'Nick has something in mind. We're waiting for him.'

'I'll go tell him you're waiting,' Stella said.

'Is he still mad at us?'

'Stella says not.'

Before they could say any more, Nick came down the stairs, followed by Bob.

'Maggie says you have an idea,' Zelah pitched in.

'Good morning to you, too, Zelah. I do have something to check out, but I need to go out and pick up - '

'Hold it right there,' Bob said. 'Where are you going, and why? And you're not seriously suggesting going out alone, after the past twenty-four hours?'

'I have something to collect, at the library in Newport. I'm happy for you to come with me, Bob. It will only take five minutes, then I shall come back here. They open at nine.'

Bob rubbed his chin. 'OK. I'm back at work today, but if this is important, I can spare the time to take you and bring you back.' He looked around at Maggie. 'Any sign of Max yet?'

'No. He and Jack were talking for a while last night. Do you need him again?'

'Possibly. I don't know yet. I've arranged for a doctor to come here to look him over. This afternoon. I didn't think he'd be up before lunchtime.'

'Thank you,' said Nick, smiling for the first time. 'I was hoping to persuade him to go to A&E today, to have his hand X-rayed. But if someone qualified can look at it, I think he'd prefer that. I gather the wait in the emergency department is still hours long and without support.'

Bob nodded. 'We're allowed in if there's a need. But no family, friends, whatever.'

'We have an hour before you can go to the library. How about some breakfast, everyone?'

They all made their way to the kitchen. The tension had lessened a little, but it was still there, in the occasional staring out of a window, being recalled to a conversation, or no-one wanting to eat much.

Maggie put toast, butter, jam, cereals, and croissants on the table, with fresh pots of coffee and tea. 'Take whatever you want, or not,' she said.

After twenty quiet minutes, Stella took Flora, who had fallen asleep, back to her cot. She returned shepherding Max down the stairs. He had one arm around Stella and the other holding onto his ribs.

Maggie pulled out a chair for him. 'You look terrible,' she said. 'Sure you don't want to go to hospital?'

'Positive,' he replied. 'It's bruising, but one of my ribs may have a crack in it. That food looks good. I'm starving.'

'Help yourself. Oops, no, let us do it for you,' she said, as he reached across the table and winced. She piled up toast, jam, and butter plus a couple of croissants on a plate and poured him a coffee. Nick was watching him, closely, and wincing.

'This is great,' Max mumbled through a mouthful of food. 'Can you all please stop watching me? I'm not a circus exhibit.'

'Sorry,' Maggie said. 'We're all worried about you.'

'What's your plan for today?' he asked, having devoured all the food on the plate and started on a second helping. 'You've only got today and tomorrow. Are you any closer?'

'Nick's going out to collect something from the library,' Maggie replied. 'Bob's taking him.'

'Right. Think I'll go back to bed, now,' Max said, supporting himself out of the chair as Nick and Stella rushed to help him. He waved them away. 'I can manage. Thanks, anyway.'

As he made his way up the stairs Maggie said to Nick, who was staring anxiously after him, 'The amount of food he just put away tells me that there's nothing seriously wrong with him. We'll tell him about the doctor later on. Let him sleep for now.'

Nick nodded. 'It's hard,' he said.

Stella hugged him. 'You get on with doing what you do best.'

Back in the office Maggie and Zelah began work on the final descendants of John Pritchard and at eight-thirty Nick and Bob left for the library. They were as quick as Nick had promised. He returned within the hour, with a long cardboard tube, from which he extracted a document that covered half the meeting table. He pinned the corners down.

They were looking at a map, an old map.

'What is this, Nick?' Maggie asked. 'I can see it's old, and I recognise Newport, but nothing else.'

'This is a map of the route taken by the Chartists from each of the three directions where they began; plus, the roads and paths by which they arrived in the town.'

Maggie and Zelah leaned over. 'There's Cefn,' Maggie said, pointing to a small collection of houses.

'It was just a village back in 1839,' Nick replied. 'It was chosen as the main place of assembly before they marched along the Risca Road and down Stow Hill.'

'When does this map date to?' Zelah asked.

'1840,' he replied. 'This is a copy. The original is in the museum.'

'What are we looking for?' Maggie asked.

Nick stood up. 'We assumed that His Lordship was Lord Tredegar or a member of the Morgan family. But what if it wasn't? We know that the word in the Will was "vault" not "fault". This suggested to me that it might not have been anything to do with Lord Tredegar or the Morgans and we know from checking it out that the family has their own vault in St Basil's church and there was nothing in it, apart from the bodies when it was moved in 1917.'

'You think it was a different Morgan?' Zelah asked. 'But why "His Lordship"? Charles Morgan was the only Lordship.'

'If you take away the word "His",' Nick said, 'we're left with "Lordship". I'm thinking that, maybe, this was a name, not a title.'

'That's a good idea,' Maggie said. 'Let's check the 1841 census. It should tell us if there is such a family.'

'Already done,' Nick replied. 'I took a quick look last night. There isn't a "Lordship".' Maggie's shoulders sank. 'But - there is a "Lawship" and that family was based in Monmouthshire.'

'Lawship's vault,' Zelah breathed. 'It makes sense. What does this map tell us?'

'The 1841 census has the family, a husband, wife, and five young children based in "Tanners Court," which was somewhere on the Risca Road. They had five servants, so it must have been sizeable, and with land.'

'Is it on here?' Maggie asked, peering down at the map.

'As you can see, the buildings along and off the road are not named. However, if we think about where the Chartists from Pontypool marched, they would have taken this route,' he traced a line from where George Evans was taken up by them, to the area around Cefn. 'They stopped overnight, some at Cefn, some closer to St Woolos church. We need to go back to the library and look at more maps, also possibly to the archives, to see what more we can find out about the Lawship family, in particular, did they have a vault?'

'This is a good lead, Nick, a great one, but even if they had a vault, who's to say where it is? Unless there's a chapel close by. And then, how would it have suggested itself as a place to bury the vase? A standing gravestone is noticeable, but a vault is close to the ground, so if it was dark, and raining, how would George Evans have even known it was there?'

'I don't know, Maggie. This is as far as I've managed.'

'What do we do now?'

'Maggie, you stay here, just in case the Doctor turns up early,' Zelah said. 'Keep on with the research, see if there's anything to be found in the final descendants of John Pritchard, just the UK ones. Don't bother with any who emigrated. And any and all information you can find about the Lawship family. Nick and I will go to the Library, to see what's there. We can't go up to the archives without prior notice, they're still operating on advance bookings only, but I'll ask my contact there to see if there's anything on the Lawship family.' Zelah headed for the door.

Maggie didn't feel inclined to argue with her. 'Whatever. You'd better get on with it. We all had.' And she turned to her computer.

'When we're done,' Nick said, 'we should go to the site of the Lawship House. Maggie, it would be most helpful if you could pin it down. I suspect it's a ruin now, but hopefully, something remains and the site hasn't been turned into a new housing estate.'

He hovered a few seconds, waiting for a response, but Maggie didn't reply or turn around, just grunted and nodded her head.

Once Nick and Zelah had gone, Maggie felt a heaviness in her chest. Her stress was increasing as the hours sped towards the deadline they had been given. Constantly at the back of her mind were two boiling issues. One: what if they didn't find it? Two: what if they found it, but it was damaged beyond repair? In either case, what would Camberwell's reaction be? As she sat back and contemplated, the doorbell rang. She went to open it, then remembered she shouldn't without knowing who was there.

'Who is it? What do you want?' Shouting through her own doorway felt particularly stupid, but safety mattered above all else, right now.

'It's John Finch and Olivia Abbott. Can we come in to talk to you?'

She opened the door and ushered them into the office.

'How are you doing?' Finch asked. Olivia Abbott stood with her back to the wall.

'How do you think I'm doing?' Maggie snapped. 'You know about Nick's son? And of course, you know about me being accused of Hugh Wilson's murder.'

Finch nodded. 'You were questioned, not accused. Anyway, that's not why we're here. We've been informed about Ian Desmond. Chief Inspector Pugh believes that Henry Camberwell was behind the abduction. Well, we've been watching him. We think he's in trouble.'

'What does that mean?'

'An associate of his, I won't say who, is threatening him. He's taken advance money from this person.'

'Dmitriev,' Maggie said. 'You told us before you suspected me. You aren't the only one watching him.'

Finch frowned. 'What do you know about him?'

'Not much. He had lunch recently with Camberwell. I know that. Dmitriev is the customer on whose behalf Camberwell is trying to acquire the vase?'

Finch nodded. 'Are you any closer to finding its whereabouts?'

Maggie shook her head. She had no intention of sharing. At least not yet, until she knew they were both free of association with Camberwell.

'I was just thinking, as you arrived, there's only a one in three chance we'll find the thing intact. It's a long shot and to be honest, I don't expect it to have survived.' She turned to Olivia. 'Do you?'

Olivia didn't react. Instead, she walked over to Maggie's computer. 'What's this?'

'None of your business.'

'Olivia, come away from the computer. Maggie, if there's anything you're doing that can help us, please tell me.'

'This,' Maggie said, closing down the screen, 'Is just research into the descendants of a man associated with Mervyn Prosser, just in case his interest in the vase was shared with one of his children. That's how we identified Ian Desmond. I'm finishing off the final ones, just to clear that line of research. Is that all you're here for?'

'No,' Finch replied. 'Olivia promised you a sketch of the vase, of how it will probably look. Olivia?'

Abbott took out a file from her attaché case and handed Maggie an A4 piece of paper.

'It doesn't look much like the one that sold for forty-one million dollars,' Maggie replied.

'They were individually made. This is the best we have from notes made by the British Museum at the time they received it.'

Instead of images of the countryside, this sketch showed dragons and other fantastic beasts, hovering over farmers and farming land.

'It's ugly,' Maggie said.

'It's still unique,' Olivia scowled.

'Do you really, honestly believe we can find it, intact? I'm not sure anymore,' Maggie said, still looking at the sketch.'

Olivia shrugged. 'The Lord knows where it is now. Inspector, we need to go,' She added, glancing at her watch.

'Yes, thanks for speaking to us. If you find anything, please keep in touch.'

'Did you come down from London just to speak to me?' Maggie asked.

'We're still liaising with the Police here. We're on our way to a meeting.'

Maggie let them out, re-bolting and locking the door. She was puzzled. Something didn't feel right. But, there was too much to do to think about Finch and Abbott. She went back to her research.

**

Nothing came of the first of the final two descendants of John Pritchard. He had emigrated to Canada and she could find no evidence of his returning, or indeed of any of his family returning. She had found twenty-seven surnames amongst those she could trace, none of them bearing any resemblance to anyone looking for the vase. One to go.

Before she set off on the final one she decided to look at the Lawship family, to discover what had happened to them after 1841, when there had been five children. By the 1851 census, another three children had appeared and two of the elder children were no longer listed, presumably either died or moved out as they became young adults. The father, James Lawship was still there, practising as a Solicitor. And again in 1861. Now there was just one child at home with James and Fanny, with James Lawship's status as "retired". By 1871 it was just an elderly James Lawship, whose status was Widower. And by 1881, another family lived at the property.

She decided to follow through with the property itself, to try to discover how long it had been inhabited according to census records, also checking the 1939 War Record. It was inhabited in each one and had retained the name of Tanners Court.

She then turned to newspaper reports, for any information from 1939 onwards. And here she found the first story that would decide the ultimate fate of Tanners Court. In 1941, during the

Second World War, Newport docks had been heavily bombed and on one occasion the area around Rogerstone had been targeted. It was reported that a bomb had landed in the grounds of the house, causing damage to the property, and the family inhabiting it at the time had had to move out. There was nothing further. If the house had been damaged beyond repair, could this have been the start of its decline into ruin? Another story came to mind, that of Fallough Hill, the case of the missing policeman in Liverpool. Fallough Hill had fallen into ruin and the current owner, a former client and now friend, Trystan Wyn Davies, was restoring it to become a hotel and spa. Fallough Hill had been listed on a website that named ruined ancient properties in Wales. She went back online, finding Tanners Court. The urban explorers' website had last been updated in 2019, but Tanners Court was still standing – just. There was a picture and a description of the property and its location.

She immediately picked up the phone and called Nick.

'Hi, I've found something about Tanners Court. It's still there, or at least it was two years ago. It's a ruin but standing. The area around it looks a lot like Fallough Hill, smaller, but terribly overgrown.'

Fantastic,' Nick replied. 'We've found a lot of information about the Lawships'. Zelah's chap in Ebbw Vale has also looked them up. There are some estate accounts and other papers, and a photograph. He's sending it all to her now.'

'Well, it was the target, or the area was, of a bomb drop in 1941, that did some damage and made the walls unstable. Hasn't been lived in since.'

'We're going to make our way back in the next ten minutes. We shall have all the information by then, so let's put it together with what you've found and see what we have.'

'Have to go. There's someone else at the door.'

'Else?'

'Yes. Tell you when you get back.'

It was the doctor, who apologised for arriving early, but now had other commitments in the afternoon. Maggie took her straight up to see Max, who wasn't too pleased to be woken up, but submitted to an examination when told by Maggie it was the best way to stop Nick asking endless questions.

Nick and Zelah arrived back just after the doctor had departed, advising Maggie to try to persuade Max to get an X-ray.

'His breath sounds are good, so the potential cracked rib isn't causing a problem, but he should still get an X-ray. There's only so much I can advise without seeing an X-ray. He should also remain quiet and still. The bruises and contusions will heal, and the finger isn't out of alignment. However, it's in his best interests to have it all checked out.'

'I'll try,' she had said. 'He's a stubborn boy, but he's old enough to understand the problems he might cause himself.'

As soon as Nick arrived he listened to the Doctor's report, then went up to see Max. When he came down, he was looking happier.

'He says he'll go, but he'd like Jack to take him.'

'Bob will arrange for someone to go with them,' Maggie said. 'Otherwise, the hospital won't allow him to be accompanied. A police escort is a different matter.'

'Yes, that would be good,' Nick said. 'Can you speak to him, arrange it for this afternoon? We're going to be otherwise engaged, and I don't want to tell Max what we're intending to do.'

'Sounds intriguing,' Maggie said. 'Are you going to tell me?'

He smirked at her back as she disappeared towards the kitchen to call Bob.

She returned a few minutes later. 'He says he'll have someone there when they arrive. I'll prod Jack into action in a minute. So, what are we going to do?'

'We're going to break into Tanners Court, to see if we can find the vault.'

Chapter 37

'When you say we,' Zelah said, 'that would be the three of us? No police escort?'

'No need for sarcasm,' Nick replied.

'Because, of course, they would be happy for us to do a bit of breaking and entering,' Zelah replied. 'All in a good cause.'

'All right, stop it,' Maggie said. 'Zelah, on this occasion I agree with Nick. Before we go, and I want to go as soon as Jack and Max are out of the house, what information did you find? And what was the info your guy at the archives sent, have you looked at it yet? Is there anything useful?'

'I have looked and I'm not sure. Again, depends on what we find at Tanners Court.'

'You said there was a photograph, Zelah?'

Zelah flipped her tablet to Maggie. 'This is the photo. It's just the children, five of them and a very ugly dog.'

Maggie took the tablet from her. It was a formal Victorian picture, all grim-faced and posed, including the dog. One of the children had her arm around its neck.

'Are you sure this isn't grandchildren?'

'Impossible to say. It's a very old one, you can tell from the style of the clothes,' Nick said. 'My guess would be 1850s.'

'Then it could be children. From the census records, there were eight in total. This photograph fits with the youngest five.'

'In the estate papers, there's a sentence that refers to Mr Lawship's keen interest in the new making of photographs. He experimented on his children?' Zelah mused.

'By the 1861 census they were all gone from home,' Maggie said. 'The youngest looks about ten or a little older here. Bit young to have left home five years later.'

'The youngest could have been away visiting. Did you check?' Zelah asked.

'No, I didn't think it was important. I can, but we should go as soon as,' she paused, as footsteps hurried down the stairs.

'You look like a right set of conspirators,' Jack said.

'Absolutely. Plotting the downfall of Henry Camberwell,' Maggie replied. 'Before you head off,' she continued, taking hold of his arm, 'I have a job for you. Max has agreed to be checked out at the hospital. Bob is going to provide a police escort. I want you to drive him down.'

Jack nodded. 'Do I have time to eat something?'

Maggie looked at her watch. 'OK, if you must. Nick, can you get Max up and dressed? By the time Jack's finished eating and driven down there, it should be about a half hour. I'll call Bob now and tell him to have someone waiting at the entrance to A&E.'

Jack took himself off to the kitchen.

Ten minutes later Nick brought Max down the stairs and helped him into Maggie's car.

Jack appeared, with a bowl of cereal, which he handed to Maggie as he got into the driving seat.

'Text us, when you know anything,' Maggie said, as she and Nick saw them off. 'Now, let's go.'

**

268

They parked Zelah's car on the outskirts of Cefn.

'There's the wooded area,' Nick said, pointing to a thick group of trees about a quarter of a mile away. 'It looks like the site from the 1840 map.'

A sign to a footpath next to a stile set in a hedge pointed across the field to the trees. Maggie took a nervous glance over and around. The area was rough grass with a flattened path bisecting it. No grazing animals.

'No killer sheep,' Zelah said, grinning at Maggie, knowing her secret fear.

'It's the cows that bother me, I can manage sheep,' Maggie snapped.

'Well, there's none of either, so let's go,' Nick said, climbing over the style and not looking back at either of them.

They walked in silence across the field. As they came nearer to the trees there was no hint of a hidden building. Nick, still in the lead, stopped at the edge of the wood.

'What are you waiting for?' Zelah said. 'Let's get in there. You can see the path.'

He nodded and took a step forward, then stopped.

'Don't tell me you're getting cold feet, not now,' Zelah said.

'No. I'm feeling the atmosphere.'

Zelah went to speak, but Maggie shushed her. 'How does it feel?'

'It's OK,' he said and started to walk again.

The wood was longer and wider than it looked from a distance. After ten minutes, they still had no sight of any type of building, nor of the wood petering out.

Then, Zelah said, 'Look, over there, to the right.'

About a hundred metres away the trees thinned and there was something solid behind them, not a building, but what looked like a barrier. They veered off the path towards it and came up against a solid fence, with a notice of warning to trespassers to beware of a dangerous structure.

'Let's walk around the fence, to see if we can find a way in. There has to be one. Urban explorer groups have posted pictures,' Maggie said.

'What if it's been repaired?'

Nick smiled at Zelah and reached into his backpack, bringing out a pair of wire clippers. 'Had to be prepared to break and enter,' he said. 'There isn't time to think about anything else.'

Maggie raised her eyebrows at Zelah, who returned the look. Nick had already started walking.

'That was a phrase I never thought I'd hear coming out of that man's mouth,' Zelah whispered to Maggie, as they followed.

'I heard that,' Nick said, as he rounded the corner of the fence. 'Here it is. Had to be here.'

A gap in the fence was just enough to allow a slender adult to crawl through, which they all managed.

'I still can't see the house,' Maggie whispered.

'We walk diagonally,' Nick said. 'This is the perimeter of the property. It's probably covered up by those bushes and trees, there.' He pointed to a thicket and began to walk.

Before they reached the spot, hints of brick appeared, and close up, they could see they were standing at the side of a house.

'OK, Doctor Livingstone, how do you propose we breach this?' Zelah said, staring at a seemingly impenetrable wall of thick bushes, with heavy branches and thorns. 'Anything in your magic bag?'

He didn't answer, but opened the rucksack and brought out another tool, this time a set of toggle loppers.'

Zelah chuckled and shook her head as Nick began to chop away the branches. It took five minutes before he had made his way through.

'There,' he said, pushing his head through the hole he had made. He forced the branches apart, making enough room to push the rest of his body through, and disappeared.

Maggie went next, followed by Zelah.

They were now standing on the edge of what might once have been a formal lawn but had become a waist-high grass and weed patch. The house itself stood a hundred yards away, broken down, derelict, half of the roof gone and weeds growing from every gutter, through the glassless windows, and up the walls. They were facing the front where the doorway was empty.

'Should we take a quick look inside first?' Maggie asked.

'No, definitely not,' Nick replied. 'It's not what we're here for, and it looks like it could cave in any minute. Too dangerous.'

'Agreed. So how on earth are we going to find a vault in this?' Zelah said, sweeping her arms around. 'If there is one, it'll be buried somewhere under this mess.'

'We have to try,' Maggie said, as the rain that had been threatening when they left the car, now pelted stinging fat globules into her face. 'How about we find the whole perimeter, then begin a walk around? If someone did put a vault in these grounds, my guess is, it wouldn't have been too close to the house. Somewhere they could wander out to, to visit.'

'As good a plan as any,' Nick said. 'Let's go.'

They spread out in a line, Nick closest to the border of trees and shrubs, then Maggie, and Zelah closest to the house remains. Walking slowly, they made their way forward, each tripping over the uneven ground, Zelah swearing multiple times.

It took ten minutes to cover one side of the house. On the second side of the house, the vegetation changed.

Looking along to the far end, Maggie said, 'This is different, cultivated. Might once have been vegetables. We'll have to be careful where we tread.'

Another ten minutes brought them to the next turning point. They were now facing the back of the house where the wilderness was even more expansive. There was evidence of an old outhouse.

Maggie shook her head. 'Nick, I don't think we're going to find anything, and I'm worried about walking this area. This would have been where they kept animals and where household chores were done outside. Heaven knows what abandoned rubbish we might trip over.'

He didn't reply. She looked up and saw that he was smiling.

'Over there,' he said, pointing towards a tree in the far corner. 'That's the only tree on this side. I wonder …'

'Worth a look,' Zelah said, 'but I suggest we go in a straight line. Nick, you can go first.'

'Thanks, Zelah. I'll take the fall for all of us.'

'Exactly. Get going.'

He made his way along the back perimeter, putting each foot down tentatively before stepping forwards. Maggie was behind him, and behind her, she could hear Zelah growling.

'You wanted him to be careful,' she said over her shoulder.

They reached the tree.

'Well, at least it's some shelter from this bloody rain,' Zelah said. 'What do we do now?'

'We very carefully spread out and begin to walk forward. If there is something, we should find a flat stone. But if you do, don't put your weight on it. Just stop.'

Zelah found it.

'Over here!'

When Maggie and Nick reached her she was down on her knees, trying to clear weeds and mud from around a small, square stone, about ten metres from the tree, close to the final perimeter.

The stone was covered in dirt which Nick, who had dropped to his knees, began to carefully scrape away.

'Words,' he said. 'There's an inscription. I think we've found it.'

'We need water,' Maggie said, standing up. There must be somewhere closer to the house where it collects. I'll see what I can find.'

She returned a few minutes later with a half of what might have been an old, rusted kitchen jug, full of water.

'Splash it on the area we've uncovered,' Nick said.

She ran the water gently over the stone and the first words appeared.

In memory of our beloved Timothy.

'More water, please.'

Maggie returned, with another half a jug. 'This is it. Let's hope it's enough.'

Nick and Zelah had scraped away more dirt and Zelah took a deep breath, as Maggie poured the water over the rest of the stone.

Taken too soon

1832 – 1839

They paused, each now kneeling, staring at the words.

'Seven years old,' Nick said. 'Poor child.'

'No,' Maggie said in a sharp voice, at which Nick and Zelah turned away from the stone to her.

'This isn't right. The rest of this family is buried either in St Woolos cathedral or in St Woolos cemetery. Why would they put one here? This isn't consecrated ground.'

'I agree. This is odd. Could something terrible have happened, to cause them to bury this one here?'

'It's not that, Nick,' Maggie said. 'I researched the whole family. There wasn't one called Timothy. So, who is this?'

No-one spoke. Then, Maggie slapped her palm to her forehead.

'Zelah, the photograph of the Lawship children. Was there anything on the back, any identification of which was which?'

'I didn't ask. Should I have done?'

'Yes.' Maggie looked at her watch. 'Almost five. Will your guy still be there at the archives?'

'I'll try.'

Zelah rang and the phone answered. 'Ben, are you still at work?'

'Leaving in five minutes, why?'

'Have you returned that photograph you showed me of the Lawship children to its file?'

'My last task before I shut up shop.'

'I'm going to put you on speaker. Now, this is extremely important. Can you fish it out for me?'

'This will have to be quick. The whole building closes in fifteen minutes.'

'It certainly is, Ben. Thank you,' Maggie said. 'It's a very quick question.'

A few seconds of silence followed, as Maggie, Zelah and Nick hunched over Zelah's phone, trying to keep the rain off.

'Ok, got it.'

Zelah nodded at Maggie.

'Ben, is there anything written on the back?'

'Yes, There are names.'

Maggie's shoulders sagged in relief. 'Can you read them out for us?'

Sure. They are Edward, Amelia, George, Charlotte, Annabel, and Timtoo.'

'That last one, are you sure it's Timtoo? How is it spelled?'

'It's T.I.M.T …hang on, sorry, it's not an O next, it's a W. Then there's something else, but I can't read it.'

'That's great, thank you, Ben. That's all. You can go home now.'

When Maggie ended the call, Zelah said, 'What was that?'

'Think about it. How many children in the picture?'

'Five.'

'Oh,' Nick said, his eyes darting around. 'Yes, of course. Maggie, well done. Well done!'

'Got it! The sixth name is the dog.' Zelah said. 'But what … of course. Tim number two.' She looked down at the vault stone. 'So this must be Tim number one. Beloved pet of the Lawship children. Taken too soon. I suppose seven isn't a great age for a dog, is it? So, what do we do next? Try to shift it?'

'No, absolutely not,' Nick said sharply. 'We don't have the right tools. If we make a mistake it could fall into the pit below, and if the vase is there, it'll be smashed to bits.'

'I'm not even sure about removing it at all,' Maggie said, standing up. 'This may be a dog, but it was a beloved member of the family. Is it right to interfere with what they've done here?'

'Then what do you suggest?' Zelah said.

'I suggest we leave it here, for now,' Nick replied. 'Let's go back to the office, talk this over. But just amongst the three of us.'

Maggie nodded. Nick stood and began to retrace their steps back to the hole in the shrubs, which he covered up as much as he could, once they were all through.

'No point anyone else, whatever their motive, finding what we've done.'

'Do you think anyone may have followed us?'

'No, Maggie, but there's plenty of evidence of kids having gone in, for fun. We don't want them finding the stone, either.'

He had covered it up before they walked away. Now, they had to decide what to do next.

Chapter 38

'We go back tonight,' Zelah said, as they sat around the table. 'Take whatever tools we need. We open it up.'

Nick looked at Maggie. 'In any other circumstances, I'd be with you. But, I don't think we have a choice. It makes me feel uncomfortable too, more than that, ill at ease. But, Maggie, this is our last chance.'

'I know. I just feel I'll be disgusted with myself if we find it or not.'

'Can you live with that?' Zelah asked.

Maggie didn't reply. What were the options? If she refused, Nick and Zelah would most likely go without her. If they found it, could she then have a say in what they should do with it? And what if it wasn't in the vault after all? She'd have done something she hated the thought of doing, for nothing.

'I'll come with you,' she said. 'I just hope it's there. What are we going to need, Nick?'

'A couple of large spades, maybe a fork, and something to hold it in place as it comes away from the ground, a prop of some kind.'

'I have the garden tools, and there are some pieces of wood behind the summer house. Take a look to see if they'll be strong enough.'

Maggie and Zelah waited in silence until Nick came back. 'They'll do fine. I've brought them round to the front. It should be dark by seven. We'll also need a torch each.'

'I have head torches, from our camping days.'

'Perfect,' Nick replied.

'Now all I have to do is tell Bob what we're proposing to do and …'

'No!' Nick and Zelah shouted.

'We're proposing to trespass. He'll be obliged to tell us we can't do it.'

There was silence for a few seconds, then Zelah said, 'Maggie, you're uncomfortable enough and this seals it. You shouldn't come with us. You can stay here, hold the fort, and not tell anyone where we've gone and what we're doing. If Bob asks where we are, it's up to you what you say to him.' She stood up. 'Nick, we should go now. We can manage between the two of us.'

'Now I feel like I'm letting you down,' Maggie said, her voice trembling.

'You're not doing anything of the kind,' Nick replied. 'You can tell Bob we have some further research to complete. All being well, this will be quick and we'll be back here by nine at the latest.'

Maggie nodded and swallowed. This was going to be hard.

**

Bob arrived home just after eight and asked where everyone was. Jack and Max had arrived back from the hospital ten minutes after Zelah and Nick left the house.

'The boys are upstairs. Max has a cracked rib and a fractured finger. Otherwise, he's OK. The hospital has given him extra strong painkillers, which sent him straight to bed and sleep. Jack is on his computer. Stella went out earlier to collect some more supplies for the baby. I went with her. She's staying with her mother for a few hours, then her mother will drive her back. She'll let me know when she's setting off.'

'And Zelah and Nick?'

'They're still doing some research,' she said, turning away from him. I'm expecting them back in the next half hour.'

'Is everything OK?' he asked.

'Fine,' she muttered. 'I thought I'd order some food in. The pub's delivering any minute. I've ordered for all of us.'

'Maggie?'

What?'

'Is there something you want to tell me? Or rather, something you're trying hard not to tell me?'

She couldn't do it. 'Yes. Nick and Zelah have a lead on a possible location for the vase. They've gone to see if it's a possibility.'

Where have they gone?'

'That's what I'm not telling you. I can't. There's a reason and you'll know as soon as they get back.'

He walked out of the room, as the doorbell rang. He answered it to the delivery van from the local pub and returned to the office. 'Come on, let's eat. Half an hour, you said.'

Maggie called Jack downstairs and they ate in the kitchen, mostly in silence, Maggie glancing every couple of minutes at the clock.

After they'd finished, she put food aside for Nick and Zelah. Stella called to say she was on her way back. 'We'll be there in ten minutes,' she said. 'I can't raise Nick. Do you know where he is, Maggie?'

'He and Zelah have gone to check out a potential lead,' she said, bending the truth. 'I'm expecting them back any minute.'

When Stella arrived, she settled the baby and joined Maggie and Bob in the sitting room.

'What time did you expect them back?'

'Three-quarters of an hour ago,' Bob intervened.

Another hour passed. The agitation bubbling in Maggie's stomach was making her feel sick. By eleven o'clock, she couldn't sit any longer and began to pace the room. Stella was white-faced, trying Nick's phone every five minutes. Bob was a mixture of anger and fear.

At eleven fifteen, he jumped up. 'That's enough,' he said. 'You're going to tell me where they've gone and I'll send a patrol out. And I'm going myself and –'

Before he could say any more, the front door slammed, followed by feet rushing across the hallway and into the lounge.

Maggie let out a long sigh of relief as Zelah and Nick entered the room. She looked at them and they stared back. 'Well?'

Zelah's face lit up in a huge grin, as Nick held up an old tin box.

'We've got it.'

Maggie rushed forward and hugged Zelah. 'I've been so scared. What happened?'

'Didn't go quite according to plan,' Nick said. He turned to Stella, who was standing with her hands on her hips.

'Sorry,' he said sheepishly. 'Had the phone on silent. And we had to do some serious negotiating.'

'You're an idiot,' she replied, but she was smiling.

'So,' Nick said. 'Do you want to see it?'

'You mean, it's survived? In one piece?'

'Yep. Completely undamaged.' He put the tin down on the coffee table and they gathered around. Very carefully, he pulled back the lid, which squeaked and groaned. Inside, was an old blanket, worn and threadbare. With the tips of his fingers, he pulled it away.

'There it is,' he said.

'Have you handled it?' Bob asked.

'Yes, but only to put it back in the tin.'

'Back in the tin? How did you get it out?'

'We didn't. Let me wrap it back up and close the lid. We have quite a story to tell you.'

Chapter 39

'When we found our way back, I was relieved to see nothing had been disturbed. So, Zelah and I set up and began to dig around the edge of the stone. It didn't take long. The stone wasn't as heavy as we'd expected, so we managed to lift one side, I held it up and Zelah moved in the wooden struts to hold it up. It seemed quite secure, so we shone our torches into the hole.' He paused.

'And, what?' Maggie almost shouted.

'There was nothing in there,' Zelah said. 'No vase, and no doggie.'

'We were absolutely stunned,' Nick continued. 'We kept staring into the hole as if something might just appear. We must have been concentrating so hard we didn't hear footsteps approaching, and a voice, right behind us said: "Oi, you, what do you think you're doing?" It was a man with a pitchfork and we were at the pointy end.'

'He looked like that professor out of Back to the Future,' Zelah said.

'So I asked him to please put the pitchfork down, that we were private investigators and had been tasked with looking for an object that might have been buried in the vault, with Timothy, the Lawship children's dog, back in 1839. Zelah, you tell them the rest.'

'He looked crazy at first, but the look changed, his head twitched and he seemed defensive. So, I knew he knew something.

I told him the object was stolen back at the time and was the property of the British state, and that we were trying to recover and return it. Then he asked: "Is there a reward?". Totally the wrong question. I knew then he'd got it, so I had to work out how to persuade him to give it to us. I said, yes, there was a reward, but the circumstances in which it could be paid would depend on how the object had been recovered. For example, if someone had found it and not handed it over immediately, they would be in trouble and not eligible for the reward. Then I asked him where it was, if he still had it, that we didn't care about how he'd found it, but if he gave it to us, we could give him the reward without mentioning his name.' At this point, Bob's eyes rolled and he shook his head. Zelah ignored him and went on. 'He asked how much. I took a punt on five hundred. His eyes lit up. But, I explained, he would have to let us have it right away. Turned out, he'd given it to his mother.' She paused and tutted, then went on. 'He looks after the place and a year or so ago, he found kids messing about in the garden. They'd found the vault, lifted the stone, and seen the dog's skeleton. They'd pulled some of the bones out. He'd chased them off, then decided to re-bury the bones, but in a different place so, if the kids came back, they wouldn't find anything. When he was digging out the rest, underneath, he found the tin, opened it, and found the vase, wrapped up in an old blanket. He didn't think much of it, but took it to his mother.'

'Have you paid him?' Maggie asked.

'Indeed I have. We went with him to his house. His mother wasn't too keen to part with it. It was sitting in her prized china cabinet, but five hundred was too much to turn down. I didn't have it all on me, so the man – his name is Owen Jenkins – and I went off to the nearest cash point and I took out the rest. Nick kept the old lady drinking tea and chatting, about our work and her family history, until Owen and I got back and I handed over the money.'

'She was a nice old girl,' Nick said. 'Delighted to have the money. They haven't had a holiday for years, so she thought they might go to Torquay for a couple of days. I said I'd also do some research into her family history for her, at no charge, of course.'

'Anyway, after more tea, we left, with the vase, the blanket, and the tin, and here we are. And there it is.'

'Well done, both of you,' Maggie said. 'Now we've got it, what do we do with it?' She peered into the tin. 'It's not attractive, is it? I thought forty million dollars would have been something special to look at.'

'Does the mechanism work?' Stella asked.

'Yes,' Nick said. 'Ida, Owen's mother, whooshed it around for me whilst we were waiting. She thought it was rather novel. I must say, I stopped breathing at the way she handled it, but it survived. She told me she liked to see the pictures as they whizzed around. Scary.' He paused and shuddered. 'It was quite a relief when Zelah came back with Owen and they wrapped it up and put it back into the tin.'

'So, now the bigger problem starts,' Bob said. 'It's after midnight. Can I suggest we all go to bed? Nick, you take that thing with you, and we'll talk in the morning about what to do next. This complicates matters even further.' He shook his head. 'We'll talk about it in the morning.'

'OK with me,' Nick said. 'I agree with Maggie, it's an ugly piece and I was expecting better. But, yes, I'll keep it by me. Us,' he added, nodding at Stella, who nodded back.

One by one they left the room.

**

Maggie joined Bob in the kitchen at six, followed by Stella with Flora asleep on her shoulder.

'Nick coming down too?' Maggie asked.

'I don't know. He's not talking. I don't think he's slept much, either. A couple of times I woke up and found him sitting on the side of the bed staring at the vase, turning it around in his hands, staring into the inside, you know, behind the outer part that moves around.'

Bob put a mug of coffee on the table for each of them, as footsteps hurried down the stair.

'Morning all,' Jack said, standing against the door frame, yawning. 'Any of that coffee left? I could smell it upstairs.'

They all stared back at him.

'What?'

'You're up early. You slept through the events of last night,' Maggie said.

'I'm opening up this morning and there's a delivery at the bar in an hour that I have to take in. What events? I heard talking, but it didn't sound like anything special was going on. And if it was, why didn't someone come get me? And Max. What's happened?'

'We found it, or Nick and Zelah found it.'

Jack's eyes widened. 'Can I see it?'

'Nick has it,' Maggie replied. 'He'll probably be down soon.'

'Does Max know?'

'No, he didn't wake up either. Whatever drugs the hospital gave him, they knocked him out.'

The sound of slow footsteps on the staircase made them all turn towards the door. Nick came in, carrying the tin. He walked to the table and put it down. He looked haggard, dark bags under his eyes, his skin sallow, his hands shaking.

'Have you slept at all?' Maggie asked.

Nick shook his head. 'Where's Zelah?'

'She decided – against my advice – to go home,' Bob replied. 'She'll be back any minute. She wanted some quiet thinking time.'

Maggie turned to Bob. 'You said last night this complicates matters even further. What did you mean?'

Bob sat down. 'Apart from the obvious – who gets the bloody thing,' he said, flicking his hand at the tin. 'I know you're all delighted to have found it, but whatever decision you take has consequences that range from unpleasant to downright dangerous, on more than one front.'

'Stop there,' Maggie said. 'This affects more than those of us here. We need Max and Gerry Quinn, and the Irish group and –' she paused at the sound of a key in the front door. 'Here's Zelah. Could you make some more coffee and breakfast? A conference is what we need, urgently.'

'What about the client?' Nick asked. 'Do you want to involve him?'

'No,' Maggie said. 'He won't be affected by the outcome. The vase was never going to be his. We can tell him what's happened, once we decide.'

Zelah agreed with them on getting everyone together as soon as possible. She had alerted Mischa Quinn in Cork in the early hours of the morning, and she and the McCarthy Miller boys were already waiting for them to call. Gerry Quinn was the last to arrive, twenty minutes later, agog with excitement. He took up the final place at the table. The closed tin sat in the centre.

'Open it up, let's have a look, then,' Gerry said.

Nick took the vase out and stood it in the centre of the table. It was just over eight inches tall, colourful still, and as Nick slowly rotated the outer central rim, the inner pictures of a dragon, a huge bird that might have been an eagle, and a gryphon, all flying over a winding path and mountains, appeared.

'Amazing, I suppose,' Maggie said. 'But it's cruder than I expected.'

'What do you mean?' Max asked, leaning forward for a better look. 'Oh, I see, some of the edges aren't finished, but couldn't that just be because it's deteriorated? I mean, it's so old, some bits must have fallen off.'

'It's more like they were never there in the first place. I can't explain it better,' Maggie said. 'But, I suppose, taken as a whole, and the fact it was made almost three hundred years ago …' she tailed off. 'Anyway, we have decisions to make, but first of all, Bob has something he wants to say.'

'I'm sorry to say this,' he started, 'but the way you retrieved this, you, Nick, and Zelah, was wrong, and likely to cause a whole load of problems. You should have alerted the police, or me at least and we could have ensured the proper authorities took it.'

'That's assuming we're planning to hand it over to the Proper Authorities,' Maggie said. 'As far as I'm concerned, we could still decide to give it to Camberwell. That's what we're here today to decide.'

'No chance of that!' Bob thundered, glaring at her. 'Then, there's the fact you, Zelah, paid the man and his mother five hundred pounds to give it to you. When they find out you lied, and the value of that thing, there's every chance they'll be furious and contact a lawyer.'

He was about to carry on when his phone rang. He looked at it, swore, and answered the call. More swearing followed, then he said, 'I have to go. A drug case is about to break open.'

He stood. 'Don't even think about contacting Ian Desmond or Camberwell.'

As soon as he left the house, they all looked at each other for a few seconds, then multiple arguments broke out.

'Stop!' Maggie shouted. 'Right at this moment, we've done nothing wrong. Well, maybe, that five hundred pounds, but in the bigger picture, I think we're still OK. Bob was always going to be against us doing anything that involved Camberwell, but it's up to us. So, everyone here has a say. It's time to speak. There are no limits, and you can each speak without – I repeat, without – being interrupted. Whatever your opinion, give it now. No-one has to explain or justify themselves.'

'What's your position?' Max asked.

Before she could answer, Mischa spoke. 'Maggie, this is the right thing to do, but before we do it, can we have some time, please? There's so much to think about. I'd like to talk to Niall, Stephen, and Zelah. I'm sure you want to speak to each other, too. Can we have an hour or so, please?'

'Yes, that's fair,' Maggie replied. 'Why don't we say two hours? We'll reconvene at ten. OK with everyone?'

They all nodded. 'Mischa, we'll call you back at ten.' She turned to the room. 'You're all welcome to wander around here, whatever. I'm going out into the garden.'

'I'll come with you,' Jack said.

'So, what do you think?' Maggie asked Jack once they were outside.

'I didn't want anything to do with this or Camberwell right from the start, so I'm with Bob,' he replied. 'You?'

She leaned over the fence, staring at the black water. 'I want to support Bob, but I'm sure that Camberwell will wreak vengeance on all of us if we hand it over to the museum. I suppose that's fear, but if giving it to him keeps us safe, then I'm inclining that way. I'm equally terrified of what Bob will do, if I support handing it over, though.'

Jack hugged her. 'Go with your gut. It's a good gut, you feed it well,' he said.

'Thanks, son. I think I'll just stay here for a while if you don't mind.'

He nodded. 'I have to go to work,' he said. 'Call me with what you decide. I'll back you, whatever.'

Maggie stayed next to the canal for an hour, at the end of which she was still torn. She valued her relationship with Bob, of course, but she also wanted her family, and her extended family, safe. She shook her head. Time to go back inside, and see how the arguments were progressing.

Zelah was in the kitchen, with Stella and Max.

'Where are Nick and Gerry?' Maggie asked.

'Nick was on the phone, I don't know who to,' Stella replied, standing up and handing the baby to Max. 'I'll go check. I have no idea about Gerry. I saw him approach Nick, right after we decided to pause, but I haven't seen him since.'

'What about you two?' Maggie asked.

'We both want to give it to Camberwell,' Max said. 'Get that bastard out of our lives. You?'

Maggie shook her head.

'Tough for you,' Zelah said, softly.

'I can't find him,' Stella said, hurrying back into the kitchen. 'Nor Gerry.'

Maggie stood up. 'Let's try upstairs. There's the attic room as well as the bedrooms. Five minutes later they came back down to the hall, where Maggie paused in the doorway to the office, looked in, and gave out a sharp cry. Zelah, Max, and Stella came running, as Maggie pointed to the table.

'It's gone,' she whispered. 'The vase, it's gone.'

Stella ran to the front door, pulled it open then slammed it shut. 'Our car's gone, too. Nick and Gerry have disappeared, with the vase.'

As they stood in stunned silence, Zelah's phone rang. She took the call with a surprised, puzzled expression, that turned to eye-popping fury as it ended.

'What was that?' Maggie demanded. 'Who was that?'

'That,' Zelah spat, 'Was Ian Desmond. He knows we have the vase. He and Camberwell will be here at midday. To collect.'

Chapter 40

'Gerry Quinn. It has to be him,' Stella whispered. 'And he's somehow managed to lure Nick away.'

'Stella, I believe Gerry is capable of being a two-timing little rat,' Zelah replied, 'but I don't believe Nick could be lured away by him. Something is off.' She put her hands up to her head as she paced around the hallway.

'Try Nick again,' Maggie said to Stella. 'Keep trying. Send him messages. If he's Ok, he'll reply to something.'

During the next half hour, the three women said nothing. Max went to sit in the garden. Maggie tried Bob, but his phone was switched off. After another failed attempt to reach Nick and no response to another text, Stella began to cry. Maggie, who had never seen Stella in any way discomposed, put an arm around her.

'There'll be a reason, Stella. He's doing something that he didn't want us to know about, I'm sure of it.'

'Why not? You're supposed to be a team. And what about Gerry Quinn?'

'That's a difficult one,' Maggie admitted.

From the kitchen, the baby began to cry. Stella handed Maggie her phone and went to calm Flora.

A message pinged. Maggie looked at it.

'It's Nick. Stella, come and unlock this, please, now!'

Stella exchanged the baby for the phone, read the message, and smiled. 'He says not to worry about him. He's fine. He'll be back asap.'

'Tell him he needs to be here by midday, that Camberwell's coming.'

Stella sent the message with trembling fingers and a few seconds later the reply came.

Tell him two, not midday. I need more time.

'What the hell is he up to?' Zelah said. 'And that's rhetorical. I'll call Mischa and let her know. She'll be horrified about her brother. All the hopes I had for him. Yes, I'll call Ian Desmond too. Let's hope he's amenable.' She shook her head and left them to make the calls.

When she returned, she found Maggie, Stella, and Max in the kitchen, looking devastated.

'We have almost three hours to wait,' Maggie said. 'I can't raise Bob. I've left him a message. Sorry, Zelah, he needs – he deserves – to know what's happening.'

'I'm not arguing with you,' Zelah replied. 'I've had enough of this.'

**

As the hours ticked by, the tension in the house increased to a nuclear explosion level. When Zelah dropped a mug which smashed on the kitchen floor, Stella screamed. Max, who had returned to his room, ran down the stairs, wincing and holding onto his ribs.

'Nothing wrong,' Stella muttered, helping Zelah pick up the pieces.

Maggie had half-heartedly tried to finish the research into the final Pritchard, but couldn't concentrate and gave up. Nothing further came from Nick.

Maggie still hadn't heard from Bob.

At one thirty they were sitting around the conference table when a car pulled up outside. Stella, closest to the window jumped up.

'It's Nick. He has someone with him.'

Maggie squeezed her fingers into fists as Nick entered with an elderly man, tall, grey-haired, wearing a three-piece suit. What was this, now of all times?

'Sorry,' he said, as they all glared at him. 'This is important. This is Professor Henry Letts. He's an expert in Chinese ceramics, at the University in Cardiff. He's going to be here for the meeting with Camberwell.'

'You decided that did you?' Zelah began, standing up.

'Please Zelah, trust me.' Nick said, in a quiet, firm voice. 'I know what I'm doing.'

She stared intently at him for several seconds, then sat down, nodding. Maggie was surprised, but if Zelah, neither patient nor forgiving, could see something, then she wasn't going to argue. Nick was whispering to Stella and Max.

Another car pulled up outside. The doorbell rang.

They're early,' Maggie said, going to let them in. She returned, not with Camberwell and Desmond, but with Olivia Abbott, who swept into the room, head held high, smiling triumphantly.

'How did you know?' Maggie said.

'You'll find out soon enough,' Olivia said, taking a seat at the table.

'Is Finch coming too?'

Olivia snorted.

'Of course not,' Zelah said. 'She's been in on it from the start. She's the snitch.'

Another car.

'This must be them,' Maggie said. This time, she was right.

She opened the door, ushering Henry Camberwell and Ian Desmond into the room. Camberwell smiled benignly at the assembled crowd, as Zelah dialled in the group in Ireland.

'They're family,' she spat at Camberwell, who hadn't yet spoken. He indicated his agreement with a gracious nod, which set Zelah's teeth on edge.

'Find yourselves a seat, you smug bastards,' she said to Camberwell and Desmond. 'Now, say what you have to say, so we can finish this off and go home.'

'My dear lady, how nice to meet you, at last,' Camberwell said softly. Before sitting he removed his overcoat and scarf, which he handed to Ian Desmond. He wore an immaculately tailored sports jacket over dark trousers, with a cravat at his throat.

'Piss off,' Zelah replied.

'Oh, I shall be doing so, but we aren't all here yet.'

'My son won't be coming,' Maggie said.

'But someone's son will,' Camberwell replied. 'Ah, I hear another at the door. Do let him in, Mrs Gilbert.'

Maggie strode to the front door, where Gerry Quinn stood waiting. He walked past her, head down, and entered the room. Mischa screamed when she saw him, but he didn't look at the screen.

'You piece of shit!' she yelled. 'You're no better than our father. After everything these people have done for you. I'm going to kill you.'

294

'Oh dear, Gerard. Your sister is angry, isn't she? Never mind. With what I'm going to pay you, you'll be able to avoid such a harridan. Come, sit next to me.'

Gerry sat and looked down at the table.

In the few seconds of silence that followed, Maggie, at the head of the table, glanced around. Zelah, Stella, and Max were white-faced, glaring across at Camberwell and his group. At the opposite end of the table, Nick and the professor appeared quite calm.

'Now,' Camberwell began. 'Introductions. A few here I don't know.'

Nick stood up. 'We've met before, Sir Henry. This gentleman is Professor Henry Letts, from the University of Cardiff. He's here to confirm provenance.'

Camberwell nodded. 'I know of your reputation, Professor. I'm delighted that Mr Howell has brought you here.'

'And I know of yours,' Professor Letts replied, scowling.

'This is my son, Max Howell, and my partner, Stella Bell. Maggie Gilbert you already know. Now, perhaps you can tell us something about the people here with you.'

'Indeed. None are unknown to you. Ian here, is a descendant of John Pritchard, as I believe you already know. As is Olivia, which you were close to discovering, Mrs Gilbert.'

Maggie gasped. 'The final descendant. You saw it on my computer screen.'

'My father and I had been searching for years,' Olivia said. 'I couldn't believe my luck when I was assigned to your case. My grandfather and Sir Henry were old friends.'

'So you betrayed your family and your colleagues,' Zelah said.

Olivia shrugged and smiled. 'For the record, I was the one at the hotel. I injected the drug into Hugh Wilson. The stupid idiot was going to back out and tell you,' she pointed at Maggie, 'everything. We couldn't have that, could we?'

'And finally,' Camberwell continued, 'the lovely Gerry Quinn. Truly his father's son. Gerry has no motivation other than wanting to be very, very rich. And, he will be,' he finished, beaming at Gerry who returned a watery, cheerless smile.

'Now, to business. Let me see it, please.'

'I will,' Nick said. 'But first, everyone stand up and stand back. 'No-one is to be within touching distance.'

He turned and picked up the tin from the desk behind his seat. Slowly, in tiny movements, he opened it, unwrapped the vase, and set it on the table in front of him.

Camberwell and Olivia Abbott leaned forward. His expression was avaricious, hers fanatical.

'Professor,' Camberwell said. 'Please confirm you can vouch for the authenticity. This is indeed a Tang Yin, made for Emperor Qinlin?'

The Professor nodded. 'Yes, I'm almost sorry to say that it is. But it's the property of the British Museum and as soon as you leave this room, I am going to call the police and …'

'Stop right there, Professor. Everyone in this room knows that if the police become involved, none of their lives are safe. Now, hand it over, Mr Howell.'

Nick picked up the vase. But instead of moving, he clasped it to his chest with a challenging expression aimed at Camberwell.

'No, I don't think I will.'

A series of gasps echoed around the room, as all eyes fixed on Nick.

'Yes, you will,' Camberwell said, not smiling now.

Gerry Quinn stepped forward. 'Nick, please, give the vase to me.'

Nick didn't move.

'You can't do it. It has to be me,' Gerry said. Walking around the table towards Nick he took the vase from him, but instead of returning to Camberwell, he carried on, past Max, Stella, and Zelah, stopping only when he reached Maggie, next to the open office door.

And for the briefest of moments, Maggie saw, with peace and relief, what was about to happen.

Gerry held out the vase, away from his chest, where he had cradled it, and smiled at Camberwell.

'Sir Henry?'

Camberwell nodded and took a step forward.

'Fuck you,' Gerry said, and let go of the vase, which plunged down onto the wooden floor, smashing into hundreds of tiny shards.

For what seemed like an age, moving in slow motion, but was only a second, there was silence, then pandemonium.

Olivia Abbott howled, pushed past Maggie, hit Gerry out of the way, and fell to her knees, trying to gather up the pieces.

Ian Desmond didn't move.

Camberwell took a few more seconds to recover himself. 'You'll pay for this, all of you,' he yelled.

And then Zelah stepped in.

'Enough,' she said, as she stalked past Maggie, muttering, 'I swore I'd never do this again.'

As she reached Camberwell, she stood before him, a foot shorter but not batting an eyelid at his rage. Putting her hand up to his throat she lifted him into the air as if he were no more than a puppet. His eyes bulged in horror and disbelief. He tried to grab at her, but couldn't find movement in his hands.

'No, you bastard, you will pay for this. I will make sure Mr Dmitriev knows you are responsible for what happened here today.' Then she leaned into his face and whispered, 'This is just a party trick, but I can kill you whenever I want to. Wherever you are, wherever I am. Whenever I want to. Believe that. You wouldn't be the first.'

And just as suddenly she let go and he fell to the floor, looking up at her, terrified. Springing to his feet he ran from the room and the house.

Zelah turned to Ian Desmond. 'I'm willing to bet you were responsible for Moira's accident. You greedy shit, you killed your own wife. She wasn't much, but you … you are despicable. Now, get out. And take that,' she swept her hand at Olivia who was still grovelling on the floor, 'with you.'

Ian Desmond needed no further heeding. He grabbed Olivia by the hair and dragged her out of the house.

Silence descended on the room.

Zelah turned to Gerry, eyeing him quizzically. 'Did you really just smash forty million dollars' worth of prize Chinese ceramic?'

'Nick,' Maggie said. 'I think you have the answer to that question.'

'Answer?' Zelah retorted. 'I don't expect an answer. We all saw it.'

'Ah, but you're going to have an answer, Zelah, and so are the rest of you. The answer is: no, he didn't.'

'What?' Stella said. 'What do you mean? We saw it.'

'It is – was – a fake,' Nick replied. 'According to the Professor here, it wouldn't have fetched more than a couple of thousand dollars, if it ever reached an auction house.'

'And you knew?' Max shouted at Nick. 'All along, you knew?'

'No, Max. As soon as I saw it, it didn't look right, but I'm no expert. That's why I contacted Harry.'

'I could see right away,' the Professor replied. 'It was too crude. The mechanism was good, but not good enough, not for a Tang Yin.'

Maggie flopped down onto a chair. 'Bloody hell.' She sprang up again, turned to Gerry, who was still standing, wide-eyed, in the doorway, and hugged him.

'You were in on it, weren't you?'

He nodded. 'I contacted Camberwell a week ago, thought I might find out what he knew, and of course, he accept me at face value, given my background. He asked me to keep an eye on you all, telling him what you were finding. Olivia had been booted out, then Ian, so I was his eyes and ears, or so he thought.'

'What did you tell him?' Maggie asked.

'Whatever he wanted to hear, of course. I made it all up. Made him think you were getting closer, but still had a little way to go. Then today, I had to do something quick, when I knew you'd actually found it. So, when the meeting broke up this morning, I told Nick what I'd done. I went with him to meet the Professor and we made the plan. It was me who contacted Ian Desmond. It seems like a long time ago. But it was only this morning.'

Maggie could feel him shaking. 'Brilliant boy,' she said. 'You had us all fooled for a while there.'

A squeak came from the screen and they turned to see Mischa, crying. 'I'd hug you too if I could. I'm so sorry about what I said this morning. Please forgive me.'

Gerry nodded. 'This is my family, now. Although the forty million was very attractive …'

Maggie let go of him with a friendly push. 'Professor, we should pay you some kind of fee, for what you've done today.'

Harry Letts held up his hand. 'No, nothing. I've clashed with Camberwell before. Dreadful man. This is payback enough for me. Although, if the vase could have been saved, I would have been pleased to take it, to study it. But, it wasn't to be. And one Chinese vase is not worth the life of anyone. Besides,' he said, smiling at her, 'I've not had this much fun in ages. Right, I'll go now and leave you all alone. Nick, we must talk again.'

Nick walked the professor to the door. When he came back, he went to Stella and Max enveloping them in a tight embrace. 'I'm so sorry,' he whispered. 'I must have terrified you both.'

'You did, old man,' Max replied. 'But we love you anyway.'

'I'm going to fetch a dustpan and brush,' Maggie said. 'I think I'll throw the pieces in the canal. Anyone object?'

No-one did. They watched as she gathered the shards together. Zelah and Nick accompanied her to the end of the garden and looked on as she tossed the shattered pieces high into the air over the fence and into the canal, where they sunk on impact.

'Good riddance,' Zelah said, as they walked back to the house, to find Bob standing in the hallway.

'What the hell has been going on here?'

Two Weeks Later

The call was taking longer than Maggie had expected. As she watched, Bob chewed at his bottom lip but didn't respond to the information coming down the phone.

'I see. Thanks for letting me know, John.'

She sat forward in her chair. 'Well? Is it true? Was it him?'

Bob nodded. 'Finch says he was identified through dental records. He's been dead about a week.'

'So, why … No, don't tell me.'

'Unrecognisable. Then again, he'd been in the water all that time.'

Her stomach clenched. She stood, walked out of the conservatory, and down the two steps into the garden. Leaning on the fence, her glazed eyes stared at the canal, not seeing anything.

'How's Finch?'

'Not thrilled. The vase turned out to be fake and Camberwell got away. Not the outcome for which he was hoping.'

'Hard luck.'

'You'll have to tell Nick and Stella,' Bob said..

'I know,' she replied, not looking up. 'Stella will be upset. She was disgusted at what he'd done, but not enough to want him dead.' She paused. 'And what about Camberwell? Any sign of him? Or Olivia Abbott?'

'Nothing on Camberwell, but it's early days. He may have gone to ground, waiting it out, or he may turn up, alive, or like poor Ian Desmond.'

'But surely it was Camberwell who killed Ian?'

'I don't know. Nor does John Finch, yet. Most likely Camberwell, or he could have convinced the Russian Ian was responsible for the loss of the vase. Likely we'll never know. However, Olivia Abbott has resigned without notice. Jumped before she was pushed, I guess.'

'Is she gone?'

'In the US, we think. There's a hunt on for her, for the murder of Hugh Wilson. Hopefully, you'll never hear from her again.'

'Hopefully?'

Bob shrugged. 'Come on, let's go back in.'

Back in the conservatory, they sat in silence, staring out at the garden, each deep in thought. The call about Ian Desmond had been unexpected. He wasn't to blame for the vase being smashed, but, Maggie thought, it wouldn't surprise her if Camberwell had somehow managed to transfer blame to Ian, and probably Olivia too.

She hadn't spoken much to Nick and Zelah since the meeting with Camberwell. Nick had taken Stella and Flora away to Devon for a break. They were due back later in the week.

Jack and Max were back at work, Max having recovered in the way young people do. They had decided together not to work for two weeks, to give themselves some down time. However, Maggie knew she had to speak to Zelah. It couldn't be put off. Zelah had travelled over to Ireland the day following the breaking of the vase, taking Gerry Quinn and his mother Michelle with her. She said it was the right moment for a reconciliation between Gerry, Michelle, and Mischa. She'd had just the one text, saying it was going well. Zelah was due back today and would be at work, with her and Nick, on Monday morning.

What was she going to say? To each of them?

First – why would Nick think she wouldn't, out of sheer curiosity, look up Professor Henry Letts? He had no profile on social media, nothing on Facebook or Twitter. He hadn't looked like that kind of man, more the academic type. There were only two pictures of him, and they appeared to be the man who had been in the office and confirmed that the vase was a fake. However, according to another page, the Professor had been in Singapore for a three-day conference that only finished the day before they met with Camberwell. Curiosity again getting the better of her, she had checked incoming flights. And she couldn't see how the Professor could have returned in time to meet with Nick on the morning of the gathering. Nick had headed off to Devon the morning after. Should she question him when he returned to work? Was there anything to be gained by it?

Then, there was the phrase only she had heard when Zelah rushed past her towards Camberwell, before hoisting him into the air. *I swore I would never do this again.* Again? And then the rest of the whisper to Camberwell: *I can kill you whenever I want to. Wherever you are, wherever I am. Whenever I want to. Believe that. You wouldn't be the first.*

Maggie had wracked her brain to think about the meaning of Zelah's words and had come up with one possible scenario. What to do? Did she honestly want to know if her suspicions were correct? What would she do if she was right? It would mean that Zelah had deliberately, knowingly, killed, in a way that only she could. The thought made her shiver and turn away, shaking it from her head. Both could wait a little longer. See what news came of Camberwell in the following days. Or weeks. Or never.

There was enough to do, plenty of work coming in. Maze would carry on. She would keep her terrible thoughts to herself. Until the next time.

Thanks and Acknowledgements

As always, producing a book involves many people without whose help, expert advice and encouragement I would struggle.

My 'first readers', Cheryl, and Rose, as always. Positive criticism, plot holes spotted and excellent suggestions for improvement.

My thanks on this occasion go to Ann Brady of Mentoring Writers, for final editing and proof reading.

Thanks also to Ali Morgan at Alicat Designs for the fabulous cover.

The Chartist Uprising and the march on Newport are one of the most important, yet little known events in British history and I am pleased that I have been able to use some historical information to tell the story. I am absolutely indebted to David Osmond of Our Chartist Heritage group of Newport, for help in checking over my historical data, righting some factual information and ensuring that what I have written is fundementally correct. I have used a little 'creative licence' in a couple of places to make sure people are where they are supposed to be, for the purposes of the fictional narrative, so if there any errors, they are mine.

Also, thanks to Carole McCulloch (CoachCarole) in Australia, for checking out my description of a transported convict.

I have again used some licence around the pandemic rules as the book is set in the first quarter of 2021 but I hope have retained the substance of what it would have been like to move around during that period of time in the UK.

Finally, to Stewart and Alice, my wonderful children, who give me support, encouragement and inspiration. And tell me to keep going when the doubts set in.

Thank you for reading this book!

If you have enjoyed it, please leave feedback on Amazon and/or Goodreads. If there's anything I've missed, or if you have any questions about any feature of it, please leave a message on my website: www.mkjonesauthor.com.

Maze Investigations has its own website: https://mkjonesauthor. com and its own Facebook, Twitter and Instagram pages. I have an author page on Goodreads, where you will be able to read my blog about 'My Writing Life'.

And if you can't wait, you can catch up with the stories of other cases the Maze Investigations team tackle between the books. These are available when you sign up for my newsletter on the website. You will receive two immediately as a thanks for signing up:

"The Missing Air Raid Warden 1941"
And
"Murder in the Family 1840s"

Following these there will be a new story with each newsletter, in the form of a report by one of the Maze Investigators.
Happy reading!

Bibliography

The Chartist Uprising in the UK, and in particular in Newport, is an exceptionally important event in the history of this country. Despite the failure of the march into Newport, the Chartist movement continued and eventually brought about the right to vote and other points of the Charter that we both enjoy and take for granted today. To ensure historical accuracy of the background material of this work of fiction, I have read and studied the following:

The Last Rising – The Newport Chartist Insurrection of 1839: David J V Jones

The Chartist Riots at Newport: W N Johns

Gwent Local History – Journal of the Gwent Local History Council No. 130 2021

The Chartist Movement in Monmouthshire: James Davies

The Chartist Rambler (William Edwards of Newport 1796-1849): David Osmond

The Chartists Perspectives and Legacies: Malcolm Chase

Printed in Great Britain
by Amazon

87168611R00178